THEY CAME TO A RAINFOREST

Published by Brolga Publishing Pty Ltd
ABN 46 063 962 443
PO Box 12544, A'Beckett St, VIC, Australia, 8006
markzocchi@brolgapublishing.com.au

Images on pages 20, 26, 42, 48, 130, 142, 216 and 230 are used with permission from the private collection of Margery Missen.

Images on page 94 are used with permission from Shirley Durham.

Images on pages 232, 237 and 239 are used with permission from Jackie Fisher.

Images on pages 6, 62 (by N. J. Caire), 114 (by Walter Hodgkinson), 160, 188, 240, 244 and 248 are used with permission from the Pictures Collection, State Library of Victoria.

National Library of Australia Cataloguing-in-Publication entry

Boddy, Doris M.
They came to a rainforest / Doris Mary Boddy.
9781921596063 (pbk.)
Pioneers—Victoria—Gippsland—Fiction.
A823.4

Printed in Indonesia
Cover by David Khan
Typeset by Imogen Stubbs

THEY CAME TO A RAINFOREST

Doris Boddy

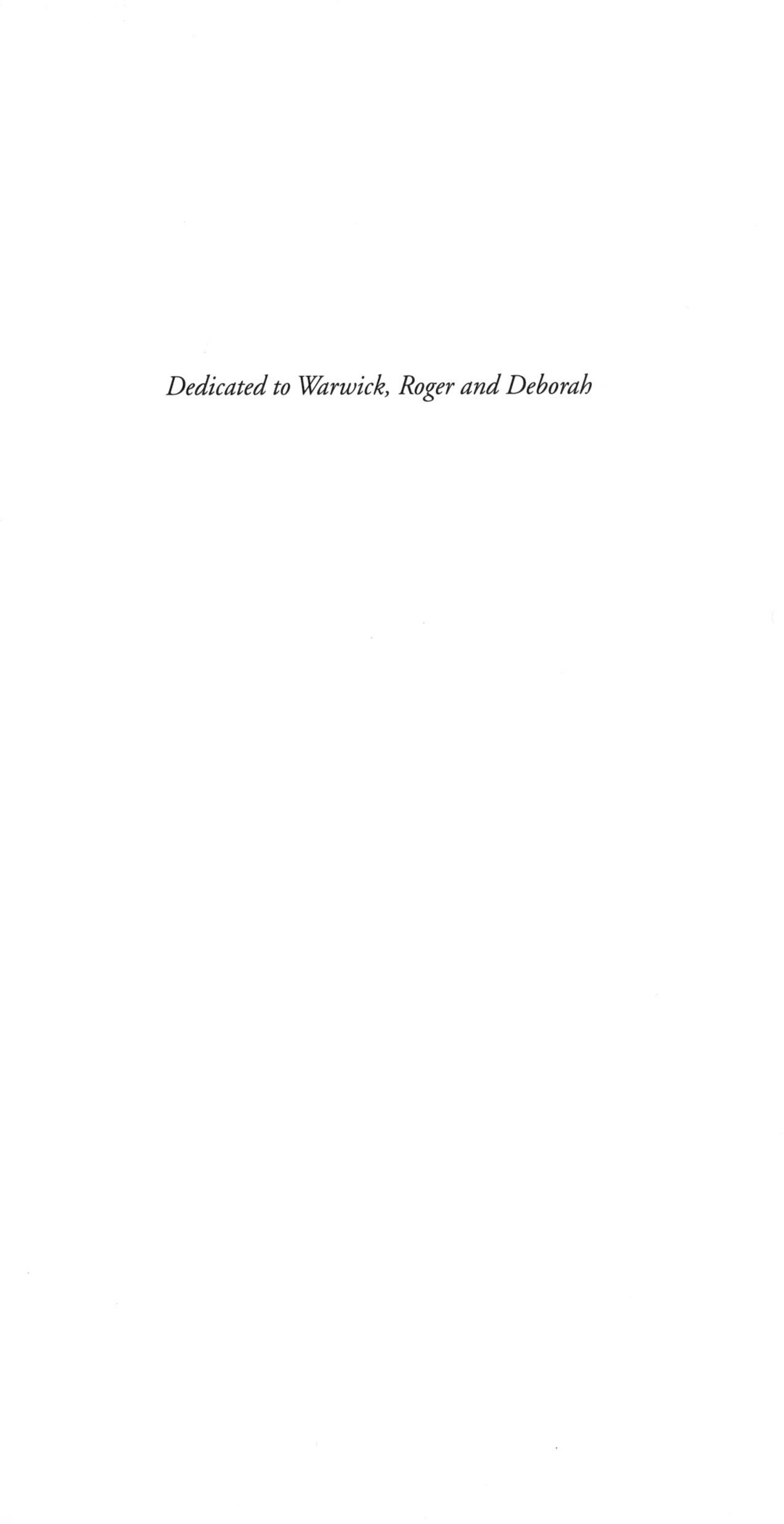

Dedicated to Warwick, Roger and Deborah

A novel based on diaries of district pioneers
who opened the Country.

The experiences are similar to those of the
founders of families whose descendants reside in
Woodside, Morwell and Yarram today.

"Is this for progress Beauty Swept away?"

… I will lift up mine eyes to the hills
from whence cometh my strength…

DORIS MARY SAUNDERS COOK BODDY

ABOUT THE AUTHOR

DEDICATED, INDEPENDENT, WISE AND INFINITELY CHEERFUL! What a description! I can hear Docie saying, "Who me?" with honest disbelief. Yet that is how she stood in the eyes of this granddaughter.

Doris Mary Saunders Boddy was a lady dedicated to a thinking, challenging life. Always believing in positive actions, words and deeds, she was a lady dedicated to maintaining her ideals and to making the absolute best out of any situation.

Independent in that she had the strength to stand alone against adversity. Independent enough to 'go teaching' in pioneering times and country. Independent of inhibition – a youthful scallywag, a bold adult.

Wise, not in philosophical or grandiose ways, but in a knowing perceptive manner. Her wisdom was born from knowing how to put people at ease. She was very adept with reality and how to direct her realities in the most positive direction, with education being an integral part of this wisdom. A great believer in the development of one's mind, she never stopped reading, writing and, most of all, thinking and commenting on human issues.

Cheerful, she had a song or quote for any occasion or conversation. The cheer came from a Pollyanna like belief in the good that could be found in each situation and so often epitomised in her writings.

"...Take heart oh dreamer, Night too has its glory. Always: there's another day. Be on your way..."

She must have had many hard times without cheer and many 'nights,' but to the world she presented a cheerful welcoming face and to the people she met, a cheerful welcoming hand.

A great lady to me, maybe here described in golden hues but I am her granddaughter and thus see her only through loving eyes.

Deborah Gill

INTRODUCTION

Doris Mary Boddy (nee Cook) came as a young teacher to the Balloong school. She married a farmer and they lived at 'Carawatha' for many years, later retiring to Yarram.

She was always interested in literature and loved to write.

Her short stories *This Old Cob*, *The Trouble With Algernon* were printed in *The Weekly Times* and a poem *The Opening Shoot* won first prize in a Melbourne Writers' Club competition.

The small book B*eyond the Ninety-Mile* records the history of many early pioneers in the Woodside and nearby districts.

They Came to a Rainforest was printed in serial form in the then *Gippsland Standard* between 5 April 1967 and 11 September 1968.

During the last twenty-five years I have often read *They Came to a Rainforest* and thought 'This should be published' but then it went back into the cupboard, together with the short stories and poems.

In 2008 two things happened. My cousin Judith Sheard arranged for an electronic copy of the manuscript to be sent to my friend Christine Lister, who offered to prepare it for submission to a publisher.

Christine's book *The Hidden Journey – Melanoma Up Close and Personal* had just been released by Brolga Publishing so *They Came to a Rainforest* was sent to them.

I was delighted when Brolga decided to publish it.

Some editing was suggested but as this could not be done by the author it was decided to publish as written.

I had all the *Standard* clippings and so was able to authenticate the story.

My thanks to everyone who encouraged me to persevere with my wish to see *They Came to a Rainforest* published.

My special thanks to Judith Sheard, Christine Lister and Brolga Publishing who made this wish come true.

My mother would be smiling.

Athylie L Gill
2009

CHAPTER 1

It was a very cold August that year in 1875. Maggie Ford stood shivering beside her garden gate, waiting for her children to return from the small bush school at Yarraman Park. Beyond their small holding backed by the magic hills of Gippsland, trees swayed like a tumultuous sea. The setting sun etched them in sharp relief, crimson and gold, but in the swiftly changing light the veiled blue of the foothills was merging into slate grey. She never tired of watching the vast panorama, yet somehow it gave her a sense of unrest, loneliness.

She glanced about and smiled grimly, realising just how much her way of life had changed. In retrospect, she saw the quiet English village, the pattern of respectability, her childhood home with the fine old farm furniture, the good linen, old and valuable china, and pure silver table appointments; all almost dim memories at times in the stress of the present. She shook her head as she whispered,

"Here I am, and I chose my way. I have Miles, my husband, and there are my little ones hurrying home, Guy, Jinny and Mary-Ann."

Still and tense as she leaned her face against the thick gatepost, her thoughts, again took her back to the past. With some regret, she remembered the consternation of her parents, when they were on a business trip to Melbourne and she, their only child, had announced her intention of staying in Australia to marry a young Irishman, Miles Ford. He had taught her to ride when she was visiting friends on a large property near Melbourne. To their horror, although well born, he earned his living 'breaking in' horses. However, despite their misgivings and knowing her to be like Queen Elizabeth I, with a quiet strength of will they knew when to 'give in gracefully', and agreed to return to live in Australia themselves. Reluctant to leave their home, still they lingered.

Her face became strained in a moment of sadness, and soon its tension relaxed, and she smiled. Across the wet paddocks, with flailing arms and legs, looking like screaming Catherine wheels, raced her children. Then, in the opposite direction with the thundering pounding of hooves, shouting of men and barking dogs, numerous horses galloped into a small holding paddock. Suddenly peace reigned again. The children stood still to watch. The horses ceased their prancing and mane tossing, and lowered their heads into the rich native grasses; the dogs, red tongued and panting, stretched out on the ground.

Miles Ford and his two drovers, having put up the sliprails securely, stood conversing, lighting their pipes and contemplating the muster. Then mounting their horses again, the men cantered down the track to the road gate. Miles unfastened his bridle from the stirrup and led his horse up to the house to Maggie who waved a hand as if to say,

"So here you are." Standing together, they turned and watched their children gleefully slipping through the puddles and wet grass in their wild scramble homewards. As she touched her husbands arm and pointed across the paddock, Maggie said,

"Mary-Ann is trailing behind, and Jinny is a poor second this time, Guy is well ahead. Did you tell him you are delivering the horses tomorrow?" Miles pushed back his hat and ran his fingers through his hair as he said ruefully,

"There's no need to tell that young shaver anything pertaining to horses my dear. He just senses things. Do you know what he said to me last week, after we returned from the last delivery?"

"I've no idea," said she with a hint of mischief in her smile. Miles continued in a fair imitation of the lad's shrill voice.

"Those horses are tons fatter now Dad. Soon ye'll be after delivering them too, an' can I be going with you? So we made a bargain Maggie," he went on, his voice back to its normal rich baritone, "but I shall wait and see if it still holds. He's a shrewd little scallywag that lad, you know."

Young Guy, red-faced, wide-eyed and skinny as a lathe, almost collided with his father's horse which reared in alarm.

"Steady girl, steady," urged Miles as he patted the frightened animal. "Guy, have some horse sense." He turned to the lad in a sharper voice.

"Och! Sorry Dad!" panted the boy. "Woof! I ran all the way from school to help you yard those horses. Why didn't you wait? There now," he looked very grim, "if I'd wagged it from school I'd bin here in time."

"Guy!" exclaimed Miles, taking a firm hold on the boy's arms as he looked down interrogatively into the blue eyes so like his own. "I remember that last week when I took you to the horse sales in Melbourne, we made a pact, a bargain, you and I. Yes?" Guy's sharp young face broke into a delightful grin.

"Yes Dad! I remember too an' I haven't played the wag once since I promised!"

"Lucky for you me lad, it is, or you would not be going to Melbourne with me."

"And," he said as he shook a tightly clenched fist almost on the tip of Guys nose, "if I ever hear of you playing truant again, you'll not be after seeing Melbourne or Kirk's Bazaar until you are a grown man and you can make your own arrangements. Understand?"

Miles was very stern and recognising the quiet strength of purpose of his father, Guy nodded. Standing with his back against the horse, he stared into Miles' face with candid eyes.

"I'll never do it again Dad. I promised didn't I?"

"Yes son," Miles nodded and turned to his horse to unbuckle the girth straps. "I'll do that Dad," said Guy. He looked imploringly over his shoulder and his skinny fingers struggled with the straps. "Can I help you take the horses to Eumemmering Creek to meet the owners tomorrow? Please, please Dad!" Maggie had a smile as she said,

"Tomorrow's a school day son."

"Oh Mum!" he scarcely breathed a moment and head down in utter dejection; he scuffed his feet in the muddy track. The little girls arrived and Maggie, with a merry wing towards Miles, took them into the house.

Guy slowly removed the saddle and set it down by the gate ready to be hung in the back porch, and then stood by his father waiting. Miles, patting his tousled head said,

"Come lad, we must feed the saddle horses, then there's wood to be cut, an' by jove; you had better shine up my riding boots an' leggings, and… yes!" He paused and pursed his lips as if considering a weighty problem, "Oh yes," he repeated slowly, "you'd better be after shining your own – the ones your grandfather gave you when…" Guy spoke swiftly.

"You mean dad, that I… I…" he gulped for breath in his overjoyed excitement, "I can go with you?"

"Yes! Yes! Now stop your blather an' be about your jobs. We'll be leaving at the first hint of light in the morning. So be off, and see that you're abed early."

Needing no second bidding, Guy took the bridle and rode the horse at a smart canter towards the stables. His father turned and walked up the garden path to the house. Maggie looked up from preparing the meal and the smiled at each other.

"Well," she said, "it's all settled, and its fair leapin' for joy the lad is, to be sure." She nodded. "There's going to be heavy frost. He will be frozen before you get to the creek."

"Not him. Excitement will keep him warm, an' it's a long ride ahead of him, but we'll be staying the night with grandfather, so he'll be right,' he laughed shortly. "If Guy had only known it, I had every intention of taking him. He saves me paying out one man's wages, as I need four men to drove those fifty-odd horses; two in front and two at the rear. Guy can ride ahead. The horses soon settle down once they get along the road, so he will enjoy scanning the countryside. He's a real farmer that one. He'll be waiting at the creek to stop the horses when we get there. The last time we lost two horses there. They swam across and got off into the timber. As things are, we need all the money we can get without paying for other chap's lost stock. Guy's a grand stock rider even if he's only twelve years old and such a little fellow," he added.

"Too young, too young," said Maggie shaking her head as she left the room with a dish of peelings.

THE BOURKE-STREET HORSE SHOW.

CHAPTER 2

THE NEXT MORNING AT DAYLIGHT MILES AND GUY, WITH THE help of the two drovers, delivered the horses to the waiting owners. The two men secured contracts to continue on the roads with the main part of the muster, and Miles and Guy rode on past Dandenong, where they stayed at Miles's father's home until the next morning. Then they rode into Melbourne, 'bright and early', stabled their hacks and set out to walk through the city and up Bourke Street to the big horse bazaar.

Sunshine danced in a blaze of reflected lights from the frost encrusted buildings and pavements, and almost dancing too like a puppet with co-ordinating joints was Guy. Eager and sharp faced, with a fine crop of freckles burgeoning across his pert little nose, like mushrooms after a spring shower, and with his sandy hair long and unkempt, he resembled nothing so much as a bright-eyed little fox. His direct gaze, however, proclaiming his essential honesty, denied the former's reputation for cunning. He blew on his fingers in a vain attempt to warm them, and looking impatiently at the city buildings, pulled at his father's old Chesterfield overcoat.

"Come on Dad! The sales'll be over before we get there. People are hurrying past us. Just look at the crowds of men up at the end of the street." Miles looked down at the boy and smiled tolerantly.

"Steady son! To be sure, I'll soon have to be running to keep up with you."

Guy hopped about as if the pavement were hot coals and looked at his father imploringly.

"But there'll be no room near the sale ring for us. Do hurry Dad!"

"Come on then. Run boy, run!" and his father raced ahead, regardless of the stares of the pedestrians.

When they arrived at the edge of the crowd, they paused, trying to find a way through the dust and confusion of people talking close together. This presented no problems to the boy. Being small and insignificant looking, he had little difficulty in darting away from his father's staying hand and 'ducking in amongst the bloke's legs', as he himself expressed it.

When Miles eventually caught up with him, Guy, looking like an extremely inquisitive monkey, was perched on the topmost rail of the sale ring, his head turning swiftly from one point of interest to another.

In the dusty interior men were shouting and horses stamping and neighing. All around, and in the numerous stalls about him and beyond the ring, a continuous murmur of conversation and the descent of high raucous laughter were just parts of a terrific din, which rose to the cobwebbed rafters of the great roof.

"Kirk's Bazaar", the lad's nodding head seemed to be saying, in his great satisfaction at just being there.

He watched the array of harnesses, trappings for every type of horse and vehicle; the drays, carts, wagons and buggies to be bought and sold. One day he would own 'the best horses ever, an' a dandy gig' he told himself, and suddenly his keen eyes took on a dreamy faraway aspect.

The auctioneer's voice rang out. Guy tensed, dreams were gone. There was a sound like the sough of a mighty receding wave and a silence charged with excitement followed. It seemed as if time itself had paused.

The sale was 'on'. The bidding was fast, decisive as the flash of a blade through the arid dust-laden air. Horses of all descriptions were led in and out of the ring in quick succession. A splendid Clydesdale gelding, neighing and straining against the halter as it played the air with its forelegs and all the menace of its great power, drew all eyes. The hammer sent its triple message...

"Going! Going! Gone!"

The boy nearly fell into the ringside as he turned excitedly to his father.

"Dad! Dad! That's the very same horse we saw sold here last week." He turned back for a second inspection. "Yes, it is too, an' the same man has bought it. Ten pounds more he paid. Why would..." the shrill voice paused and the boy recoiled.

"Shut your mouth, you young whipper-snapper, or I'll break every bone in your body." Guy looked up at a man whose great shoulders were moving like wings of a hovering eagle-hawk as he shook a ham of a hand at him.

"Garn", Guy mocked, but took the precaution of edging behind his father. From that vantage point, he concluded that the irate man was not as fierce as he sounded.

"Easy man, easy!" said Miles.

Then the other whispered. "Great Scott alive, Mate! Keep this kid quiet, or there'll be the devil to pay here. Please!" He touched Miles' shoulder with swift entreaty. Miles gave the boy a warning look, and the stranger said, "Good man! Thanks! I'll come back and tell you all about it when the sales finished," nodding his head in a friendly manner he left them.

But Guy had lost interest in the stranger and his problems; he was keenly watching the magic of the continuous stream of horses being bought and sold. He climbed on the rail of the sale ring again, and sat there, erect and tense as a pointer dog watching the quail in the shooting season.

The crown was thinning, the morning sales easing. When they ceased, he sat a while watching the people and listening to scraps of conversation on the morning's transactions. They left the building. Then he noticed his father and the strange burly man talking together, and went across to them, confidently grinning. Seeing him, the man patted his head none too gently and said,

"Hello, young-feller-me-lad!"

"Still mad at me mister?" Guy asked cautiously.

"No! Your Dad an' I are going to have the best dinner in the City. Want to come?"

"Yes please, sir!" said Guy quickly. So they turned and left the dusty saleyards.

As they walked along the busy city streets, Guy's puckish face was very intent. He had no difficulty dodging people or keeping up with the men, but his thoughts were on the morning's sales. Almost with the insight of an experienced horse dealer, he was reviewing events.

Suddenly he peered up into the men's faces and saw that it was no use, then, to seek answers to the things that puzzled him. He would wait. He slowed his steps and walked behind them, watching the passing scene. They paused at a fine city hotel and opened two great glass doors, heavy with polished oaken woodwork, then looked back and beckoned him.

Wide-eyed, head turning rapidly to catch every aspect of a grand new world, he walked almost on tiptoe. Such luxury! He caught his father's sleeve, whispering,

"Ee-ee Dad! Ain't it fine?" and his eyes opened wider as if they could not even then, take in all the newfound splendour about him. "Gee! Dad! Look at those big lookin' glasses an' the leather chairs, an' shiny table."

Then he breathed out slowly as he studied the large red-patterned carpets, soft to the feet as the moss in the gullies along the creek at Dandenong. It fascinated him as he stepped gingerly across the archway leading to the dining room.

"Look at all the white table cloths, an' the sliver an' the flowers."

"We're in luck boy. Shhhh! Here comes the waiter. Read the card an' pick out your fancy young fella," added their host. Guy did just that.

The dinner was to him a feast to remember and Miles commented,

"Hunger being a wonderful sauce, it was well seasoned in every way." The years increased its magic to Guy.

As they returned to the saleyards, their new friend told them his name was Joe Crow, adding,

"That's not my real surname, but it does me now. I'll tell you this, but keep it under your hat." Guy looked at his father's hat as if to say,

"That old hat wouldn't even keep Dad's head under it much longer." His father read his thought and laughed as he took it off and ruefully tried to bring some line or shape to it.

"He doesn't think much of keeping anything under this Joe, but go on, your secret will be safe with us."

"Strike me!" muttered Joe forcefully. "I know that. I can always tell a good chap when I see one." He whispered, "Me name's really Crowherd. Ain't it bloomin' well awful?"

"Well! Joe Crow's a jolly good name," said Miles, very seriously, and not even with a twinkle in his eye to show his amusement.

Guy was not interested. His little head was still intrigued with his own problem. He could wait no longer. On a sudden impulse he walked in front of Joe and stood there looking earnestly up into his face. In his eagerness the words just tumbled forth.

"Mr. Joe! Why did you buy your own horse for ten pounds more than you paid last week?" Guy paused. "An' why were you mad at me?"

Joe's eyes almost closed as he chuckled, twitched his big wide hat around his tousled head and answered,

"I get mad easy, I do. That horse? Ah! Yes. So at last you ask me. I thought it would come soon."

"Go on please Mr. Joe. That was a funny thing to do. You…"

"Now, now! Guy that's enough," interrupted his father. But the boy edged away and pretended not to hear and Joe's laugh boomed out over the heads of the pedestrians who paused momentarily to stare.

"Great Scott alive! Sheer roguery that! Don't ask me boy. Och! Yes, I'll tell you. Get along. We don't want all the city listenin' to us," he said somewhat irately.

As they walked, Joe talked and they listened.

"I'm a saw miller. I came to buy strong horses for logging; big staunch horses with plenty of pull and fire in 'em."

"Do you always buy them twice, Mr. Joe?" Joe shrugged.

"Well I s'pose I must explain or you'll bust, youngster." He turned to Miles, "He's a bright kid he is, an' he'll give us no peace 'til he knows. Well, here we are at the saleyards again." He looked at the great watch tucked firmly in his waistcoat pocket. "H'm! I've got ten minutes to spare before the next draft of horses is offered. Come over to this bench an' I'll tell you." So they seated themselves and the crowd of men gathered around was so dense, that they themselves, strangely enough, had complete privacy.

"Cripes Mister! I thought you were a horse-dealer, not a saw miller."

"Now, now! Don't be so impatient," remonstrated Guy's father, but Joe laughed good-humouredly.

"That's a good one that!" was Joe's reaction in his customary vernacular.

"I do want to hear about that horse Dad," Guy shook his head at his father.

"Yes, yes! I'm coming to that," said Joe. "It was just a bit of skilled juggling lad. I bring my worn out horses down here, put them out on agistment for a while, and then sell them. The lot I sold today was a sorry one, so I put the big Clydesdale up for sale to make the market, see?" He leaned over the boy, "I was bidding on him myself because I want that horse, and I wasn't going to let anyone else have him. The big Clydesdale gave the market a rise. So I sold my other horses at a good price. A good day's work, yes?"

Guy looked at him with his head on one side, "Oo-oo! So you're what my Grand-dad calls a shyster."

"Guy!"

"Well, he is Dad!"

Joe stood up and looked over the heads of the crowd towards the sale yards as he replied, "You're a smart young fellow. Perhaps you're right, but I must hurry. Come now. The horses I want to buy are almost due to be offered. You'll come Sir?" He turned to Miles who agreed, saying,

"Yes, we'll watch your bidding, then we must hurry to be off. We have ten miles to ride and the days are short, and," he added, "my name's Miles. Don't Sir me." Joe nodded.

Again they worked their way to the sale ring and it did not take long for him to complete his transaction. As Miles and Guy saddled their horses before they separated, Joe told them that he too would be "shoving off at the crack o'dawn. Got to find a paddock to garage 'em for a day or so." Guy turned to him and tugged his sleeve,

"We can graze 'em Mr. Joe."

"You can?" Joe looked inquiringly at Miles, who replied,

"Yes, the lad's right. We have small paddocks where we agist horses for a living."

"Great Caesar! That's just into my hands mate. Will you take these horses I've just brought? I would like to leave them for a while to spell before they go to the logging camp."

"Yes!" agreed Miles. "That will be quite convenient. We have a paddock that has been free of stock for some considerable time and there's a very good sole of grass there now. We delivered our last muster of horses yesterday, so I promised Guy we would watch the horse sales before we returned home. He loves even the smell of a horse." He looked proudly down at his son, "He should be at school..."

"Hate school!" interrupted Guy truculently.

"Yes boy, and so did I once," said Joe. "Never regretted anything so much as all those days I played the wag. Lack of schoolin' kept me a poor man, an' it's no use hating even that. We can't go back."

"A poor man Mr. Joe? But you have all those horses. How can you say that?" Guy leaned across to Joe, wide-eyed and open-mouthed.

"Horses ain't riches boy. They're pretty poor property sometimes. Take it from me. An' riches ain't everything in this world neither. Listen 'ere! Its' brains and learning how to use 'em the right way that add up to the most in the long run. I'll tell you what!" Joe caught hold of Guy's stirrup strap and looked into the sharp little face of the boy, "You go to school an' learn all y'can, and in a couplea years I'll help you get all the horses and things you want. See what I mean?"

CHAPTER 3

"BY JINGO! IT'S STRANGE HOW THINGS HAPPEN, 'TIS INDEED. A bloke's been joshing his brains for weeks about holding paddocks for his stock an' along comes a likely youngster an' fairly puts 'em in his hands. Right where I need 'em most too, on the main track from the loggin' forest."

Joe rubbed his gnarled hands together and a wily satisfied grin spread over his face. Still muttering to himself, he strode away to his drovers to tell them of his new location.

The new draft of horses was duly delivered to Miles Ford's property and Joe followed a few days later, driving two high stepping light-delivery horses, tandem in a spring cart loaded with stores and tools for the group of timber cutters, bullock drivers and their families at his mill. Another profitable transaction!

He was made welcome by Miles, and 'young Guy' was delighted at being given permission to ride any horse he could saddle up. The two men spent much time inspecting pastures or just leaning over the slip-rails yarning. Maggie did her housework with a very subdued air. At the table, the men continued their discussions and her smile became very scant and wintry as they sought to include her

The family jinker

co-operation in any issue. She virtually refused to be involved. She had formed the opinion that the big bluff man's plans were not altogether altruistic and watched the proceedings with circumspect eyes.

As Miles expressed it later, 'the upshot' was that Joe was to take over all the grazing rights of the Ford pastures for his stock travelling to and from the markets. In addition, he was to buy one field on which he could build a shelter for his teamsters to rest overnight, and to store surplus goods. This opened the way to a much more prosperous future for the Ford family, an issue Miles was at some pains to assure his wife, but she refused to comment. Miles, having exhausted his patience, looked into her closed face.

"Maggie! Have your say. You're not with me. Come! Come Lass! Sliprails between you an' me I just can't tolerate. If you don't speak, how can I be going along? You're not easy in your mind? To be sure, you go quiet when that's so."

Miles voice was gentle.

As she replied, his face relaxed. "It's true. I'm not happy in my mind about that Joe. As I see him he's a violent man if roused, and much too close a dealer for you, an essentially honest person."

"He's a big bluster, shrewd, and with a strong sense of the best side of a bargain. Yes. All the same he's a kind man and he admires strength of character in others. Young Guy looked him straight in the face and Joe told him what he thought of him and I firmly believe Joe will be his friend for life." Miles patted Maggie's thin shoulder as he said, "Don't worry Lass, Joe will be a friend of us too. I like the old scallywag."

So Maggie accepted the arrangements perforce, and a new routine. The bullock wagons, loaded with sleepers, rails, palings and building timbers made the Miles Ford holding a recognised stopping place.

Maggie, rather reluctantly, at the drivers somewhat lucrative request, provided them with meals in the large kitchen. They noted no faults in building or furniture. The food was good. They were content. In fact, everyone was satisfied with the arrangements but Maggie.

Their property was not large and Joe saw to it that every part of it was made to yield a certain profit.

"Even the grass is not allowed to show its fresh beauty a day before the grazing stock trample it into the mud," she brooded, and she grudged the few remaining trees being ruthlessly felled for firewood or fencing rails.

One day she stood with Miles watching the children as they rode the horses along the track, and then turning towards the house, she frowned as she remarked,

"Why did the earliest settlers have to use that skillion type of building? All over the country it seems to be the pattern. They are so ugly!"

Miles turned and looked at the little unpainted cottage. The shingles on the roof were silvered, and a greenish spread of lichen covered some. The hazy glimmering light was a nimbus around them and the bleached walls. Maggie's eyes opened wide in pleased surprise and a smile brightened her grave face as she said impulsively,

"How strange! I've hated its ugliness so long, and now its' lovely. Look at that light. Its fanciful I know, but the whole place seems to be smiling at us." Then a cloud cast its shadow as it passed slowly overhead, and the moment of beauty fled. Sadly, she said, "It's gone. That was just a mockery."

Miles put his arm about her shoulders saying in his quiet way,

"You're tired girl. Your days are too busy, and when that is so, horizons become limited. Look over the top of the house, over the mud and disorder. See the undulating country, and the magic of the distant hills and forests?"

Maggie's eyes followed the direction of his out-thrust hand. Past the maligned cottage, over near paddocks with the dew-wet grass shining in the sun and far on over the undulating country to the dark rim of the forest-clad horizon they swept. With elated awareness they dwelt on the distant grandeur of snow-capped mountains. Maggie trembled and stood tensed, listening. Somehow, there was music all about her, faint, on the wafted tones of the distant horse and cattle bells, bird songs and even the sodden earth bubbles bursting in the warming sun; a merging of sounds, sweet to her previously unheeding ears.

She breathed heavily and the tension and petty-fogging things that had troubled here were no more. She was ready for the future. She turned with,

"Come! We'll go into that ugly house I've grumbled about and I'll make you a cup of tea before you leave for the muster."

Miles smiled down into her face as he said facetiously, "So the moment of discontent is over?"

"Yes, and the task of living and loving is going to be just fine," she replied and they walked through the sunshine back to the kitchen where the big black kettle was boiling gently as it swung with slow rhythm on the crane.

Seated at the snow-white deal table, they drank their tea. Maggie talked on various matters and Miles absently traced the grain of the wood; long lines of it. Then he reversed the movements of his fingertips.

"Miles! You haven't heard a word I've been saying. What are you thinking of?" He looked across at her; shook his head as if to clear it.

"By jove, you're right. I was thinking. See this table." She looked startled,

"Of course I do." Looking like a small boy caught in mischief, he explained, "While I traced this grain, I thought of Guy."

"Of Guy?" Miles went on unheeding of her query.

"I rubbed with the grain and it was a smooth and pleasant motion, across it. Well watch, see how my finger has to rise and fall? Going with the grain, the movement was unhampered." He looked across the table at her as he said gravely, "Surely you understand why I say that of Guy? Against the grain is a symbol of what his entire life will be if we don't recognise his natural bent. A student he will never be. Walls will never hold him for he is a part of this wild immensity, this untamed land he was born into, and we must bow to it."

There was a potent silence in the room, but for the falling apart of the crimson-gold coals in the fire, and outside the muted sounds of animals, birdcalls and a rising wind. Maggie caught her husband's hand, and holding it firmly said,

"Go on. There's more to this. Guy isn't the contented boy he used to be I admit. Too much restless activity, if you like. But this 'against the grain?' Well it sounds like nonsense to me." Miles shook his head slowly.

"He's going to school each morning since we've been more financial, yes, most reluctantly. His mind is on horses and land, nothing else."

Dray at Reedy Creek

CHAPTER 4

A MONTH PASSED. THEN ANOTHER, AND MAGGIE'S FEELING OF unease faded in the sequence of happenings in the family life. Joe Crow and his teamsters and stock came and went, an accepted pattern in the routine of the days.

On one trip, Joe was more talkative than usual, highly excited too. He and Miles conversed until the early morning, but as he left for the marketing of his stock, well before daylight, Maggie did not see him.

Miles, she noticed, was very thoughtful at the breakfast table, which was so unusual that her curiosity was aroused.

"What is it that holds you Miles?"

"To be sure, it's a weighty problem that's after holding me. Hard an' fast it is too," he replied in the brogue he lapsed into with any excitement. "And Maggie, girl, I'll be losing no time in the tellin' of it to you. Indeed an' I'll not."

Watching him in deep interest, she shook her head as she said,

"I know. You have little need to tell me. That Joe! Ah!" she sighed as she thought. "So! It's come and I knew it had to, with Joe always filling Guy's head with dreams of land and horses."

But Miles was not to be denied of the telling. Briefly, Joe had made it possible for him to secure a large run, by buying their holding at a good price, and in addition, had even found one in a good locality.

"But I must be off with some stock now and we'll talk it over thoroughly tonight." He hurried off to saddle his horse and was soon cantering to the paddock. Watching him as he so easily rode his long-striding hack, Maggie's eyes shone in an amused smile. She knew his mustering was not so urgent and recognised that he, in his quiet way, was leaving her to realise that he had made a decision; and, as it was, thus it would be. Notwithstanding Maggie's reluctant understanding of her husbands little scheme, it was successful. She, at least, resigned herself to whatever was ahead.

"But," she squared her firm chin even more, "I'll not be allowing him to be thinking it's an easy victory to be deciding before I'm in the knowing." She smiled impishly for she was not really perturbed. Speaking her thoughts aloud she said, as if excusing Miles, "He knows I'm not immutable," but only the tiny brush wrens tapping ceaselessly on the windowpane heard her. She watched them and said humorously, "And little you care anyway, you wee brown shadows."

That night, when the excited children were asleep and the house was quiet, Miles and Maggie sat by the fireside, discussing their plans. The room was hazy with smoke and the acrid fumes of the kerosene lamp. The hours passed, and the almost empty lamp was causing only a yellow corona on the table, but they noticed neither. Maggie, stirring and sighing deeply, said,

"It's an act of faith. That's all it is. Such a tremendous undertaking. It's, it's just…" she was momentarily at a loss for words, then she said harshly, "mad, but," she added after a pause, "you're a very fine madman despite this act of faith." She laughed tremulously. Rising, he looked into her face while caressing her head, and replied,

"Indeed isn't life itself just like that?" Bending to tap the ashes of his pipe on the hearthstone, he added, "We've had many changes since we married, girl, but this time we'll be set. Just you wait an' see."

"Yes, I'll wait," she countered with slightly taut lips, "and I surely will see."

Miles's answer was,

"Look through the window, it's nearly another day." Everything had been discussed, and a new day certainly was dawning for the Fords.

For the next month, everything in the Ford household revolved around arrangements for the new enterprise and everyone certainly had much to do, even little Mary-Ann who was the least enthusiastic member of the family. Jinny and Guy were eager to hasten the adventure, so were most helpful.

At last the day came when all was ready. Many times Maggie had been distressed with horror at so momentous a change. When Miles had told her that the new holding was a vast run in a virgin rain forest, she was aghast.

"It's crazy. How will you ever pay for it?"

"You forget we have a considerable sum of money put by from the sale of this property. The first payment is ready, and we have paid for the stock. Guy and I'll be taking delivery of them the day we leave."

"And the next payment?"

"The returns from the sales of wool and natural increase will assure that. Then, there will be fat cattle to swell the exchequer. So please, girl, try to have faith in the future at last. I have." She smiled up at him, realising that Miles, like a man following a star, would not be turned aside. At last her fires of indecision and doubt had vastly been diminished by this man who was so intrepid and determined to build a future with so many hazards in the 'magic hills of Gippsland'. All was ready.

Joe had arranged for one of his teamsters to manage the holding Miles had bought, and was there finalising matters. Miles and Guy had left to take delivery of their sheep and cattle. All the furniture was packed on the spring cart and bullock dray; the latter to be driven by the lad they hired, Sidney, a fine husky farm lad. Their supplies, stock and feed and all other possessions were loaded on the bullock wagon, which was to be their 'place of refuge', as Miles had facetiously stated, until they arrived at their destination.

Joe had volunteered a driver to guide them on their way. He had left to be ahead of the travelling stock.

Maggie stood alone, and looked around the bare kitchen. Pushing her hair from her face with both hands, she turned and walked through the rooms. She returned with slow steps, paused beside a small old sea chest, and finished packing some food and a few cooking utensils. Taking a firm hold, she carried the awkward burden to the door, placed it on the crazy step, which almost subsided into the sodden earth, and with a sight, stood a moment, just looking – looking at practically nothing, until Sidney came and hoisted it on top of the loaded spring cart. So! She thanked him and he strode back to his charges, two bullocks hitched to the dray, took up the long whip and, with a nod, signified he was waiting to leave.

Jinny and Mary-Ann, young faces shining with rare delight, rode their ponies to her and also waited. They watched Maggie, looking like an out-sized ant in her slim-waisted, long black frock, as she climbed nimbly over the wheel of the spring-cart. Seated on a large trunk, she beckoned to them to ride to the road gate. With set mouth, she looked down at the shabby cottage that had been their home, brushed a hand across her brightened eyes, lifted their reins, and Paddy, the once lively coach-horse, moved into the collar. Sidney shouted to his bullocks and without a backward glance they moved forward into a problematical future.

The little girls went gaily ahead. They had no problems. This, to them, was high adventure. All the days to come were theirs. No hurry! That night, they would sleep under the stars.

"Wonderful!" said they.

"If the rains hold off," returned Maggie. But it certainly did not 'hold off'. The tracks were greasy quagmires and progress was slow. Towards sunset, which was really a dim yellow glow on the horizon, they saw twinkling lights through the water-weighed trees.

"The campfire! The campfire!" shrilled the children.

"Thank goodness," muttered their mother.

"By Jingo! Tucker!" shouted Sidney. Doubtless, the tired animals would have expressed their feelings even more vociferously – if only they could!

Jinny started the tired horses with a shrill and lasting "coo-ee-ee…" Calls far in the mass of heavy timber and undergrowth brought welcome answers and soon Guy rode to them through the gloom. The girls arrived at the camp with him, but Maggie and wary old Paddy trailed in the rear.

"Come-on Mum! Hurry your nag, dad an' I have pitched bark tents for tonight. Smell the chops he's grilling?" Guy shouted. Then he rode back to her.

"Where's the bullock wagon?" said she, peering around the campsite.

"Dad says the driver's a 'hatter' an' he cooks his own grub. He doesn't want to be with us. Funny chap!" answered Guy with a laugh.

Maggie was silent a moment. Secretly, she was well pleased to be alone with her family. With her usual circumspect attitude to life in general, she would not allow her young son to gauge her feelings. She looked over her shoulder as she remarked,

"Sidney's a long way behind."

"He'll be along soon, I s'pose," Guy casually answered. "Come on Mum, do hurry." Soon they were all together at the campfire and Miles looked around, well satisfied. Grilled chops and 'mum's oven scones' made a fitting end to the day.

Above: Reedy Creek fire place

Excited and restless, the children lost no time getting into their improvised bunks, warm under possum skin.

"It's good to lie here, hearing the rain outside," remarked Jinny. "I can hear the wood-pigeons hooting. Listen!"

Mary-Ann crouched her little body quite under the coverings.

"That dreadful howling! Foxes? Ough!" she murmured fearfully.

"Foxes! Rubbish! They're dingoes, mostly dingoes. Put your head under the rug an' go to sleep!" called Guy.

Saddle-sore and weary, despite the muted clamour of the distant wilderness and the nearer noises with their fear provoking, the children were soon dreamlessly asleep.

"Guy's going with the grain now Lass," said Miles with deep satisfaction. But Maggie feigned to be asleep.

Morning and the sunshine gave brilliance to the world about them. Trees, scrub and even the grasses bent to the earth with the weight of the raindrops; a fine spectacle of dazzling lights. The stillness gave an atmosphere of awe and the giant trees, meeting in a green canopy above the heads of the travellers, passed sunshine down, leaf-by-leaf. His head backwards, watching and listening, Miles said,

"The trees seem as if they're waitin' for something to happen."

"There's no poetry about it all for me. Be assured something will be sure to do just that," and Maggie with a slight shiver, drew her jacket close.

But Miles was not discouraged. He moved closer to her as he said, "The air's so pungent with the scent of dank ferns and moss. See, the gum blossoms are full of honey. Smell the musk leaf!" He plucked one and bruising it, held it to her rather scornfully tilted nose. She had to smile but plucked a wattle bloom, just to confound him with,

"This is sweeter".

"Try the wet dog-wood," called Guy as he eyed the little play whilst lacing his boots.

"Dog-wood be danged," said Miles. "It stinks! Go on, get on your horse and let's be off with the stock. It's short enough the days are. With the heavy going on the tracks, we've no time to be after wasting, no time at all. Gad!" He turned to Maggie with teasing smile. "Sure an' it's a fine world it is, Lass!" and with parting advice and a shrill whistle to the dogs, he and Guy left to round up their stock.

Maggie knelt on a sheet of bark as she wiped bacon grease from the breakfast plates with bunches of kangaroo grass. Down in the gully a sudden peal of laughter rang out, and then protests. She heard Jinny's shrill voice giving instructions to help her up the slippery bank of the creek, and more laughter came from the tangle of trees and ferns. She listened and a smile widened in her mouth as she said aloud,

"Seems as if Jinny has slipped with her bucket of water. She's a careless one that. She never looks where her feet are going."

"It's jolly hard to stay on yer feet anywhere this morning, ain't it? Missus! Here's the water for the dish washing. Jinny's all wet. She fell into the creek."

Maggie turned in sudden surprise.

"Why Sidney! Where have you been all night?"

"Well, Missus! It got too dark to see the tracks, so I camped. I just arrived at the creek when Jinny fell in."

"But where did you sleep?"

"Ha! That was no worry. I just put your kitchen table alongside the dray and made a roof of bags. Slept on the top of the table, I did."

"You slept on my table!" Maggie was horrified. Her lovely smooth, white table!

"S'alright, Missus, I took me hobnail boots off."

She put aside the pile of plates and stood up. There was nothing to be said, she gave him breakfast.

Smiling as if he had performed some major feat, he went across to the fire and filled the black bucket with clear water from the creek in the gully. The dishes were washed and packed, and Maggie set the big lumbering boy to tidy the camp and load the cart again. When Jinny had changed into dry clothes, she and Mary-Ann set out to catch up with Miles and Guy; Maggie on the spring cart, and Sid with the bullock dray followed.

The pattern was set. Each day through the bogs and overhanging wetness of the huge bulks of sassafras, mountain ash, red gums and wattles, they plodded ahead. Some days they barely covered six miles – other days they almost did ten and were jubilant. Ten miles a day!

"One hundred years later, how would that register?" Maggie wondered as she looked about her, from her uncomfortable vantage point on the top of the spring cartload. The beauty and peace around soothed and relaxed her. She faced the future with hope and Miles' inevitable, "Next year things will be better! Next year!" It brought a wry smile to her still face.

There were many delays; some quite negligible; but when an axle developed a gaping crack, there was dismay. With the aid of fencing wire, a stout sapling, and strong hands, it was brought back to safety at least.

"These things, they say, are sent to try us," remarked Miles, biting hard on his pipe stem.

"Oo wants ter be tried?" was Sid's swift reply. No one answered as they set the animals in motion. They at least are refreshed, thought Maggie as she watched Miles and the young folk move away. As they travelled on, Maggie, alone on her heterogenous load, had no time to think.

Suddenly, loud coo-ees and shouting startled her out of her

quiet lethargy – Jinny had become separated from the others ahead. Missing!

"Of course it's Jinny."

"What happened?" she asked Guy, her voice husky with anticipatory, fearful thoughts, swift as the striking tongue of a serpent.

"It's Jinny! We've lost her! We've lost her!" Mary-Ann repeated the grim words as she rode with Guy towards Maggie. The child persisted hysterically until Guy shouted,

"Be quiet, for the love-o-Mike". Then he explained to his mother the reason for his sister's distracted cries.

In a frenzy of fear, the child turned her pony as if to return to the menacing gloom of the forest, shouting,

"I must find her!" but Guy caught her bridle, and Maggie persuaded her to dismount, and although greatly shocked herself, assumed an air of serenity. Taking Mary-Ann's hand, she said quietly,

"Come little one! We'll light a big bonfire and Jinny will see the smoke and soon she'll be with us again!"

Sidney ran from his bullocks. They were wise in their bovine stupidity. They would not move until they heard Sidney's harsh "hup hup" or the screaming whistle of the bullwhip. Maggie watched him mount Mary-Ann's pony and gallop after Guy. Suddenly, she saw the world about her with hate in her heart. For the branching trees became the clutching hands of an appalling enemy, reaching out for her loved daughter, Jinny; gay laughing Jinny.

All day Miles and the boys searched, calling, calling, and when they could no longer see, they returned, and spent an apprehensive, sleepless night, and Jinny alone in the forest! At first light they saddled their horses and set out again, but had scarcely penetrated the bush when they saw her advancing through the messmate, the mountain ash giants. The pony stepping carefully through the dense, low growing scrub sent a long 'hinny' to the other horses. Everyone shouted. Jinny was with them again!

"Things 'er pretty good now ain't they?" said Sidney with a wide grin.

"Let's be hurrying back," said Miles, and Guy said,

"You duffer, Jinny!" They lost no time returning to the camp. The strain was broken. Maggie and Mary-Ann embraced Jinny frantically and then, woman-like, Maggie set about preparing a much-delayed meal.

Standing at the fire, a sturdy, but unkempt little girl, she answered their questions. There were no recriminations. There had been too many tragedies of children lost in primeval bushlands.

"Go on Jinny, you're wrung our poor hearts. Be tellin' of your brave adventures" and Guy sitting on his heels at her feet in mock humility added, "an' tell us of the screamin' banshees." Then he rose and said more forcibly, "Think of the time we wasted to save you from 'em!" Laughter cured their tension.

"Be quiet!" said his father, but Jinny went on unheeding, breathlessly.

"When I found I was lost, after riding in circles for so long, I gathered some stringy bark and tied my pony to a sapling. Then I hid in a big hollow tree and before daylight I saddled up and just gave the pony his head. I should have done that yesterday." Then she 'broke' and cried in sudden reaction. Miles motioned for all to leave them as he drew her to him.

"There! There me darlin', you can't be havin' the wisdom of the ages an' you not so far off bein' a baby". He wiped her eyes and she smiled at him. So they ate and rested in utmost contentment.

Later, when all was ready to start off again, Miles gave dire warnings for future behaviour,

"Above all, keep together!" Each day he repeated the injunction and Guy irrepressibly quipped,

"Cripes! We'll call the run 'keep together' – when we find it," he added.

"If we ever DO," said little Mary-Ann. Miles looked down in

sudden sympathy at her pale little face.

"Yes! Me darlin', we'll find it. I know it's a long time and a long travellin' an' leppin' about for a little lass. To be sure an' it's yourself will be lovin' to be drawin' pictures of the grand things you'll see there, even prettier flowers than that." He took her little slate and smiled encouragingly at her childish efforts.

Two more weeks travelling with the little cavalcade pausing at times for the stock to feed, brought them almost to their journey's end. Then Mary-Ann became ill, so they made camp. The horses hobbled, were allowed to graze and logs were drawn around the fire. The days had lengthened and summer was approaching. Mary-Ann rather reluctantly, travelled on the spring cart with her mother. Forward without further incidents went the Fords and all their possessions.

CHAPTER 5

At last the odyssey was over. Out of the wildest country of their entire journey they crossed a bridge made of logs from fallen trees, to face a small, gently undulating and well-grassed flat between two rivers.

"There now! Will you just look at that," said Miles, slowly and solemnly. Ahead of them towered the mountains they had so often seen shining in the distance; a grand mountain, with the sunshine glittering as if it were a cap of diamonds it wore on its tiered summit. "It seems as if it had stored up all the snows of past winter and just for us to see its flaunting beauty. Bedad an' it has. It's just fantastic."

"Fantastic! Is that its name?" repeated Mary-Ann. They all looked down at the entranced face of the child and Maggie answered softly,

"Yes! That's its name to us, Mount Fantastic!" And for all the years ahead, that was their name for the most beautiful sight of their long travels.

"Yes, an' this is our run, right here. There's the miner's hut yonder that Joe Crow said would serve for a home awhile." Maggie looked aghast. A deserted hut of one small room! A family of five and a working lad! She shook her head and said emphatically,

"We'll camp as we've been doing along the tracks!"

Miles, watching her face, smiled faintly. Yonder was the teamster who had brought the bullock wagon ahead with their stores, so he rode off to speak to him. He left Maggie to organise to her liking. Thus, he knew, she would sooner orient herself, and only then would everything be right.

"Bedad an' she's a fine one, my Maggie. A man's just got to be going easy that' all," he muttered, as he cast his eyes around in utmost joy. This was their holding? Eight thousand acres of splendid land, eighteen miles from the nearest township, at the foot of a snow-topped mountain which fed the swift flowing rivers, and there all about them was the rainforest to conquer. When he returned to his family, he was highly delighted to listen to Maggie's decisive voice. He stood well back, listening...

"Come! Come!" she said swiftly. "Get the cart unloaded. Over on that rise is an ideal place for a home. If we place the tents along side that spreading red-gum tree, it'll protect us from the wind. That," pointing to the hut, "will do for a cowshed."

So, for some days they lived in their tents of bags and bark, but working together from dawn until darkness set in, Miles, Sid and Guy soon had saplings stripped and a store of bark, sand and pipe clay for the building of their house.

A week later they all stood happily around, as the framework, with its creamy shining laths was ready for the daub. Everyone helped and soon there it was, a fine house; bark roof, slab doors, and wattle and daub walls.

All very primitive, but Maggie's pride in her kitchen glowed in her face for all to see. The sun streamed into the wide doorway and lay like a golden pathway right to the huge cobblestone fireplace; cobbles brought from the creek in the gully.

Impulsively, she turned to her husband and said,

"It's so big. I'll be happy here. It's wonderful – earthen floor and all, and I like it just as it is. Certainly a big improvement on bag gunyahs!"

Miles smiled as he said facetiously, "Guy, Sidney and I dyed our hands to the bones to strip bark from those great trees to make this palatial home for you. And," he added with more intent, "it always appals me to be destroying these lovely trees; destruction in hours of a century of sunshine and life-giving earth. Yes! Maggie! Every time I strike a tree with my axe, I shudder, feeling that I am murdering a living object. Bedad perfection destroyed for man's advancement. However!" he laughed tersely, "Even feeling as I do, it seems to be the same, now and always. Sheets of bark for walls and roofs of huts, palings, fencing posts, firewood! We take an' use them all. At least!" he paused to tamp down his pipe, "I'm surely thankful."

"And so am I," Maggie said seriously. "This house, with bark walls and roof and sapling timber is a home. Even a palace isn't that, often."

Miles face lit with a delighted smile, as he replied, "Later, when we have cleared and fenced more paddocks to hold the stock and have sown more pastures, perhaps we'll build a more gracious one," and he looked around at the results of weeks of toil with pardonable pride, "in time."

Maggie interrupted him swiftly. "Time Miles! We have all the time we need. As long as we go along with it, our problems will solve themselves." He moved closer to her and taking her hand in his, said gently,

"You are resigned more to this isolated and not very cultured life and its problems, girl?"

"Problems! Problems!" There was a rush of feet; Guy had arrived in a state of commotion. They turned in swift alarm as the tall, slim boy threw himself on a form made of saplings against the wall.

He was pale and shivering as he repeated, "Problems we've got!"

Maggie, without speaking, turned to the fireplace and swung the crane to position the kettle over the flame. Miles said quietly, his keen eyes studying Guy's face,

"What's the trouble lad?"

"Those blasted dingoes!"

In gasping periods, the sorry story was told. The boys, Guy and Sidney, had left at daylight to trail cattle through the forest. So much was unfenced on the run that the cattle strayed and were difficult to muster.

"We were just on top of the high hill paddock and we saw the cattle down in the gully among the acacia and dogwood. We shouted to them and they moved to a grassy flat. We were riding the horses down the steep slope, when a pack of dingoes rushed the whole mob. There were so many, they looked like a run of yellow flame, with the sun on their backs. They're so disgustingly fat now, the brutes. The cattle huddled against a little hill when they couldn't run anymore. The big fat brindle steer – you remember him dad?"

"Yes son! Be tellin' of it!" Guy was almost in tears of anger.

"They… they got him down an' ate him while he was alive. Ough! How I hate those bleedin' brutes! Anyway, we drove them off with stock whips and brought the rest of the cattle back to the stockyards. We'll lose 'em all if we don't do something!" Tense and disturbed, Miles stood silent awhile.

"I know what we'll do. We'll go to the township next week and get some staghounds!"

"Staghounds! Oh! By Jingo! We'll scarify those yellow devils. When do we go?"

"We'll go tomorrow. Bedad! There's always something to plague a man! Dingoes eat our animals. Kangaroos, paddy-melons and then emus eat our crops. Wombats break our fences. Things happen, difficulties, hardships, and we must manage as best we can. Begorrah! I'm after wondering where it'll all end!" He paused and his face showed signs of the frustrations of the past. Then he shrugged his shoulders and said with force, "Dash it all, I dare say things will work out in time." They were all at loss for words and to turn aside the moment of troubled thought as he smiled as he said, "I'll read some Irish poetry to you tonight." Guy picked up his hat and having work to do, muttered as he walked to the door,

"Gran'pa would say 'goddlemighty' to that I'll be bound, an' so do I."

That night, by the pale light of tallow candles, which filled the room with murky fumes, Miles read his beloved Irish poems aloud, while the dingoes' howls in the near distance rang through the sharp night air, and Guy, dreaming of the future and the havoc he planned for those very brutes, heard his father's voice as but a dull droning.

"Poetry! Ach!"

The staghounds were brought to the holding and became a profitable investment. They diminished the size of the yellow packs.

"Yellow cowards!" Guy exclaimed in fury as he watched them slink into the distance at the sound of his hounds baying – but stock were still ravaged.

The days were busy ones. Cattle had to be trailed far into the forest and Miles and the lads had much difficulty in drafting their own branded ones from the numerous strays and wild cattle. Guy, separated from Miles and Sid, had to camp out one night and packs of dingoes howled around all night, despite the large fire, and 'all the dogs with the others'! Even with the kills by the hounds, there would be snarling packs of fifteen or twenty each morning at daylight, when he set out to round up the horses for the mustering. They would advance to within yards of him if the hounds were absent. Being an expert with the whip, he kept them at bay, seething with impotent rage with every lash. They were venturesome despite their cowardly natures.

Once, the lads had to camp in the forest. Tired after a long day's riding they had slept soundly and were chagrined to find their saddles and whips well chewed when they awoke. Poison baits? The wild dogs became alert to them. Afraid of the staghounds in daytime, they still killed at night. In a year's tally, over half of the drops of calves missing, killed by dingoes and, added to natural deaths, the returns were calamitous.

"I daresay we're lucky to get any young stock at all," said Guy.

"Yes," said Miles quietly, "but what's left will not pay our way I'm afraid."

He looked across at Maggie and noted her ageing head as she bent it low over a dish of dough she was kneading. Living conditions were deteriorating. The roads were impassable, being winter. Their bullocks were in poor condition on the snow-covered slopes.

"It'll cost fifteen pounds to get a bullock wagon load of supplies from the city, Maggie," he said. "Make up your order. We'll scrape up the money somehow. That last draft of cattle we sent down to the sales brought the bare pound a head after expenses were paid. Breeding cattle is the only possibility, even with all the killings. Things are not going to be easy until we can fence more land, or the prices rise and warmer weather comes. Most of our sheep are gone. Things seem to get progressively worse. There's not much we can do about it all really."

After a pause, Maggie said, "I took the box of butter to the township in front of the saddle again this week. Butter's two shillings a pound. Little enough! Still, it's something!" She stood beside Miles and looked up at his careworn face. She was calm in her strength of purpose and the needs of her people roused her to action. But it disturbed him. He took a deep breath as he turned away, saying,

"Maggie! This shouldn't be. This is a hard life for any woman, especially for you, brought up so differently."

They were completely still and silent awhile, then Maggie replied tersely,

"What can we do? We're all here, caught in a trap. This rainforest is ruling our lives!"

"Yes! Perhaps you're right. But changes are on the way!"

"What do you mean?" Maggie spoke in surprise.

He replied huskily, "There's been a deal of shouting an' cracking of whips along the tracks some distance from here. As I rode through the trees I met a bloke who was trudging to the new diggings. He told me there's a big rush on the way. The place is called Walhalla – Walhalla! The home of slain heroes' souls!" Miles looked very disconsolate as he said bitterly, "It'll be the end of this beautiful land!"

"Not on our run, surely?" she said, horrified.

"Yes!"

"Then stop them Miles. Stop them!" He shook his head.

"I might just as well try to stop that rushing creek in the gully. Perhaps some good will come of it."

She spoke bitterly, "You certainly can discipline yourself my dear!" He frowned as he replied,

"There's no jubilation in my heart when I think of all those people tearing up, violating the countryside. Gold! A lure it is!"

Thrusting his hands deep into his pockets, he walked slowly to the door. Standing under the lintel, his eyes stared grimly towards the dark mass of forest-clad hills. With a brief nod to Maggie, he left for the stables.

Some days later, she saw him standing motionless on the bank of the creek in the gully. He was there so long that her curiosity was aroused. She left her tasks and approached him. Deep in thought, he did not hear nor sense her standing by, still as the giant Blackwood tree beside him. She waited. Head bent back, she watched the flight of a flock of red mountain parrots. Then, the gang-tang of cockatoos sent their harsh call in passing. Still he lingered. The air was tangy with perfume of gum blossom and moist earth, and with a feeling of tranquillity she stepped silently to a mossy log and waited.

She heard him mutter, "Pipeclay shale, quartz! Be gosh!" Shaking his head, he studied an object in his hand. Turning slowly, he saw her there. His eyes opened in wide surprise. "Maggie! What brings you here?"

"Mere curiosity," she answered gaily. "I had to come just to see what was holding you!"

"This." He showed her a piece of quartz. "That speck is gold. I know there's been much gold found in yon mountains, but hoped there would be no alluvial gold here. I'm after bein' perturbed!"

"But why? If gold is found here it will solve our difficulties!"

"Nonsense. Are you thinking to have the prospectors almost at our back door? People staking claims, rushing pell-mell from one shisha no-good shaft, to dig another, then leaving the countryside a tortured mass of mullock hills? I know enough about gold to know also, that there's not the place to find it in payable quantities. This, the prospectors will not accept. I'll not be havin' my land ripped up, not if I can do anything about it. Say nothing of this, even to the family."

He dug a hole in the soft earth with the heel of his boot, stooped and inserted the piece of quartz. He covered it well and tramped down the soil. To Maggie's secret amusement, he took a grass-covered clod, placed it carefully and patted it down. With set mouth and hardened, slitted eyes he faced her.

"Let's be going back to the homestead."

Uttering very few words, they approached the house, but Miles turned off towards the stables. Maggie returned to her household tasks.

It was of little avail. Miners had been coming and going to the hills beyond the run for years and, like a recurring fever, the gold lust invaded men's minds, with its insidiously demanding, spasmodic urge.

Fortunately, no one discovered gold near the Ford home.

"Tis lucky we are," dryly commented Miles. "Gold! Confound it an' its doings. But..." he turned with a sudden humorous grin to Maggie, "I could be after doin' with some, all the same!"

Bob Vincent

CHAPTER 6

DESPITE THE MANY DIFFICULTIES, THE HOLDING HELD MANY pleasures for the young ones. There was tobogganing and sledging races on the snow slopes; hacks to be broken in to saddle and harness for the Indian market, bought cheaply and sold with small returns; black-berrying; fishing; swimming; and hunting for swan eggs which they made into prodigious omelettes. All contributed to enliven the isolated way of life. The men greatly improved the homestead; enlarging and whitening the wattle and daub or pise finish with fine pipe clay from the creek. They had even given it the name of Maggie's past home. 'Rock Allen' it became then and always.

Maggie though, was unpredictable. When troubles upset the routine of family life, she was the strength and binding for every eventuality. Then, when all was running smoothly, Maggie, with time to think, going about her various household activities, would become quiet and quieter, and Miles watched with wary eyes.

She was trimming the wicks of the oil lamps one morning as he entered the kitchen. He stood beside the mantle shelf, filling his pipe and telling her of farm matters. She did not seem to be listening. Suddenly she remarked wearily,

"Kerosene's low and we've used thee last of the tallow candles. After tonight, we'll have to talk by the firelight!" There was a hint of hardness in her voice.

The window was open and a sudden flurry of wind blew her hair awry. Impatiently she leaned and closed the window, then, after slowly washing her hands she commenced her butter-making, beating the thick yet obstinate cream with an awkward ladle made by herself from a piece of pine wood. Her silence was becoming oppressive to Miles, and he stepped across to her.

"Here! Give me a turn!" He held up the ladle, and examined it with speculative eyes. "Shame on me, eh wife?" he smiled down at her. "Never mind! Next year maybe, things will be better an' it's meself that will be after buying you the best churn that ever came to Gippsland if I have to carry it on me shoulders the whole eighteen miles from the town. Next year – maybe," and without thinking, as if to add emphasis to his wishful offer, he slapped the ladle heavily into the curdled cream and scattered the sour smelling stuff in creaming arcs about them. "There, me love, its rich rain we're getting!" he laughed.

But Maggie was exasperated as she looked around the be-spattered window and surroundings. This was the final match to her smouldering black mood. She stamped her foot at him in red-hot temper,

"Next year! Next year! I'm sick and tired of the very sound of the words. We should call this property 'Next Year!' Pah!" she glared at him with a convulsed face as she continued, "I daresay I'll still be trudging the rough tracks to the little shanty store to sell my eggs and butter for our necessities while you men are slaving your lives away up those dreadful hills in the thickest part of the bush country. Miles! Miles! Is it all worth the struggle?"

She plunged her hands into a pail of water on the table and rubbed them across her burning face. Miles watched in deep concern. He realised that she was going through one of her moods of deep depression. The monotonous round of back breaking tasks in the ill-equipped outback home; the lack of other women's company, and the absolute contrast between this and her former life all contributed, but as time went on the moods were less frequent. Grandfather often said,

"Faith an' begorrah, Maggie's no nagger. Y'wouldn't hear her whinging around a man's neck. A fine woman she is to be sure. She can crack hardy like a man." Miles remembered this with wry conviction, but he knew this was a severe mood and he realised that recent happenings had brought it about.

Fully recognising the events that had engendered Maggie's outburst, Miles realised as he had read in one of his few books, that "the most fruitful and natural exercise of our spirit, is conference." So, quietly and forcefully, he discussed matters from all angles, knowing well, that with her strength of character and fair-mindedness, she would eventually condition herself to their life as it had to be.

Then, he saddled his horse and rode to the far paddocks to check the stock. As he guided his mount through the silver tussocks, his thoughts were very earnest.

"Is it all worth the struggle?" Maggie's words recurred with the persistency of the beat of a trip-hammer. Many times he too had secretly wondered, "Is it?"

He tensed and felt dejected, but then only for a short space of time. He looked up at the mountain in the far distance. The stock was quietly grazing and he reined the horse to a standstill. There, with giant trees gently swaying and the noise of flowing waters mingling with animal and other sounds, a sense of freedom from the rest of the world helped to resolve his troubled thoughts. Only one subtle uneasiness remained as he thought of Maggie. He remembered how a few months past she had been seriously ill, desperately. In fact, it seemed that her life was ebbing. Only her recovery was of any importance to her family. The planning, the working and the teasing, every activity ceased.

It was a time of fear, of tension and silences. No drive!

A baby was born. It died. There were no questions for there were no answers. When Maggie recovered, it was as if everyone breathed again. To Miles, even the rustle of the forest trees became a mighty sound and all was still. Then, his whole being filled with thanksgiving. However, the bereaved mother expressed herself freely in her grief and exhaustion.

"So tiny, so perfect! And it didn't live. My little one! Had a doctor, a nurse, or even another woman been here to help you Miles, I would now be holding him in my arms. This dreadful marauding forest! Pitiless! Cruel. It's trying to destroy us. We should never have come here. Little Mary-Ann once said that it doesn't like us being here, and I reproved her for being fanciful. Now, I begin to think that children's eyes see clearer than ours. We must leave this rainforest." Miles, trying to cheer her said,

"What? Let it chase you out?" But it was not the time to be facetious. She repeated her tirade so often that one day he said brokenly, "My dear, he was my little son too". In a sudden realisation she looked at him, held out both hands and said,

"Yes! Yes! I'm sorry. Forgive me, I'm so tired."

Remembering so clearly, he gently shook the reins and rode briskly back to the homestead.

She was still in a state of tension but busy. He gently touched her shoulder and looked with utmost understanding into her face as she turned to him.

She spoke in husky tones, "I know I should not say these things, but so much has happened to us that it makes one wonder, why? At least. Depression has been driving me for days. It's like an ominous cloud that hovers until it insidiously thrusts itself into one's very soul, a cloying presence until something really happens, something frustrating or tragic! Then it holds and one's imagination does the rest."

He held her shoulders, to stop the trembling. "Say no more, girl. I know what's tearin' you apart. Too well I know." His face was pale and his clear-cut features sent Maggie's thoughts off on a tangent. It reminded her of the marble carvings in the English churchyard. It was just too much.

In a frenzy, she exclaimed, "Those little graves! All over this country they're dotted, our own small one amongst them! I keep thinking of that little mother out there. It breaks my heart." Maggie sat at the table and dropping her head on her arms, cried bitterly.

During the past week, a girl wife, living in a miner's shack, had died at childbirth and was buried with her babies in her arms…

Maggie exclaimed, "This cruel land! How many more must needlessly die in its taming? Sometimes I hate it so. Miles! Let us return to the Old Country back to my people, to home, to the small village with its ways of peace and completeness. Here, it's so crude, so lonely and sad. Is all its beauty worth its ruthlessness?"

Miles held her close and did not answer. Then they heard the sound of bells approaching, bullock bells; Maggie pushed him aside with a choking laugh.

"This will pass. Here come the others. The dinner's burnt and I'm being futile, so weak. Oh dear! I'm right now!"

Miles stooped over, and with what, upon closer inspection, they saw was a greasy blackened oven cloth, wiped her face. It streaked heavily, and tragedy turned into soul-cleansing laughter – and they faced life together again. But even moods could not shape their future.

1
2
3
GENERAL STORE
POST OFFICE
Port Albert
FISHERMANS PARADISE

CHAPTER 7

THE FOLLOWING YEAR, LATE SUMMER CAME WITH BLAZING SUNshine and blistering winds of great force, bushfire winds. Smoke and heat haze obliterated even the mountains.

"Anything can happen," said Miles as he stood in the doorway, and peered grimly toward the forest gloom. They were all tired, having taken turns in the moonlight all night, ploughing firebreaks with a single furrow mouldboard plough and the ancient horse, Paddy.

Returning to the boys as they ate their early meal, he said, "Saddle up and bring all the stock to the flat along the creek, as close to the homestead as possible." He went to the slip-rails and opening then, he hurried the lads away to the mustering.

It was scarcely daylight when the horizon became aflame. With Maggie, Jinny and Mary-Ann, Miles gathered all available sacks and, racing to the creek in the gully, they frenziedly soaked them all in the small puddles, all that remained of the once gurgling creek. Drought!

Grimly speechless, they watched the flames flying from tree to tree and coming nearer with the speed of a terrific wind. Birds were circling wildly. Dingoes, kangaroos, wallabies, even wombats, rushed frantically about. Flying squirrels, making queer noises like 'syrup, syrup' were so futile in their charging from limb to limb that they dropped tragically to the receiving fires beneath. And on came the flames.

Harassed and almost exhausted, Miles gave his family terse, clear-cut instructions. "When you boys return with the stock, we will stand well back out of the way." He then showed them the positions they were to take. "Then, if we work with these wet bags, and branches too, along the fire-break we'll try to burn back to the fire. Understand?"

"Yes! Yes!"

Forcing a gay smile, he said, "We'll all save the homestead." "Maybe!" he added silently.

Turning away from Maggie's searching gaze, as if to test the amount of saturation in the quickly drying sacks, he thought grimly,

"It's little chance we have of saving anything with this scorching wind, charged as it is with gas and flames." He sighed deeply and turned his reddened eyes towards the hell beyond. "If only Guy and Sid were here, the whole lot could go. Nothing is as precious as young lives."

Then he turned to the others with a stern look, and repeated his orders.

"We must all run to that dip in the gully and stand in the water with the wet bags over our heads, if the wind blows that way. Understand?"

They nodded silently. Maggie was moving like an automaton as they dragged heavy buckets of water from muddy holes, up the hard clay banks of the once flowing creek. They were haggard, burning in the awful heat, but quietly and efficiently preparing for the onslaught of the ghastly fire.

Suddenly a loud roar sounded. Then through what appeared to be a wall of fire galloped Guy, and ahead of him a mob of cattle, horses and bush animals, all fear maddened. Wild bulls from the mountains added to the panic and trampled the sheep, as they headed for the creek bed, and halted, eddying in a thundering melee. The firewall at their rear became a low grass fire, for nearer the house the timber had been cleared well. Still the red cloud advanced.

There appeared to be faint chance to save anything except their own lives. The cowshed burnt as matchwood, and was soon just a spread of white ash in an area of black.

They raced across the burned grass, beating with branches as the flames danced towards the house.

Although drought had left little to burn, fire just went before the wind in great clouds of gas and flame. It was like an uncontrollable beast approaching its prey. It locked its flaming tongue around the house. Lath and plaster was not such an easy victim as the tinder-dry bark of the cowshed. Branches and wet bags in the hands of frantically determined fighters brought a need of success.

Then, of a sudden, the wind dropped, and drops of rain fell like blessings on their poor burned faces. Soon it fell in torrents and they held up their heads, exultant, laughing hysterically. Thankful!

Their home stood. Part of it was burnt,

"But," said Maggie, "We still have a kitchen. We've much to be thankful for."

"We can sleep just anywhere so long as there's you and Dad, all of us – and a kitchen," added Guy, with a mocking grin. He looked around. "But cripes, where's Sid?"

They looked at the blackened horizon in consternation.

"Poor Sidney. Wherever can he be?" said Jinny. Guy said swiftly,

"He was riding after the stock with me until we got them through the timber to where the fossickers were working last year."

"Get your horse, Guy. We must find him, dead or alive," said his father.

Constantly, for three days and nights, with the help of many men from long distances away, they searched for Sid. Rain had washed the tracks. Carcasses of cattle, sheep, bush animals and those of the fine horses they had bred and 'gentled' for sale and export to the Indian market, were tragic guides. The ground was burnt to the sub-soil, and the heavy rain had washed the burnt grass to the cracked earth. Sun again hardened it. Sid had his dog with him. It never left his side for somehow he had a way with animals.

They found the dog, badly burnt, footsore and pitifully whining beside a small mullock hill some frustrated miner had left at a scrub-concealed shaft. But, where was Sid?

"Sidney, Sidney!" The men's immediate reaction to sighting the dog was to send the call in voices strained with undefined fearful imaginings.

"Sid…" and the little dog answered with weak, but joyful helpings. Avid for action with a likely reward, they tore away the Manuka scrub beside the mullock and there was the gaping mouth of a shaft.

With red eyes and swollen from their ordeal by fire, they peered into the gloom beneath. There on a rocky ledge, just awakening from a traumatic stupor, was Sidney! After a short time he answered their relieved greetings in a characteristic manner.

"I'm surely glad you found me. Did you bring any tucker?" he spoke weakly.

Immediately their compassionate feelings changed to laughter, which ceased in sudden concern when the weak voice said,

"My horse's there." They then saw the unfortunate horse further down, pathetically cramped amongst shale and wash-dirt. He turned his great expressive eyes upward as if imploring release.

Some of the men rushed away to a wagon, equipped with spades, picks and block and tackle, taking care to avoid the treacherous overgrowth which hid the numerous shafts. There were many in the locality. Rotting windlasses or crude huts were warnings. Some shafts were from six to a hundred feet in depth; some with narrow openings, others very wide. Fortunately, Sidney and his horse had crashed into a wide shallow one.

He was soon hauled to the surface and carried off on a bush stretcher. The horse was a different proposition. As many men had rallied to the search, there was sufficient aid, so they arranged to make a wide excavation, but it took more than a very full day to clear the rubble and gain a position for use of a block and tackle to raise the emaciated animal.

There were no bones broken and one searcher remarked, "They're tough young animals, both of 'em. They'll soon pull up," and the willing helpers nonchalantly dispersed.

Sidney and his horse recovered rapidly. "Good tucker, that's all we need," said the youth as he wolfed Maggie's home made bread and great chunks of farm beef.

The Rock Allen family had a considerable reaction to their ordeal as they took stock of the damages. Maggie, as usual in emergencies, rose to the occasion as she said laconically,

"It could have been worse. We're all alive. We have a cow to milk and poultry for eggs and killing."

"Yes! An' our big kitchen," repeated Mary-Ann.

"That's right," added Miles, "an' our axes are sharp as ever. Boys!! I daresay the first thing to do is to harness the bullocks that are left. Lucky we are to have a team still. We'll drag all the dead stock together and dispose of 'em."

Sidney grinned widely. "How're we gonna do that boss? Yer can't burn 'em. There's no stockin' around."

Just for a second, Miles paused, and then he said crisply, "It's a trick you've shown us, Lad!"

"Me boss?" he blinked with eyes like an owl's suddenly exposed to daylight. Miles continued, "We'll haul the carcasses to the deep shafts and dump them."

"Golly!" Sidney rubbed his head around from ear to ear with a grimy hand. "That so? Then I guess I'll be off an' yoke up Bluey an' Stumpy an' the two old polers. That oughta do, with Rudolph an' Nosey. Hup, Hup!" He jumped about excitedly and looked like an outsized frog as he bounded away, laughter following his fast disappearing bulky frame.

"I'll help him to gather up the tackle and ropes," said Guy and glad to be doing something definite again, he left the house whistling merrily.

Turning to Maggie, Miles remarked, "It's good to have some cheer around the place. When we finish with the work out there in a few days, we'll take those sharp axes I've mentioned an' be after stripping some bark and splitting timber back there on the run a few miles off, where the fires stopped. We'll build a temporary shelter alongside this kitchen. Soon you'll have a house again. Back where we started, we are!" he ended, somewhat dejectedly.

"Yes! Yes! Now! You just get along after that crazy Sidney, or he'll probably end up with the bullocks and carcases in some shaft!" Maggie spoke half-maliciously of set purpose. Miles relaxed as she continued, "Jinny and Mary-Ann will help me do some clearing up around here while you're away. Come, girls. We'll pick up the burn sticks." So, to hide the aversion she felt for all the disorder, she gallantly followed them outside to their tasks. For some time they gathered burnt things and stacked them ready for removal. Suddenly, Maggie realised that Mary-Ann was not with them. They had been so busy and happy to be making good headway, clearing away debris to speed the foundations of their new rooms, that they had not noticed the child leaving.

Mary-Ann was quite and fanciful. They were used to her slipping away to quiet places to play her games of fantasy. But, this time, their calls did not return the usual childish reply. Her mother decided she had made her escape from the ugly burn surroundings, and lured by a bright bird or flower, had wandered further than usual. They hurried to the slip-rails leading up to a steep hillside. Climbing, they called urgently and became alarmed.

At the summit of the hill, they paused and stared in disturbed silence. In the distance they saw a cart or jinker with two people waving strenuously. They watched and uttered sighs of relief, for, seated beside a big bearded man in the approaching vehicle, was Mary-Ann. Her face was bright as a sun-kissed sunflower, as she called to them in gay excitement. The horse halted and the driver shouted in a husky voice,

"Hey! Hey! Maggie! Here's your lost bush maiden!"

Momentarily, she was speechless. Mary-Ann sank back in the seat watching her somewhat fearfully, but Maggie's eyes were on the man's face as she exclaimed,

"Oh Joe!! Joe Crow! I'm so thankful to you! It's fine to see you again, after all this time, and you come as usual, with goodness in your stride. You knew it was our baby, Mary-Ann, you've found?"

Joe grinned happily. "Of course I knew this little one, and," he sprang on to the track still holding the reins, "is this tall golden haired one the plump little girl who used to bring the chips to make a scone fire?"

Jinny shyly advanced to shake hands, and Joe gave her a smacking kiss on the forehead.

"Jump up into the jinker lass. You drive this horse; he's gentle as a dove. Your Ma and I will walk up to the house. I've a lot to talk about."

But Maggie turned to the jinker and reaching up to Mary-Ann took her hand and held it firmly as she said,

"Why did you run away? You did, child, I know. No!" She held up an arresting hand as Mary-Ann attempted a denial. "You have been a very naughty girl." Maggie was unusually stern. "Tell me! Why?" Maggie looked severely at the child, "Mary-Ann! You deliberately left while Jinny and I were very busy, knowing that we would not notice and call you back. Why did you behave like a wild young paddy-melon?"

The child pressed her hand to her mouth as she recoiled further on the hard seat of the dog cart. Her eyes were wide open and beautifully shaped, yet had a defiant gleam as she replied,

"It's all so ugly now!" Her voice was shrill and she thrust her small hands forward, pointing at the burnt country. "I hate it, I do! Yes, truly, I hate it there. I don't like the black on my hands either, so I ran away." She was verging on hysteria.

Maggie held up a warning hand and spoke gently, quietly, yet firmly. "That's enough dear! Yes! It's all very unpleasant but soon those forest trees on yon hill will be covered with soft, young shoots and the black paddocks will look as if they're veiled in green. We all have eyes to see, Mary-Ann. You must learn not to run away from ugliness, but face it!"

"But Mummy! It all frightens me" said the child tearfully.

"No! You were just a little coward. To be afraid sometimes is natural, but to be a coward is wrong. Now! Off you go, and be sure to help Jinny unharness the horse when you get to the stockyards." Jinny raised the reins and the horse trotted smartly to the sliprails, then on to the track. Maggie turned to the waiting Joe, and talking together, they followed slowly. She looked harassed as she said,

"Mary-Ann has a fast growing habit of choosing the easy way, escaping from reality. So young too! Its character forming I'm afraid!"

Joe gave a short laugh as he said, "Mary-Ann will make her own way in life, and I assure you she'll get by. Now, don't be concerned. There's no need. Tell me, where's Miles? And how's my young friend Guy?"

By the time they reached the house or the remnants (and a sorry looking scene it was), Maggie had answered his many interested queries. He made no comment as he looked all about with his hawk-like eyes. She watched him as he hung his wide-brimmed hat on a six-inch nail driven into the wall near the kitchen door. Then he rubbed his hands over the flaking particles of scorched wood.

Grim-faced, they walked inside. Maggie made tea, and as she poured it, she heard whips cracking, and the familiar 'Hup! Hup! Gee-oup!' bullocky talk.

"Here are the men," she remarked as she glanced through the window. She opened it, and leaning forward watched intently. Looking most perplexed, she walked over to Joe at the table. He was steadily munching homemade bread and blackberry jam with very evident enjoyment. Her voice husky in surprise, she exclaimed, "those are not our teams. Jinny has stabled your horse and she and Mary-Ann are going across the house-yard to them. Loaded wagons? Timber? Yours Joe?" She moved the chair and sitting here, holding her hands until they whitened, she watched him with questioning eyes, waiting.

But the big man looked at her and a wide grin made his mouth look, as Guy had been heard to remark, 'like a torn pocket'. He continued spreading bread and jam, with assumed concentration. As she waited, her tired brain dwelt on all the happenings that had almost sapped their morale over the years, and she felt ashamed. She shook her head to clear the upsurge of tears when he said,

"You're not to be troubled Maggie. There's always tracks through the wild bush you know!" His words somehow gave her release and Joe listened in deep interest as she murmured,

"All day, my rebellious thoughts have been driving me mad. I was picking up pieces of our destroyed home and trying to be thankful for the little that was left, but at the back of it all, with every burnt stick I handled, was hate for this life. Where, I asked myself, will this dreadful, eternal battle elude us all? What is to become of my daughters? Are they to become old before they are young, working against setbacks like these? I was down in the depths."

"Perhaps it was self-pity. I see I know. Joe! I lost my grip, and now, you are here; already I'm better. The sun shines. I feel like a lost one coming out of an evil cave into the bright daylight. You are so welcome Joe, and here I am drooling!"

Joe put down his cup. "My goodness Maggie, it's glad I am to be here. Never before have I seen you like this, but you had much to make you down-in-the-mouth."

Then Maggie laughed with trembling spontaneity. "Down in the mouth! Oh dear! I must not do it again. So doleful! I'm sorry." She ended seriously as she brushed back her hair with a well shaped yet toil worn hand and took the teapot from the great hob to refill Joe's cup. Then they heard a clump of heavy boots and men's voices mingled with laughter of young folk as they paused at the doorway. She hastened to place cups ready for them. Joe rose swiftly. The door opened and Miles, his face showing his pleasure as shaking hands, they stood a moment in silence.

"Joe! My very good friend!" was all Miles could say, but Joe's booming voice filled the smoke stained kitchen with its hearty tones.

"Well! Well! Here I am. To be sure. I've been having you on my mind this many a day and meaning to come along an' see how you're making out on the run. Too bad it took a bush fire to bring me. Too bad! Thought I'd bring along a load of timber at the same time!"

Miles shook his head in protest. "Joe! You must let me make things clear to you. I'm nearly broke! This is almost the last straw! This beastly fire! That's the bare bones of truth. I can't hope to pay for that timber. You must turn your men and oxen back with it! I appreciate…"

But he paused as Joe caught him by the shoulder and said softly, "Come outside. We'll talk things over. I never could bear to make a bargain between four walls and with folks looking on. I talk to the trees y'know and, holy mackerel! Man! They calm me soul an' square me judgement. Yes, out here in the great gum forest!"

Miles smiled in spite of himself, but made no more to go outside. "Yes, Yes! Joe, but..." with a wide grin, Joe interrupted, saying,

"One fool at a time Man! An' as I'm the biggest, well, I talk first. See 'ere now. Nothing in this world is free. They tell us it is, but Man! You've got to use effort even to walk up to a blue gum to lean again' it an' speculate, ain't that effort. Power of yer legs, you're using up?"

"Don't split hairs Joe!" said Miles with evident impatience, to hide his feelings.

Joe, sensing Miles' nervous reaction, hastened to explain.

"Right! I'll come to the point! Over on that load of timber is my nephew. He's pored over books until he's as lean as a starved cockerel. I want you to help him here until he's fit an' strong. He aims to be a lawyer, but now he's a mightily sick boy. So I told my sister that I shall toughen him up or kill him off." Smiling broadly, he went on to say, "That's why I brought the timber. There's another load on the way with stores also. So you see, I intend, with your permission to help rebuild this house and add an extra room for Charles Day, that's his name."

Miles stared at him, lost for words. Then he laughed shortly. "To be sure Joe, you would talk your way out of hell to make a heaven for others. All I can say is thank you".

Joe turned the subject to his nephew. "This Charles! Just leave him alone for a few days and you'll find he's quite a good lad, quiet and dependable. I don't think he likes work, mind you. But keep him at it. No matter if he dislikes it, so long as he does it," said Joe, winking wickedly across the room at Maggie.

"Can he ride?" she asked to show interest. Joe grunted,

"Ride? He can ride a horse with a bushy tail. That's his limit."

"A bushy tale? What…"

"He means a branch Maggie," said Miles with a laugh. "He'll soon learn our way Joe."

"You'll have the lad then?" Joe looked from one to another. They both agreed, "Then it's a bargain."

"You still love bargains Joe."

"My word! Now, I guess we have things to do. We must unload that timber first!" Joe strode across the room and took his hat as he opened the door. Jinny, Mary-Ann, Guy, Sid, Charles Day and Joe's two bullock drivers were standing outside talking.

"Miles! Tell them tea is getting cold," urged his wife. She watched them and turning away thought, "Surely this will be the end of all the unfortunate things that beset us!" The others trooped into the kitchen and Miles and Joe left them to their sounds and silences of talk and food.

While Maggie was providing the hungry young folk with a meal, she was in a reflective mood. She heard the noisy clatter of voices and the clink of dishes as a bothersome accompaniment to her thoughts. She crossed to the doorway, dodging the haphazard placing of chairs and elbows, and paused under the lintel. With creased forehead and contracted eyes, she studied the scene across the house-yard. Standing by one of the wagons were Miles and Joe Crow, their heads and hands moving vigorously as they talked.

She caught her breath as she thought in silent, solemn curiosity, "I wonder what ideas Joe is expounding to my poor Miles. Joe's a sound man and a specially good friend to us, I admit, but," she decided somewhat grudgingly, "he's good to Joe, himself too!"

She frowned at her involuntary disloyalty and, as if to rid herself of such uncertainty, she resolved the situation in her own way. "Joe is essentially and solely a man of action. He plans well ahead, and always appears successful. Miles plans with dreams. Although he too is a man of action, he fails so often. Little he dreams of failure, unfortunately!"

Sighing softly she turned back to her world. With a swift glance about her, she noticed that the girls, Jinny and Mary-Ann, were very happily engrossed in the presence of extra people, laughing at the exchange of humorous anecdotes. It was amusing to her to watch Mary-Ann trying to enact the pose of a great lady and her courtiers from one of her storybooks.

Maggie felt fleeting regret. "Perhaps I was harsh with her for leaving the burnt place today. I, myself, have often wished to escape from this forest country. We judge others by our experience of life, I daresay."

Determinedly, she took the big black kettle from the crane and, filling the awkward tin dish with hot water, she set about the washing up. This was no time to be moralising.

Bullock team with wagon

CHAPTER 8

THE NEXT WEEKS WERE VERY BUSY ONES. JOE CROW AND HIS men stayed a while. Great sheets of bark had been stripped and used for temporary sleeping quarters for everyone – bark huts! Steady progress was made with the re-building of the homestead. This time, sawn timber was used instead of the slithery, sappy saplings. It was a well-built commodious home with a large living room, the fireplace of which occupied one end wall in its entirety.

Sidney had remarked when the last cobbles had been smoothed over, "The Saints preserve us! It'll take a bloomin' tree for a back-log. Are ya goin' to roast a bullock?"

"No lad," returned Miles, "When you hoist up some more boulders from the creek, we'll make some dashed fine hobs and you can sit on them 'an roast your knees, maybe!"

"Golly!" said the big lad as he stared open-mouthed at the great cavity. "We'll just about have to train old Paddy to put on the back logs!"

"Get along wid ye!" answered Miles in exaggerated brogue, at his pleasure in the approaching end of their labours. Joe Crow's mill-sawn timber was offered as a gift. But Miles meticulously made up his accounts and gave Joe an I.O.U., which the latter had to reluctantly accept in view of Miles ferocious insistence. "A man's got a right to his independence you know!"

And Joe agreed. However, he gained the point that he and his men would assist in the work. "Great Scot alive Man! Aren't you going to make a man of my weakling nephew Charles?"

So they agreed. "Quits!" and the matter lay.

So, Phoenix-like, the Ford's homestead rose from the ashes. It was a large house, spacious enough for all Maggie's needs as a mother and housewife.

One of Joe's teamsters gave Miles a very comfortable chair. "Made it out of a beer barrel, I did, and I even made the polish for the wood from 'black-boy' leaves, cushioned it with good Lincoln wool too! Just you sit in it Boss!" He spoke with some embarrassment, yet evident pride in his handy work.

Miles sat in it and sighed luxuriously. "It's a chair fit for a king bedad," he replied, his pleasure showing in his merry eyes. It was a treasured possession; his very own down through all the years; a token of good fellowship and a masterpiece, in its own way, of a bushman's craft.

For some days before Joe and his teamsters returned to the saw-milling area, he and Miles rode around the run for hours. "An eight-thousand acre run takes a deal of ridin' the pigskin," Joe was heard to comment. When they returned to the homestead, Maggie could not fail to notice their avoidance of her intent gaze. She was intrigued but silent. She could wait.

Life eventually settled into its familiar routine. The girls were set their daily lessons, but the call of the outdoors almost defeated Maggie's efforts. Within a few months Joe returned. Again, he and Miles rode the run, and talked to early morning hours. He left shortly, and nothing said!

One morning, Maggie was trimming a newly pressed cheese, when Miles entered the kitchen and stood watching her. The morning sun was thrusting through the window, touching and burnishing the neat coil of hair piled high on her head. He was so quiet that at last, she looked up at him with questioning eyes. Completing her work, she patted the big cheese in satisfaction. He leaned forward and breathed in the rich odour.

"Ah! In faith it's going to be good eatin' to be sure."

She watched him, and with inscrutable face she said, "What is it you have to tell me?"

He grinned rather uncertainly. "Maggie! It's a shrewd one you are!"

"It's well I know the signs," she returned in assuming nonchalance.

He laughed as he linked his arm in hers and firmly, yet gently led her to her chair at the table, saying, "Sit ye' down my dear. I came to talk with you while the others are away in the paddocks. In very faith, there's so much blather with the young folk around the place that we two never seem to have a word alone. Getting too silent you are. You think but don't talk. It's no good between man and wife."

"Miles! You talk and I shall listen, for I know you have much on your mind. I've been thinking it's time you should be telling me what you and Joe are planning!"

"Planning...? Yes! Yes! But I'm all confused – yes! Confused!"

"Then," Maggie laughed with gentle sarcasm, "maybe you should bring out your Irish poems. Do you remember how you could fold away your problems and read them to us? After a time your thoughts cleared and doubts settled like dregs in the coffee pot? Then you made your decisions!"

He took her hand and held it. "Yes! I well remember too, begorrah, that a certain fine lady opened a door an' peeped into the future to give me a lead!"

"Now! What have you to tell me?" She looked at the room, frowning at the thought of her unfinished tasks.

"Don't hurry me, Girl! Just listen. Somehow, with all the doings and turmoil we have lost touch. We go no with our work, seeing the waiting tasks ahead an' just take each other for granted."

"It's just being there, knowing it. That's the secret!"

"Anyway, overwork, tiredness or family shouldn't be rubbing off the magic of our essential selves. You've disappeared into your silence. Come back my dear!"

With a gentle hand he smoothed back his thinning hair and softly she said,

"If it's trouble we're well seasoned, we can face it. Confusion? Well! I daresay we'll untangle it with time and patience!"

He rose. "Lets get along outside. We'll ride around the property while I tell you of the way of things as Joe and I see it all. I'll get the spring cart and you get your sunbonnet!"

He crossed to the fireplace, took the big black kettle, filled it, hung it on the crane, and swung it over the fire, which he stoked back safely. With a merry grin he looked at her saying, "There now! The youngsters can be after getting a meal for themselves for a change!"

So Maggie was soon sitting on the board seat of the cart and away they went, bumping over the rough uneven ground. As they reached a far hilltop, Miles reined in the horses. The wide expanse before them was dominated by their Mount Fantastic.

The scorched trees were covered in the re-growth of soft green foliage. Swaying gently in the breeze, they gave the forest a weird illusion of myriads of ballerinas bowing, pirouetting and retreating. In the brilliant sunshine, the whole panorama was breathtakingly splendid.

They sat in silence. There were not words enough, for somehow this was a supreme moment. With gentleness he touched Maggie's shoulder,

"Here is the answer, God! Everything has yearned or hungered for seems to reach out from all that beauty!"

But she was silent, just watching the trees that covered the mountains, rimmed the steep escarpments and deepened into the gorges to be lost in the darkness. The rustle of wind gradually increased and the trees went into an increasingly mad frolic.

She moved at last. "Turn away!" So they drove beside the creek in a lofty valley, and, wile they determinedly talked of mundane things, the wispy mists veiled the high places.

The spirit of the immensity around them stayed and the frets of every-day living just vanished. But it was not to last, for Miles said abruptly, yet reluctant to introduce the subject,

"We have a decision to make. I must surrender the lease of the run. Perhaps I should never have taken such acreage. It appears that my ideas are larger than my capacity. Distances, pests, stock thieves, stock that gets lost in the forests, or mate up with wild ones, fires, floods. They're all too much for a little Irishman like me," he needed with a wry grin. "We lose most of our cattle each year, sheep too. At least we fatten the dingoes an' crows in very faith. So! That's my confusion Girl!" He looked into her face and said, "Maybe we should return to the city".

She lifted her eyes to the towering mountains. "No! No!" Then with a sudden realisation, she knew she loved this land and here she would stay. And Miles!

He laughed in joy. "Such a woman!" Now the way was clear. "Bedad, we'll select land too. Maybe we have pre-emptive rights. Maybe!"

Miles lost no time in selecting his, "Three hundred an' twenty acres of this fine land, begad, right here at the homestead. Now I see my way clear. Now I'll work every acre of this precious soil. Yes! Every ounce of it shall be payin' its way. Now, we can fence the paddocks an' the botheration of all the wild things of the forest will be over.

Post an' rails in the far paddocks. Yes! We'll mortice the posts from the best trees an' shoulder in the rails. Begad! They'll be here in a hundred years time for our grandchildren to see how we could work, we the ones from yonder countries. Imagine that now!" He looked around at Maggie, his face serious at the prospect of the years ahead.

Maggie was watching him with love-filled eyes, and she nodded gaily, "It's the Irish of him we're after hearin', he's so happy, excitement is possessing him!"

Miles stared at her, momentarily abashed at her imitation of his accent. Then he laughed with them. Still elated. "You're right Girl, an' it's excitement you should have too. You with a selection of three hundred an' twenty acres of your own. A foine block it is, right against mine. The only thing that riles me is that you're not old enough to select a block too, young feller," to Guy later.

"I'll soon get over that, Dad. Joe told me he has dummied some blocks and will let me take over one of them, right on the run here."

"Dummied? No bloomin' fear! You'll get your land in your own good name. I'll have no dummying, no truck with it. Confound it! Now get off with ye an' help Sid move some bits of furniture. It's your mother who's busy preparing a room for your grandfather. He's got a block alongside ours' so is coming any day now."

"Is he going to live here always?"

"Sure an' he is. Sure an' it's glad I am," returned young Guy with a pert grin at his father.

"Get off you young spalpeen" exclaimed Miles, a semblance of anger tightening his lean face, at his mocking son.

In a short time Donald Ford made the long trip from the city with all his possessions and received a heart-warming welcome from his people at Rock Allen.

Donald Ford, a man of many parts, as shrewd as any bush lawyer, active, honest as the noon sunshine. Aggressively honest. When Miles told his father of Joe's land dealings, the old man stood in the doorway, hat in hand, ready to catch his horse to ride around their survey pegs and plan with his son how best to work the smaller holding. He was impatient to be off, but the story appalled the staunch old man. He moved nearer and stood resting on the table as he studied Mile's face.

"Is this true?"

Miles nodded. Grandfather shook a wrinkled finger emphatically. With eyes flashing under his unkempt beetling brows and looking like a fierce mastiff he exclaimed,

"Trust that land hungry old shyster of a saw miller to find a way of getting what he wants by hook or by crook! Hm! Well! We'll be afta waitin' to see what comes of it. Bad cess to him an' all," and he thumped one fist into the other in dire disgust, and stamped away outside.

In the earliest days of selecting Rock Allen the Ford home became as Mile's father irately expressed it, "Alive, too much alive. Great Scott! This place is just a dumping ground for all those dang fools of selectors. Just look at that conglomeration. Drays, spring carts, wagons, even sledges! This place is like Kirk's Bazaar. How you bloomin' well stand it I don't know!"

The old man shook his head and uttered around, "C'ark," a noise resembling nothing so much as the 'squark' of a debilitated crow.

His son looked around and realised that it was a very apt description, "Kirks Bazaar."

"Still," he said, "Dad, you must realise that, as this is the only clear acreage for miles around, and as the selector's blocks are well into the forest, there are no tracks. How far, I ask you, could a wagon go once it crossed yon plateau? It will not be long before all these vehicles and possessions will be on the new selections."

"Hmm. Well! I grant you that" returned old Donald Ford. "They are all so danged sure that it's the best soil they have ever seen that they're working like tigers. They expect to be independent in less than not time. Gad. P'raps they will too, if they keep on grafting."

"Yes. They seem to be a bunch of honest, hard-working folk. These working bees help. They get together some how to help each other. Guy, Charles and Sid have taken bullocks and pulleys today to one block. It's just a turn of the wheel. We might be glad of their help one of these days."

His father grunted. "Why? I don't know. Haven't you enough for them to do here, with Maggie wanting benches for all those milk dishes, instead of breaking her back bending over boxes?"

Miles turned swiftly, "By George, you're right dad. Come on, you and I will be at it now!"

With a secret smile he led the way to the wood heap to get the axes. So Maggie's big flat dishes soon had a rough bench to rest their weight upon, in a slab-built bark-roofed dairy. This she painstakingly whitewashed while the men were out in the paddocks ploughing, clearing, fencing, grubbing stumps or sowing crops. Little she saw of them except when they came to meals. But Grandfather! Wiry old grandfather, active and often irritable, yet was of much help to her. He was like an old warhorse scenting battle. Born on a small farm in Ireland, he had migrated to the Colony in search of gold.

"Only gold I got was sunshine," he declared. So like thousands of others with little money in their pockets, he had gravitated to the city. There, he married and brought up his family on the wages he received as a driver for a big flour-milling firm. He was happy enough, for handling horses was his delight. He had the urge for land and his chance came to get back to the country when Miles suggested he select for some of the run.

"All you need to do is potter. We'll do the work," he had told his father.

"Potter be danged! I'm good for a dashed long sight o' years yet.

It's not puttering around I'll be doing. To be sure, it's break in your horses, I will, and fence with any fella. Aye, an' split palings too." And indeed, the tall, lean man was as good as his word.

Charles Day stayed with them for some months and it was 'Old Donald's' secret delight to take him out for a day's light work. 'Light Work'. The lad with his background of little exercise and much study was, according to Donald,

"Green as yon sapling. He'll toughen". He said tersely, with set purpose and wicked gleam in his old eyes. Toughen, he certainly did. But the first stages were torture for the 'poor lad, and him so gentle and quiet' protested Maggie.

"Gad, we'll be after makin' a man of him in this grand country to be sure," said Grandfather as he rubbed his gnarled old hands together in impish glee.

CHAPTER 9

Although Miles Ford was elated about his family selections, he had an unspoken regret for the great expanse of country he had of necessity relinquished. Tentatively he had envisaged the thought of moving to another district to again lease a large run, but the new law which said that squatting leases were not to be renewed settled that idea, and selectors were gathering throughout the forest country.

At Rock Allen there was so much to be done in the more intense farming, that in the dawn to sundown routine, Miles speedily lost the yearning for land beyond the limit of his sight. Winter came with wind-blown flurries of snow which speedily and silently whitened the rainforest country. All so inexpressibly lovely! But to the new settlers, most trying, for it hampered their progress.

Grandfather grumbled. "It's perishin' cold an' makes a man achin' hungry. In fact, its needle cold on my old joints, an' there's more rain than forest!"

"Maybe you should go back to the city Dad," said Miles quietly, as they sloshed through deep mud with Guy and Sidney to the barn.

"Stuff an' nonsense," was the old man's irate reply, and he was very quiet as they oiled and mended harnesses and overhauled the rolling stock.

The long winter with its enforced idleness in most spheres frayed tempers. "Confound it all!" Miles muttered, his lean face, crinkling in frustration, looked like dry unoiled leather.

At last! One morning Guy burst into the kitchen greatly excited, calling, "Come and see. The clouds have lifted from the mountains and the sky is all clear. No wind either." Everyone left the breakfast table to hurry to the porch outside.

"See our mountain! Mount Fantastic," added Mary-Ann as she ran to the garden gate in a merry dance. "It's all gold." Indeed it was, for sun gleamed over the heights, gliding the tiers of snow tipped hills, rippling like liquid gold down to the darkness of the gorges.

"A taste of glory it is in faith," said Grandfather as, standing on the doorstep, he thrust his beaky face over Miles' shoulder. "Come on boys. Let's saddle up. The rain's gone, the mists are clearing and if the wind doesn't spring up from the wrong direction to bring them back we'll have…"

But Maggie interrupted her husband's hopeful words with, "Look! Look up there on the brow of the hill. Someone's coming."

Miles turned his gaze. "Great Scott alive. However did they get through all the mud an' slush in this weather? Sheer madness to even try!" They all watched intent and puzzled, speculatively, like an audience waiting for the actors to play their parts and unfold the plot! Steadily and slowly the strangers approached. A spring cart driven by a woman with a child beside her, followed by two horsemen, their mounts slithering down the track toward the sliprails.

Miles, with a slow grin spreading over his face remarked, "It looks as if we're to have another addition to our Kirk's Bazaar!"

Grandfather peered even more intently through his busy, overgrown eyebrows and watching him, Jinny thought, "He looks just like our little terrier, he's so alert", and put her hand over her mouth to hide a sudden mirth. Maggie went quietly back to the kitchen, and the only near sound was a clink of dishes and the stoking of fires.

She called, "Miles! The poor souls will be drenched and freezing. Bring them inside here, the kettles boiling,"

Simultaneously, the men moved to the house-yard gate. Guy opened it and beckoned to the stranger. But the small cavalcade halted and the people looked down uncertainly.

Grandfather was muttering softly, "Them horses. Livin' hat racks I call 'em." Then he said aloud, somewhat viciously for he had interest only in the animals, "Come along! Come along! Get up to the house, and unharness those poor brutes. Starving they are. Get them to the stables. God-a-mighty! What a way to have your horses!"

Trying to smooth the rough reception, Miles smiled as he repeated, "Yes, come along to the house. It's welcome you are." But the woman sat there on a high seat appearing tired to the point of exhaustion as she looked apathetically at the child beside her. The horse appeared as if it would willingly have stood there, head almost touching the ground, until the crack of doom.

Guy solved the situation as he walked to the animal's head saying, "I'll lead him." So everyone went back, and paused at the small gate right opposite the kitchen door, where Maggie and the girls were waiting taut and expectant.

At last the woman moved and spoke. "This child is too weak to walk."

"Give her to me," said Guy unhesitating. He sprang on the step of the cart and took the small child in his arm, lowered himself gently to the ground and walked into the house.

The child stirred, turned as if to gather warmth from his young body. Guy looked at the pale little face. "Poor kid!" he muttered, and somehow without realising what he was doing, he held her closer, and then pressed his face to hers – in all the pity of his young manhood. Colouring deeply, he pushed his way though the doorway and placed the child beside the big fireplace. "There you are. I'll send the mother in to you." The little one stirred.

"She's not my mother," she said faintly.

Guy was not listening. He hurried away.

There was a murmur of pity when Maggie took hold of the child's scarred blue hands to warm them. Her mouth set. The woman and the two men came in and huddled around the big fire at the side of the colonial oven.

Soon they were warm and fed. The family stood by curiously, although Miles suggested they employ themselves somewhere. Old Donald sat back on the slab bench, looking sternly around. Maggie poured a cup of tea for him, and then sat beside him waiting. No child was going to be ill-treated without her knowing the reason why. She studied the woman's face. Surely such a woman would not be the culprit. She looked kind, in spite of her exhausted state. The men? They appeared to be decent, hard working.

"Father and son," she surmised. Then she crossed to the child and exclaimed as she started to undress her, "Shall we bath her? She's so chilled!"

The strange woman looked at her gratefully. "That is what she needs, but please be careful."

The child, warming, said with much spirit, "I'm clean enough. Don't need a bath. Take me back to our wagon," she begged, as she looked fearfully about the strange surroundings.

Soothingly the woman spoke, telling her she would not leave her. "These are good people," she whispered.

So Jinny and Mary-Ann, wide-eyed and silent, brought the big tub to the fireside and proceeded to pour the buckets of water into it. Then they stood by aghast as the few clothes were taken off and the child moaned.

"Look at this," said the woman as she revealed partly healed weals on the tender young back. The men gasped and turned away.

"What houndish beast has done this?" exploded Grandfather as they left the room.

"Time for explanations later," said Miles succinctly, without even a backward glance at the newcomers.

The sun had vanished, the mountains were enveloped in misty clouds and rain was again dripping form the eaves and sad-looking trees in the distance, when the men returned to the house.

The child slept soundly in the barrel chair beside the fire. Maggie and her visitor, Patience, were busy with the dinner preparations. Miles glanced with satisfaction at the long table ready for the extra people. The strangers, Gerrard Treen and his son Rhys, with appreciative gleaming eyes looked at the plates of conventional outback fare being carried to each place.

Roast beef, juicy, rare or crisped, flanked by great floury browned potatoes, mashed swede, turnips with their tops cut fine for greens and pumpkin, all with the golden butter shining through the curling steam – and they certainly were hungry!

"Fall to, folks," said Miles genial as everyone was seated.

"What about a blessin?" said Grandfather, and Maggie glancing around the table, thought,

"I'm glad to have these people here. It's a fine way to start a friendship with Grandfather's blessin'"

All the same, there was a constraint in the conversation as they ate. Miles alone knew anything of the people before their arrival at Rock Allen for he and Gerrard had a previous exchange of views. They all ate with enjoyment and Sidney, finishing the last infinite morsel of suet dumpling and treacle sauce, looked across at Jinny with a wide grin as he said,

"Good tucker like this'll stick to my ribs while I'm breaking in the mealy-nose colt for Charlie ere' to ride."

He rose as if to leave the table and Miles, secretly amused at the implied thrust at Charles, the city lad's poor horsemanship said,

"Sit ye down. It's too wet to be riding the young horse. You can hear our guests' story with us, right Gerrard?"

"Yes," said the other, and his wife added,

"And will you tell them about the little one also?"

Gerrard rose, pushed his chair close to the table and walked across to the fire to look down at the sleeping child. "How is she Patience?" he said as he straightened his back.

"She's sleeping naturally at last, a deep contented sleep, it seems to me. Such kindness!" Turning to the others, he outstretched his hands in a somewhat theatrical movement, yet with utmost sincerity and as he moved toward Maggie, he said simply, "I do thank you."

There they were, all eager to hear the account of the new farmers doings – the Fords, Miles, Maggie, Guy, Jinny and Mary-Ann, Grandfather, and with eyes and mouth wide open, Sidney the hired hand, and a little aloof and self-contained, Charles Day, the law student, rapidly regaining health in the life of the high country. He was, however, just as intrigued as the others.

Taking his seat again at the table, Gerrard Treen spoke with a quaint inflexion of Welsh. "As you probably have noticed, we're from Wales, a tough and to us at times, a hungry country, but our country even though we left it, and still love the memories there. We had a little money and thinking of a wider future for our son, we came to this land of opportunity. Two years we were in the Western District and much experience we gained, and," his round cheerful face creased in a rueful grin, "We certainly paid for it. You see? Our little store of money went one way; we went the other. But we were happy enough really, as we lived through the busy years. Eventually, we decided to select land in the high country, this wet country. The soil appears to be rich. We hope it will prove so. We selected two blocks, Patience and I, which gives us six hundred and forty acres. We realise that the price is high in hard work and courage to go on."

He squared his broad shoulders. "You see, we have never owned land. We rented. That's unsatisfactory. We cleaned acres and acres with our bullock team and the forest devil, all for another man. So, we cut our losses and left. We had a team of sixteen bullocks, a tilted wagon, cattle, a few horses and a spring cart. I built a house on the wagon. Three rooms, a kitchen and two bedrooms. We furnished them with our bits and pieces and there we were, ah! Right!"

"One fine hot day we set out." He turned to Miles with a slow shake of the head. "Right did I say? The devil must have tucked his tail in that cosy little house we were so proud of. Trouble! All the way it's been with us. However, here we are, with Old Nick about to cut his capers and be off, we hope!"

Gerrard paused and rubbed tobacco slowly with the heel of his thumb into the other hand, then pressed it into the bowl of an old black pipe. Patience said, as she watched him with gentle tolerance, "My husband never talks until that pipe is full and drawing, like silk through your hands."

So they waited. A butcherbird sent a shrill message from a near stringy-bark. Rain gently dripped from the eaves and weak sunshine gleamed through the mottled sky.

"Listen!" whispered Jinny to Charles Day. "That's a sign the weather is clearing. We'll be able to go for a ride this afternoon." Charles smiled dubiously.

Mary-Ann scowled and Grandfather, looking pained, croaked, "Easy there, don't spoil a good man's story."

So, with the clouds of smoke almost veiling his face, the 'good man' continued. "To make my story shorter, I'll tally off our troubles. First, the bullocks were not in very good fettle and grass was scarce. They got weaker."

"Couldn't you moonlight 'em Mister?" put in Sid.

Gerrard grinned. "To tell you the truth I was often tempted to do so. Once we had a lucky break. The bullocks broke a fence trying to eat along the line of it and they all got into a fine pasture and had a good feed..."

Sid chuckled. "Accidentally done on purpose. I'll bet me Blucher boots!"

But the other, disregarding the subtle indictment, went on with his story. "Before the moon came out and I found them, I was about to say. Later two bullocks got down and we had to kill them. They were too weak to go further. So we decided to make camp."

"Old Nick made you pay for the moonlighting, huh?" Sid was really enjoying himself. Again Gerrard ignored him. Miles's mouth set in annoyance.

"It was beside a river. Rhys went and bought hay from a farmer. I made a yard for the fowls and let them out of the crate. That night it rained; the river rose and drowned them all. Three ducks were left, so that was a lucky thing for us. Patience was happy, I assure you. We stayed there about a month. The grass grew rapidly and the stock thrived. We picked up our traps and on we moved. With the humid weather, much of our food had to be thrown away.

Patience said, "Give me a bag of flour, a bag of potatoes and kerosene. We'll manage."

"An' manage we did. We broke the axle, the wind blew the cover off the wagon, but we got it back, torn certainly. However, we patched it up with old dungarees and moleskins. You see, we have learned to be expendable. Nothing stopped us for long."

Gerrard paused, walked across to the window and smiled as he looked at Jinny.

"That butcherbird of yours gave a wrong forecast. Look. It's raining again, sleety rain too." She hung her head shyly. Guy brought some messmate and banksia logs, and soon the great fireplace glowed with splendid coals as Gerrard continued with the account of his family's odyssey from the Western District.

"Approaching Melbourne, we made camp on the roadside. I surmised, we were a day's journey away; bullock wagon pace," he added with a wide grin spreading from mouth almost ear to ear, "So I rode ahead to advise the city fathers of our long, slow-moving cavalcade, and to discover the most suitable day and time for us to travel through the city as there was no detour."

"This is preposterous,"said the Mayor as he bristled with civic dignity. "Pass through this city with a herd of cattle! It's out of all reason. Absolutely. Man! You just go back to where you came from and stay there!"

Gerrard paused to puff at his pipe while the others watched in silent expectation. Continuing quietly as he held his pipe in a balancing motion of his broad hand, he looked around and stood erect, with his chest forward in imitation of the self-important Mayor and his tirade. "Ridiculous! You certainly will not be permitted to bring a herd of cattle, a mob of sheep, a stupid house on wheels and," he puffed in outraged pride, "To say nothing of a sixteen teal bullock wagon."

"There! There!" agreed his councillors.

"Go back to where you came from," said they Mayor again.

"There! There!" again said his men.

Gerrard gave such a realistic, humorous recital of the meeting that everyone laughed. "The Mayor expanded his chest and tried to look even more important than he felt, which was rather a difficult process really."

"So," said he. I did likewise. I looked him in the eyes and said, "Mister! You have to live. I have to live. Everybody has to eat. All I want is for you to set me on the path to help you and the people in your city to eat. I have land waiting to be cleared, to grow grass and fodder to feed my cattle and to produce beef and butter. I'm only a little man in the scheme of things, but as you know, many bees make a hive. There will be more selectors coming to you soon with the same request. There's much more country being opened up in yonder mountains."

There was a twinkle in the ponderous Mayor's eye when he said, "Mr. Treen. Bring your cavalcade, it is our wish that you produce and bring food to the people in this city." So we smiled at each other, then, they came two days hence, a bullock wagon drawn by sixteen huge bullocks. A spring cart driven by a woman and a herd of cattle driven by a mere boy, a long drawn out procession! It could only pass through when the streets were deserted. They mayor insisted that it must be arranged secretly.

Like flame along a well-saturated oil wick, somehow the story spread. "The night we arrived at the outskirts of the city, the crowd met us even there. As we moved slowly along, it grew into a mob. The cattle which were so quiet, so used to the gentle handling and living of the past months, were terrified. They milled around and then went berserk. When daylight came, they were scattered far and wide over the highways and by-ways. Two days it took us to gather them together again."

"How did you manage with the bullocks and wagon?" Guy queried.

Rhys, the son, a lad of nineteen, took up the story. "Oh! They were too quiet to stampede. Dad and I had to go after the cattle and so we had to promote a new driver." He turned to his mother with a gay laugh. "Only a new chum, but Dad said, "Needs must when the devil drives," and he ordered Ma from the spring cart and there she was, a bullocky."

"Yes," said Patience, "And the devil certainly did drive those bullocks, he also got into me I'm sure. I was so mad at everything; I sent them on and nearly lassoed every bystander along the way as trying to crack the whip. It paid though. They soon gave way. I guess it was a sight worth seeing, a bedraggled woman nearly trying herself in a bundle with a knotted bull-whip, walking beside sixteen oxen drawing a big tilted wagon, and an old horse hitched to that, drawing a spring cart loaded well over the wheels."

Gerrard and Rhys watched her in sudden deep interest. As she paused, Rhys said, "Go on Ma. Tell 'em the rest of the story."

Patience looked around in sharp realisation of being the centre of attention. She was a shy woman. Self-consciously she pushed her hair behind her ears and rubbed her hands over her flushed cheeks. Gerrard went to knock the ashes out of his pipe on the hob of the fireplace.

She whispered, "Shall I tell you about the little one? You remember, we decided she's to be ours?"

"Yes! Yes! It's the right thing to do," he said.

Patience spoke softly as she turned to her listeners. "All that day I travelled on the road. I camped beside the fast running creek towards sundown, unyoked the bullocks and fed them and the horse. Then I filled my billycan at the creek and climbed into the wagon kitchen to get myself some food. I was tired, so I decided to rest on my bed awhile. I noticed it was more untidy that usual. I drew back the coverlet and there, coiled up, white and shivering like a frightened ill-used puppy, was a little girl. So thin she was, that she scarcely made a rise in the bed, so pitiable that, shocked and surprised as I was, I could not speak." Patience's eyes filled with tears. She could not even then speak for a while.

Then Maggie said softly as if knowing out of her own humanity just what the answer should be. "And what did you do Patience?"

"I gathered her up in my arms and loved her. The poor lass was so frightened she lay there without unflexing one muscle. I asked no questions. Quickly I made a fire and then I warmed her with stones dropped into my billycan of hot water and wrapped in flannel. I gave her warm milk. Then, when I had my tea, I got into bed with her and held her close. All this, and scarcely a word spoken. At last, she relaxed and slept. Love was unknown to her, I'm sure."

Looking around, Gerrard and Rhys saw questions in everyone's eyes. Patience stood over the fire to push aside some coals, then looked at her husband and shook her head. He understood. She had her say.

He turned to them with hands outspread and said, "Who she is or where she came from we know no more than you. We do know that she ran away in terror, such terror and treatment that no child should ever know."

There was little of interest or detail that Gerrard could tell of the child who had stowed away in their wagon. "When we questioned her, she trembled and said in great distress,

"Don't send me away, please," she pleaded, "Those terrible people will claim me again. My father in England sends them money. Hide me. Hide me. I'll be so good." She wouldn't even say her name. So we hushed her, said we would keep her safe and we've named her Rebecca. She has a pitiful bundle tied in an old frock, a few papers and trinkets which we will not even touch, and she has closed her mind to the past. Apparently."

"The story might be told some day. If not, then we remain content to leave it just there where the small one wishes it to be. She has her life ahead which we'll make as happy as we can. She will be our daughter."

Old Donald rose, thrusting out his long arms as if to defy any contradictions.

"Let any varmint say one word outa place to this little stowaway an' it's me that'll know the reason why. Too colonial right I will. Them that harm the little ones should be flogged. Yes! Well an' truly flogged. It's a flippin' crime!" He paused for breath, then added in broken tones, "The pity of it!" With a deep grunt, he took his hat from the stool where he had mistakenly sat on it, pushed it on his head almost to his ears, and in the potent silence of the room, he strode outside.

There was nothing to be said, and in a short time, Gerrard and

Rhys rode back to their wagon. Patience was persuaded to remain at Rock Allen with Rebecca.

The next day, not a cloud scudded across the mountaintop to shadow its snowy crown. Underfoot conditions were deplorable. The high slopes had murky sludge and barely a blade of grass emerged to supply the needs of the wandering stock, the lost herds of cattle. At daylight, a loud continuous uproar aroused Miles. Springing from his bed, he opened the window to look towards the mountains. Dressing hastily, he ran to the gunroom and then woke Guy and Charles. Across the paddocks, the confusion of sound grew in volume, and simultaneously a mob of wild cattle, a bellowing melee, broke through the hazy distance.

"The scrubbers from the bush! Quick lads! Sidney!" he shouted. They gathered cartridges and loaded guns. "Go for your lives. Those brutes'll soon be through the belt of timber an' nothin'll stop them, not even fences or sheds," Miles shouted desperately.

Everyone, even Maggie, Patience and Jinny rushed outside, armed and ready to shoot. "Shoot the old bulls first," called Donald as he ran puffing, amongst gasping, his trousers hitched with one brace and one arm in his sleeve. "Them varmints do the damage, 'specially the old bulls." He gave Charles a sudden push. "Go on boy! Get yer eyes on the sights. Don't stand an' wait for a ride on that Satan's horns!"

Caught in the mesh of a conflicting net of events, Charles was momentarily static. Reacting involuntarily to the old man's call, he put the gun to his shoulder, fired and more to his own surprise than anyone's, he shot the 'most rampaging varmint of 'em all.

"Gad! He'll be a good country lad in no time now, too right he will," said the approving old man later. Sidney shot the next beast. Eventually the mob turned tail and fled, bellowing furiously and tossing clods of earth over their bony backs. Many were shot.

"After all this," said Guy, "there'll be plenty of meat to salt down or smoke. Grilled steak, too! Good?"

"Blimey! We'll be havin' corn junk for weeks ahead now I guess!"

"If you don't like that Sid, there are always spuds," returned Guy with a merry wink to Charles, who was watching and listening as they walked slowly to the house, their heavy blucher boots squelching into the watery boggy earth.

Intrigued, Charles, looking across at Guy, remarked, "You appear to find nothing to fault in this back country way of life?"

"You're certainly right. It's all I ask for. Everything! Making a farm, breeding good stock, clearing immense trees, growing crops and grasses, gentling brumbies. Everything!"

The youth stood erect, and then waved his hands all about in circular movements as if to take the whole world in his vision of the future.

"It's a wonderful challenge. Even the conflict! You see, Charles, everything's fighting us; the elements, trees and scrub animals, even the soil. We're just little humans against virgin country, but it's great."

"Man against primeval nature, and you're exhilarated by it all," added Charles.

"Yes, and like my father, I hate to drive a saw through a living tree. It's a strange thing though." He paused awhile thoughtfully.

"There really are so many things not in my law books to learn alongside a mountain and a rainforest."

Each busy with his own thoughts, no-one spoke until they reached the kitchen door. Then, almost as of one mind, they turned and looked across the paddocks at the gruesome heaps of slain cattle, then back at each other and nodded in friendly fashion as Sidney said,

"I reckon we're quits. The city feller did as well as us bumpkins."

Somehow, in his rather dull brain, he realised that they had all reacted as a team in an emergency. Laughing together they clapped each other's shoulders, and went on their way. Breakfast was especially good. They looked across the table at the little girl, Rebecca, and tried to make her speak to them. No. But she had slept well through the night, and her sharp little face relaxed as she scissored her fingers through the fur of the possum skin rug around her.

Sometimes, she spasmodically clutched the strands and shrank back into the chair. So, at a sign from Patience, everyone ignored her presence. She slept again, and was carried back to her bed.

Gerrard and Rhys returned from their wagon, where they had spent the night, and as they drank their tea, Gerrard said, "We must push on today. The weather looks more promising."

"Yes," said Miles, "but there is no hope of driving a wagon over this sodden country, or even riding a horse any distance."

Gerrard looked very disconsolate. He said glumly, "As I told you last night when we arrived at the slip-rails, our wagon's bogged back there on the track some miles away. I made a yard for the stock and our home's on that wagon, so we'll all go now!"

Maggie stared at him as she rose from the table and said urgently, "You can never be thinking of taking that child to camp up there in her condition. Why! A chill now would kill that little thing!"

Maggie, watching Gerrard's face change in a moment of indecision, repeated her protest. "You surely do not mean to take Rebecca back to the frozen hillside. Leave her here with us." She turned to Patience with gentle insistence. "My dear, you really must see the necessity of staying here with the child. Her well-being is the main issue at present, and..." she added persuasively, "it's such a long time since I've spoken with another woman, of women's interests."

Gerrard looked infinitely more cheerful so Patience, undecided, knew he was pleased. But she was drawn both ways.

Miles solved the problem. "Can you ride, Patience?"

"Yes." She looked quizzically at her menfolk, and Rhys laughed heartedly as he said,

"Ma rides three ways. Up, on, off! You understand? She's from a city. Dad taught her to milk a cow, but, put her on a horse an' you'll just never forget the sight!"

With quiet, amused sounds about her she looked confused as she remarked, "Maybe I shall improve," and joined in with the kindly laughter.

"That settles it then," said Miles. "You stay here and Guy, Sid and I will go to the camp with Gerrard and Rhys. Perhaps we will move that wagon."

"It's an awful mess," Gerrard explained, "bogged to the axles."

"Then," said Miles, going to the mantle-shelf for his pipe, "the best thing to do is to get on the track. Saddle up boys," he said to Guy and Sidney. "The days are short an' we sure need all of 'em."

However, the lads stayed for more tea. Jinny sitting quietly by, touched her grandfather's arm, "Are you going with them?"

Old Donald passed his cup to be refilled, saying as he took it, "I hope there's still some tea with a bit of colour in it. That was like dish water. Humph! Water bewitched an' tea begrudged."

"I'll make a fresh brew just for you," she replied, and whisked away with a swing, like a sprightly young wagtail flitting from one insect to another. "This should improve his humour," she thought, as she watched him vigorously stirring the tea nearly out of the cup.

He sipped it slowly and then, with an explosive breath he exclaimed, "Ah'h! You brew good tea Lass, God's blessin' on yer soul. Put the teapot on the hob. I might want another cup." She knew the wily old man was just tantalising her, and turning back to him, she repeated her question. "I heard you the first time young lady. Of course I'm not going up yon hill. A bloke needs webfeet to be goin' out this weather. I'll be keepin' the fire warm!"

"Then," she said swiftly, "I can ride your hack?"

"Oh! Dash me buttons! Take the horse an' ride him hard. He's getting too spry with not enough work. Watch out for the water-channels as he jumps, or you'll go right over his head if you don't stick to the pic-skin!"

Mary-Ann's shrill voice came across the room. "It's Charles who takes the headers. He's an awful horseman. I saw him go right over old paddy's head."

"Be quiet, you nasty little beast!" hissed Jinny. "Come on Charles, we'll round up the horses."

So hand in hand they walked up to the yard to the harness shed for bridles. Sidney, watching her with smouldering animosity, deposited his cup with a heavy thud, stepped over the form at the back of the table and, without a word, left the house.

Maggie had seen the young people's exit with some dismay. Grandfather, nursing his teacup with both hands, missed nothing. As she took his cup he patted her arm saying gruffly,

"Don't peer into the future, lass. Let the young people be; let 'em be. You can't see the wind weather it blows hot or cold. All you can do is feel. You warm up or strip off. See? Watch the clouds. They come, they go. That's the measure of life too."

With clouded eyes she looked down at the old man sitting there with the set gaze of one who contemplates the mystery of life in its very existence. He started as she said,

"You noticed something Grandfather?" For a moment there was silence. She continued, "You're so wise, but dear man, I fear the future."

"Let things bride Maggie, that's best." And grinning in a somewhat impish effort to lighten her mood, he added, "Bedad! I must be getting some wood for your bakin'." Crossing to the wood-heap he muttered, "Lads and lasses. Dash it all! That's where all the trouble in the world starts. In faith, it's good to be old!"

When Miles, Guy and Sidney arrived with the Treen's at their camp, the cattle were milling frantically, bellowing to the resounding echoes from the hills. Gerrard and Rhys hastened to open the roughly constructed fence. The hungry animals stamped into the bushland, and although they found only silver tussocks and sparse native grasses, devoured them rapaciously.

Miles inspected the stockyards and turned aside to Gerrard saying, "The cattle could very easily break out of here at night an' its goodbye you'll be afta sayin' to them!"

"Yes! Yes! I see what you mean. This's a wild country. We'll make a dogleg fence and wire it well. The country will be kinder to you than humans, for there are horse thieves and they certainly enjoy beef steaks!"

"Yes! Yes! I understand. Wild country holds men of all kinds," commented Gerrard. "But horse thieves! Imagine that!"

A grim smile hovered around Miles' mobile mouth, like the wings of a questing bee, as he watched the other's mystified face.

"Fact!" he said crisply.

"But how do they dispose of the animals? The owners would recognise their own brands."

"That's the thieves' least concern. They over-brand, mutilate, or leave the brands and sell quickly over the borders from mountain hideouts! Good money!"

"Then I see that Rhys and I must take turns to guard the stock at night until the weather takes up and we can move on. Our selection is through trackless forest country, and as we need to hack our way, there's too much to do. It's a long time we'll be travelling to arrive." Then he said humorously, "If we do the nearest job, the far one will come nearer. So let's strengthen the fences here!"

With the Ford men's help, this was soon done.

The next day, Gerrard and Rhys packed swags and set out with packhorses to pull out trees with their strongest bullocks.

Through days of rain, wind, sleet and snow, then periodic brilliant sunshine, with the men working from dawn to dark, the track to the Treen's selection was almost cleared. It was, as Sidney declared, 'tough goin'. Huge trees had to be felled; dense scrub cut, burnt or pulled away by the bullocks; beautiful bushland, of necessity, swept away. But there were thousands of acres around that track, and ahead was the ultimate of the Treens – their very own plot of land; their future; their chance to cry 'Eureka'.

For the last few miles Gerrard and Rhys worked alone, for the other men who came to help had their own selections to clear. The September winds had dried the surface of the waterlogged earth so Gerrard could bring his wagon home as far into the forest as the track allowed; then the whole cavalcade, and Patience and Rebecca, were once again part of the scheme of things. Each week the two men picked up their swags and turned their faces to the task of clearing the over-growth of lichened scrub, tree ferns, bracken entangled with dodder, ancient of still green, withes of clematis, and various species of mosses and other primitive plants. Overhead, forest gums an sassafras almost hid the sky. At noon they paused for lunch.

"Hungry Rhys?" asked his father, as he watched the boy unpacking their dinner.

"Hungry? I could eat an ox!"

"Well there's plenty to eat here. Mum sees to that. Bread, corn junk and tea. No treacle, thank goodness! I hate the beastly stuff!"

Gerrard smiled. "When all the food in the wagon's finished, we must live off the land. I'm told there's splendid honey in those yellow box trees, an' we'll not starve. No more treacle either!"

At last they arrived! After some searching, they found their survey pegs, almost hidden in the luxuriant undergrowth, and followed the sub-division lines.

"Soon," Gerrard remarked, "more land-hungry folk will be selecting in this vicinity, so it's best we know our own fencing lines."

But Rhys was not within hearing of his father's prediction. He was standing with his head back, listening intently. Then he forced his way down a steep incline to disappear temporarily. Almost immediately he called in high-pitched tones,

"Come down here. There's a little creek. Fish galore!"

Gerrard hurried down, shouting, "Within our lines too. Good! Good!" and hands on hips he looked around in great satisfaction as he said huskily, "Boy, It's a fine heritage you'll be building. There's no tradition in this land similar to that of centuries of great deeds, tragedies, works of art and literature, as in the old world. But there's a silent grandeur and hope, hope of increasing greatness, and a potential richness." Gerrard's short rotund figure had a sudden dignity as his eyes hazed, lost in a grand vision of the future. Momentarily the subtle charm of the wilderness and mystic loneliness of his environment possessed him. With a slow smile, he turned, picked up his axe, saying, "Come along. There's much bark to be stripped for the buildings." The spell was broken and with squared shoulders the intrepid Welsh Neo-Australians set about their self-appointed tasks.

Of Rebecca's past, the Treens learned no more. She strongly refused to tell them her real name. "I like 'Becky' best," was her invariable reply. She became part of the family and the life of the forest and quickly accustomed herself to its ways. She was an avid reader and delighted the Treens with her reading aloud as Patience kneaded bread or did her mending, and the men greased harness on wet days.

One day Patience said, "Maggie told me that the earliest settler built a church, a big bark-roofed, bark-walled building with, of all things, a huge open fireplace extending the width of an end wall. Once a month, people travel long distances and meet there on Sundays, bringing their dinners. As the minister preaches, dinners sizzle at the big fire. They have morning service, then dinner, then afterwards the adults talk and the children play in the bush when it's fine and indoors when it's wet. Then, there's an afternoon service, tea and back to their homes. Some travel on sledges as the hills are too steep, others on horseback, in carts or in bullock drays or spring carts."

"So long as we gather together, the ways are immaterial," commented Gerrard with satisfaction. "I shall look forward to these church days. For the women there must be a great release from constant rounds of housework, meals and butter making."

"Butter! They make it and shape it an place it in shelved boxes, then with these on the saddle or sledge, they take it to the nearest township."

"How will I take mine?" asked Patience with a quirk of her lips. "Not on horseback, I'm sure."

Gerrard replied, "Eggs and butter help to pay off the holdings, so I daresay you and I can get to the market in the bullock dray – one day in the far future."

"I should like that," said Patience, "But I would much prefer to travel on my old spring cart," she added, with a quiet smile brightening her serious face.

Tarra Valley Park

CHAPTER 10

THE WEEKS WERE AS DAYS, THE YEARS AS MONTHS, FOR LIFE WAS so busy that the forest settlers did not notice the steady progress of time – and the once lonely, isolated run as Miles took it up, had become a close knit farming community with all the human virtues and defects.

Along the rich river flats the timber was cleared. It had been a colossal undertaking; slow work for men who started out with only their hands, willing hands and great hearts, to make a living for themselves and a future for their families. Giant stumps stood out in cleared paddocks like mourners in a vast unreal parade.

Sunburnt grasses or green crops waned and danced around them. The great mountains in the background looked down in all their majesty, snow-capped and gleaming. Protective armies or disapproving critics?

Bark huts gave way to skillion cottages and these in time, to larger, more aesthetic homes. The settlers and their families were allied with the elements, for the rich mountain soil was the arbiter of their lives. In the long winters, snow covered the tracks and flooded creeks, and rivers enclosed them. The children knew no other life. Summer was a reward, a glory of richness and beauty.

Cool green valleys were shaded by huge tree ferns and towering trees; birds, flowers, scented shrubs, must and wattles clustered below. Wild fruits and berries flourished, there for the seeking and taking. In the cold sparkling rivers and creeks, black fish abounded. No one went hungry, either bodily or aesthetically.

Old Donald, still, in his own words 'wiry as a cat's sinew' looked around at the wonderful growth of grass and shook his head. "Hm! Rolling fat cattle and not a decent tree left on some of the codger's places. Sheer vandals, that's what they are, no soul."

"Yes Grandfather! But their bank accounts look much healthier," said Guy.

Grandfather scowled. "Yes, they'll probably be the richest folk under the sod, if that's satisfaction, and their tombstones are the dead stumps on their properties, hundreds of 'em."

"Oh you are a disgruntled old man today. What's eating into you?" asked Guy.

"Och! I don't rightly know. I've been riding around the countryside an' scarcely can I see a fine tree except on the track. Maybe it's the years playing up with me. I'm just sad. What's that you're saying boy?" Guy hoping to divert him waved a letter. He stood awhile in an almost regal pose, holding it high in the air and his grandfather eyed him keenly as he said with a certain grim facetiousness,

"Why do you point that flippin' thing to the sky as if you were old Croesus' messenger presenting gifts to the Oracles?"

Guy's eyes opened in puzzled surprise as he said, "My goodness Grandfather! You've been reading that ancient history book again. Sometimes I wonder which world you live in, this one, or that of the times they call B.C." Then laughed mirthfully. "Come back old timer, we want you right here." Old Donald glared at him, momentarily at a loss for words. Guy, sensing some confusion in his manner, said hastily as he passed the offending missive across, "It's a letter from Joe. Joe Crow."

"Begosh! Is that so? What does the old shyster say?"

"He's coming over from the saw-mill, and you're to be ready to try to take him down at dribbage."

"I'll jolly well take him down a few pegs on the board."

Grandfather gloated happily at the very idea. Together they stood looking around, and then Donald studied Guy as he stood beside him, straight and supple as sapling, with his lean and freckled fine-boned face, beaky nose and sandy hair still giving him the keen fox-like look he had as a small boy. There was also the inquiring glance, just as when he had queried Joe Crow's enigmatic dealings at Kirk's Bazaar. At eighteen, he greatly resembled his father and old Donald also.

"Come on! Let's get back to the house. I must find the cribbage board," said he, hastily. Guy agreed, and affectionately patting his Grandfather's shoulders, they walked together to the kitchen of the homestead.

Jinny was alone and busy, sewing at Maggie's still gleaming-white table. Her eyes widened as Grandfather told of Joe's coming. Then she said happily,

"Yes, and Charles is coming too. We're going to the dance in the bush school, and the Treen's are bringing Rebecca over."

"Oh, no they're not," said Guy swiftly. "I'm going for her right now. So long." He stood under the lintel then returned to touch Jinny's sewing. "What's this yellow stuff?" he teased.

"It's my frock! Water-waved silk too!" and she held it against her slim form and waltzed around the table.

Grandfather clasped his hands. "My, oh my! You'll be the prettiest lass at the dance, I'm sure, with that golden hair an' those big, big eyes. So, Charles is coming? Now just why?" he asked, with his usual wry grin wrinkling his leathery face.

"How do you know?"

"Yes! Go on Jinny, how do you know?" Guy forced the issue. But Jinny walked slowly up to her Grandfather and, kissing the top of his head, said softly,

"You guess!"

"I'll tell," said Guy, winking provocatively, knowing full well of Charles' letters and those his sister wrote when everyone was away and the house was silent.

But Jinny held a threatening finger at him. "If you don't be careful Guy, I'll tell something I know!" and she turned in sudden alarm as he caught her and threatened to toss her hair. "No! No! Please don't," she cried. "It took me hours to make those roll curls," and she whispered, "Rebecca's dress is here. Rhys left it today."

Grandfather heard. "What? Is that lass going dancing too? Too young, too young!"

"Oh Grandad, you're old fashioned. Becky is nearly fifteen and she's the best dancer in the hills," said Guy.

"All right, don't scowl at me lad. I'll agree. I'll agree! Arrah! I think it's best I go and look our for old Joe, or you youngster's will ride roughshod over me," and he fumbled under the chair for his hat.

"Wait, Grandfather! I'm coming too," said Jinny. "I'll saddle your horse when I catch mine. I promised to meet them," she said quietly.

With a mocking laugh, Guy turned to go but with a final quip, "Now that Charles has passed most examinations and is nearly a lawyer, he should be too busy to visit the back-blocks. So make the best of your time, Jinny!"

"Don't say such things, Guy," protested Jinny, blushing furiously. Then the door opened and Sid stood there.

Sid had developed into a very large person, very fleshy, slow moving, yet strong and willing, still curious. He leaned forward, his head turning from one to the other.

"What's that yer saying to 'er, Guy?" He had really overheard. With an easy nonchalance, Guy told him of Charles' visit, and then went outside towards his horse, already saddled.

"What's that Charlie fellow comin' 'ere for? City coves like 'im ain't any use 'ere." Then he looked at Jinny and slowly the truth of the matter entered his brain. "Charles and Jinny! Oh, no!"

His face seemed to swell and become dusky red. Into his eyes, his little eyes which almost disappeared in the flesh around them, came a baleful light. He turned and walked through the open doorway, muttering,

"So them letters were from him. Should've known, I should!"

Jinny held her breath. She rushed to the window and watched him stride away with heavy tread and clenched fists. "Oh, Grandfather!" she turned and went across to him. "That Sid. He's so cross these days. He was always so good tempered. He's changed and I don't understand."

"What does he say to you Lass?"

"Nothing! Oh, just nothing. He looks at me, as if he wants to talk, but he only says something cross or grunts. It's strange," and Jinny frowned as she picked up pins and threads of cotton from the floor.

Grandfather shook his head slowly as he spoke. "Where are your Mother and Dad?"

"They went down to the creek. The black fish are biting so Dad persuaded Mother to go with him for a while."

"H'm! Well, get the horse Jinny. I'll be with you at the stables in ten minutes."

Jinny closed her workbox with a firm snap and carefully gathered her sewing into its right folds. Smiling across at him, as walking towards the door, he paused; leaning with two hands on the rounded edge of an old bentwood, chair, she said with barely concealed excitement,

"My pony is hard to catch. She's so mischievous, she dodges behind the clump of Manuka and then wades into the little billabong down by the creek!"

"Then, my dear, get after her on my old hack with the stock

whip. Just crack it at her heels. She'll soon gallop to the stable yard. Now, be off girl, or old Joe will be here before we reach the plateau. Nice welcome that is!" and he hurried away, his long, somewhat bandy legs, looking like a pair of pincers, against the late sun.

It took Jinny a few minutes to clear up her sewing and leave the table free. The kitchen, apart from the occasional crackling of the fire and the louder tick of the old Ansonia clock, was unusually quiet. Suddenly Sid again appeared at the door. He stood there, just looking. So long he remained silent, that Jinny had a queer prickling feeling, 'all over the top of my head', she said later, and she spoke somewhat impatiently.

"What do you want, Sid? I'm in an awful hurry. Don't just stand there!"

But his frame edged towards her. Suddenly, for the first time in her life, she was afraid. He looked different, his lips were drawn back over his strong white teeth and his eyes appeared as two dark black spots, shining like the berries of the nightshade, yet alive.

She moved away, but said kindly, "Don't look at me like that, Sid. What's wrong? Let's talk about it, but do hurry as Grandfather and I are going to meet Joe Crow and Charles!"

Sid shook her fiercely. "Him! He ain't getting' you. I want ya! I'm going to have ya! Ever since I came here I've bin waitin' for ya' to grow up. See? I'll – I'll kill him before he can have ya! Mind. I'm..." he took her by the shoulders, "I'm a better man than that."

Then came footsteps, quick, light footsteps up the path toward the kitchen door, and Maggie's voice, "Jinny! Hurry! Grandfather's waiting, the horses are at the stable gates."

She paused at the doorway. Sid turned and, head down, brushed past her. Glancing back at Jinny as he paused under the lintel, he scowled fiercely. For a few seconds the two stood wise-eyed, dismayed. Then Jinny told Maggie of his behaviour. She leaned her head against her shoulder and cried softly, more from fright than anything else.

"Oh Mother! I was so relieved when I heard your voice. That Sid was terrible, he's in a raging temper."

"Hush my dear!" said Maggie soothingly. "We'll talk about it later. Get into your skirt and we'll help you saddle the horses. Grandfather sent me. He saw Sid coming towards the house. See? I'm out of breath too. I ran from the gully." Maggie's face was pale, her lips set firmly.

Wiping her eyes Jinny said, "The kettle's boiling, Mother. Have a cup of tea. I won't be a minute," and gathering up her sewing regardless of its crushing she ran from the room.

"What now?" muttered Maggie. "So it's come to a head. Grandfather and I thought things would pass over. I couldn't believe it of that slow-moving Sid. Oh dear! What will we do?"

Then Miles came into the kitchen, and, putting his basket of fish on the table, he turned and noticed her perturbed air. Miles knew there was something very wrong as Maggie's composure was not easily shaken.

"It's Jinny? Sid?"

"Yes!"

He shook his head, "Come on, girl, let's clean this fish for dinner. Let things be until Jinny leaves."

Maggie just had to speak, and told him quietly, briefly. He was furiously angry, but controlled. "We must not have disturbances while Joe is here, then I'll fix things."

Jinny, much subdued, entered the kitchen. Head held high, she was resolved not to cry again. "Come on Mother! You said you would help me saddle up. I'm still going with Grandfather to meet Joe and Charles. He wants me to be his girl, and now I know that's just what I want to be. Sid has made things clear for me!" She looked at them, expecting opposition. "They think I'm just a child," she thought, but with serious faces they studied their fast growing-up daughter, and said no more about Sidney.

"Come on darling," said Maggie, and Jinny, the tension eased, caught her mother's hand. Together they went outside into the sunshine, followed by Miles to the house gate, where he remained watching them. He saw Jinny rub her golden head against Maggie's. Then she mounted, and took the leading rein of Donald's horse. With a wave of the whip, she rode off. Maggie, watching her thoughtfully, turned and walked slowly back to Miles. As they stood together at the gate, they saw Grandfather take the reins of his horse and spring into the saddle as lightly as a much younger man. Then side-by-side they cantered up the hill and away over the plateau.

Miles and Maggie went into the house and set about preparing the luscious black fish for the pan, discussing Sid's behaviour as they worked. Miles, his eyes narrowed, and nostrils distended, said quietly,

"I'll just walk over to the hut and speak to Sid."

"Then," she said, "be careful. You know, you have often remarked how the unfortunate folk of limited intelligence, when angered, are sometimes violent. It's kindness Sid needs, and understanding."

"Yes! I know all that," said Miles, whose hands shook as he filled his pipe. He stood beside Maggie, looking down at her, and somewhat impatiently exclaimed through clenched teeth, "I'll manage Sid!" He paused beside her, puffing his pipe, then went off without a backward glance or another word.

As he walked towards the hut he thought over the times when Sid had almost driven him to distraction with his slow muddling and prying ways; how he would at most times shake his head and take him with a certain amount of philosophy – 'well, that's just Sid'. But this he could not overlook, and he went on with forceful strides.

Sid had lost his anger and was a pitiable object when Miles had finished with him. He begged to be allowed to remain with the family, and promised not to speak to or approach either Jinny or

Charles Day until permitted.

"I'll not tell Guy of your behaviour and will caution Jinny also that she must not, and," said Miles on leaving him, "if you go to that dance tonight, keep away from my daughter! In the morning, you and Guy are to go to the mountain and look for the cattle that broke through the fence of the hill paddock. Understand?"

"Yes, Boss!"

"Fine! Now get on with the milking. I'll help you tonight. I see Guy has gone off through the forest."

"Yes, Boss," said the abject Sid.

CHAPTER 11

"IT FAIR DISTURBS ME!" GRANDFATHER SHOOK HIS FROSTY HEAD vigorously as he listened to the account of Sid's behaviour. "It's not surprised I'm being. To be sure I'm the one that's been watching him when he thought no one had eyes to see. I should have spoken. Yes, I thought when the young shavers went to the local hops an' met all the girls, Sid would get more sense. Not so! Not so!" he struck his skinny thighs as he moved closer to Miles. "Send him packing. Send him packing!"

Miles looked at him with narrowed eyes, "I think things will be alright for a while." Then he added thoughtfully, "But miracles just don't happen. We'll keep him so busy that the soles of his boots will spark on the cobbles!"

Grandfather's face lit up at the idea, and then he became serious. "He thinks he's in love with Jinny. It's concerned ye are? An' well ye might be. Take my word, its action that's needed right now."

Miles nodded. "Love should be a glory, like sunshine on ripening wheat, but it's so often like rocks crashing down a beautiful gully. Yes! Sid must go!"

"We're not telling Guy about this business until they return from trailing the lost stock in the mountain!" Grandfather nodded his agreement.

"That's good. Good! I should have warned you months ago!" The old man looked utterly disconsolate, but Miles patted his shoulder saying,

"Never mind Father! Things will probably right themselves!"

As if to thrust aside all unpleasantness, Miles, head back, sniffed the air like a hound scenting its prey. He looked round with a mischievous gleam in his eyes.

"Mm, Mm! Do you smell anything? Something is tickling my palate."

Grandfather turned his head toward the house, and then he almost jumped into action. "Yes! By Gad! It's the blackfish frying. Let's hurry or that old shyster Joe will eat the lot!" and shaking his head, Grandfather strode ahead of Miles, hungrily inhaling the delectable odour. Miles paused to hitch the loop of wire over the stable yard gate and followed him.

The next morning, Maggie was up before daybreak to cook breakfast for Guy and Sid. They set off with sufficient food in their packs for two days of searching in the mountains, in case the stock had wandered further than they expected.

They rode away in good spirits. When the sun was at its zenith, they paused beside a small mountain stream, attending to their hacks, and were just about to boil the billy when Guy sprang up, tipped the contents swiftly over the fire and gathered up his pack saying,

"Look at those men down the valley on the flat! Quick, Sid, move the horses. I'll get your pack. Get into the undergrowth there behind that rock."

In a flash, they had hidden their packs and had tethered their horses. Then they scrambled up a small escarpment and lay there on their stomachs, looking and watching every movement down in the little green valley.

"Cattle thieves! Look, there are our cattle, and some of the neighbours. They have them all rounded up ready to take away!"

"They must have a camp somewhere around," whispered Sid. "They're skinning a beast for tucker… they've got spades. Wonder what they want to dig? Let's go and see," he said in hissing syllables of excitement. He moved to rise, but Guy held him.

"No! There are sure to be men at their camp. We will wait until they have their lunch, then we can get behind the cattle and disturb them. Listen!" he whispered, "Do you hear a dog barking?"

They listened intently. Guy was visibly excited as he turned his head towards the direction in which they had come. "Sid, it's your old dog. By Jingo! He'll stampede those cattle and send them back into the forest! Keep down, you fool! Those men are dangerous. You know very well the evil reports of the gang of cattle and horse thieves. They're killers!"

"Huh!" breathed Sid. "We could get on our horses and run at 'em. There's only four of the varmints. Get a waddy each and we'll down 'em!"

"Don't be mad. Can't you see the guns? We want our cattle, not heads full of lead! Don't be such an idiot, and for heavens sake, keep quiet or that confounded dog of yours will come here!"

Sid, quietened, again lay on his stomach peering through the thick ti-tree scrub at the men on the flat below. He could have been hypnotised, so deeply interested he became. The four strangers who had finished skinning the beast and cutting it up were loading their packhorses when, again, in the distance, the old dog barked.

The cattle, restless after a sharp mustering, raised their heads and commenced to bellow and disperse. The men seized their guns and stood tense and alert. Looking all about them, they sprang on their horses and gave chase.

"Apparently they think there's someone with the dog, and are looking and wanting to shoot," Guy muttered. Sid put his two fingers in his mouth to give his familiar whistle.

"You stupid gomeril," exclaimed Guy, and Sid, the sun blinding his eyes, turned and received Guy's clenched fist, 'fair on the nose' as he himself later resentfully described the encounter. He certainly could not have related it at the time, because Guy's 'fair on the nose' punch was so weighty that Sid was rendered as silent as the log against which he fell. Guy, hidden by thick scrub, standing on the crest of the ridge, watched his cattle madly thrashing through the timber, with the strangers trying to follow.

They appeared to be more concerned to sight the men, who in their opinion, were travelling with the dog that had stamped the cattle, than the real culprit – the dog – fortunately for him.

How wrong their conclusions were, they discovered too late. The cattle were lost in the dense undergrowth, and finding nobody, the thieves returned and speedily loaded their horses with the rest of the illicit meat and left the scene.

Guy quoted facetiously, "He who fights and runs away lives to fight another day, and the rogues will certainly return," but no one had heard him. He turned, and, not very gently, splashed water from a mountain stream over the unconscious youth. Waiting for him to recover, he listened intently, but the only sounds, were the distant lowing of cattle, occasional bird songs and the trickling of water.

Sid stood up and looked resentfully at Guy as he wiped blood from his quickly swelling nose. "You didn't hafta do that to me. What did I do to you?"

"You silly fellow," Guy said shortly, "You're lucky to be alive. A whistle from you and those men would have shot both of us. Your dog would have led them here if they had not found us first."

"Oh, yes! So it would!" said Sid, with a stupid stare and began to laugh as if it were some entertaining story. Then he rose to his feet and peered down towards the spot where the men had skinned the beast. "Wonder what they were doing with the spades. Reckon we'll look around!"

"We will not. We came for our cattle, not to put our necks in a noose or to catch cattle thieves. Come on, let's get our horses and get away from here at once. If we hurry we'll probably have the cattle mustered before those men return. I'm sure they're only hiding, I wonder where their camp is."

So they reached their horses and rode silently back the way they had come, and in the direction the cattle had taken. They halted suddenly. In the distance, down a steep gully, they again heard the dog barking.

"That's my dog, Brownie's bark," said Sid.

"Well keep quiet for goodness sake. Those men will hear it and perhaps follow the sound.

Frowning darkly, Sidney turned to Guy as he again gave his order, in impatient desperation. "Yes! It is your dog Brownie barking over there, but if you make the slightest move to whistle him, I'll darned well knock you cold again. Yes, an' roll you down the hill into the creek. You silly ass! Have some sense. Can't you understand those thieving no-goods will follow him to us?"

Sidney glared at him, a malicious grin tightening his thick lips. "An' you an' who else will knock me cold? What'll I be doing?"

"You'll… Och! Brother! What rubbish is this? Come on! We'll skirt around that rise and sneak through that confounded tangle of ferns clematis streamers at the edge of the creek. See that old dead blue gum? From there we'll climb again and find the old trail we used years ago? Remember?" Sid gave a brief grunt.

"Umph!" as Guy continued, "That trail under all the scrub leads to Dead Dog Hill. It's a short cut. Those chaps don't know about it or it would have been tramped well down."

"Brownie's stopped barkin' He's gone home p'raps."

"Maybe," muttered Guy as leading his horse, he moved carefully forward. "Shake a leg, Sid!"

He looked back irately. The big lad ignored him as, bridle over his arm, he was eagerly unwrapping a package from his swag. Guy paused, "Oh good gracious! We forgot to eat our lunch. We'll eat as we go, or the others will race us to the cattle."

So they went quietly along the edge of the fast flowing stream, paused to water the horses, and, lying flat on the mossy bank, they too drank the sweet water. On they went, pushing back the jungle growth of ti-tree, ferns and Manuka; walking and stumbling more than their horses on the steep hillside. At the top, they emerged and there, grazing quietly on native grasses and tussocks, were the cattle. Delightedly they mounted their hacks, relaxed in the saddles and counted the bottley mob. All irritability vanished.

"I reckon there's over a hundred of the flippin' things."

"Yes," said Guy.

"There's Treen's bull. He went bush last year," said Sid, watching them with open-mouthed satisfaction, "And there are our steers. Yes, all there but the big baldy!"

"Reckon that's the one those fellows were skinning. Anyway we've got a good haul. There'er about twenty wild cattle with that mob."

Sid's eyes glinted with strange excitement. "Lucky for us!"

Guy was too intent inspecting the cattle to agree. "If we go quietly, I think we'll be able to drove them all together and get them into the stock-yards at home. Your dog's gone home, an' it's just as well. So long as the beasts aren't startled, the droving will be easy!"

So they went quietly and slowly and the herd moved ahead of them. Suddenly it was dark. "There's no twilight here, so we'll have to rest until the moon rises," said Guy. Sid was already dismounted, looking for food and ready to tether his horse.

Soon he was sprawled on a patch of fern and slept. Guy, resting his head on his saddle, lay there listening to the myriad voices of the bush. In the far distance his hated enemies, the dingoes, sent their mating calls, and closer, frogs croaked their unceasing cacophony. Wood pigeons and mopoke owls' monotonous calls mixed with the chirping and sleepy tones of numerous small birds.

All the sounds around him, even the monkey-bears or koalas crying, did not disturb his thoughts. They were like discords, which fading away, blended into harmony. Although he had danced most of the previous night on the rough hardwood floor of the little bush schoolhouse, he was not sleepy.

Out there, in the warm summer evening, waiting for the moon to rise over the great heights of the yellow box messmate and sassafras trees, his thoughts dwelt on the day's adventure. Then back they took him through the years since he had come to the rainforest as an eager small boy. All the doings of the clearing, a home in a strange forest! Then the past evening! And, Becky! Ah! Becky! He rose and looked at the fleeting clouds gradually paling with the rising moon. Standing there, he somehow felt as if he were in another world – a world of sombre trees and sudden quiet – as if everything had sung itself to sleep. Yet, he had the feeling of being surrounded by living things, breathing in the silence, asleep, with he, one solitary human, trying to puzzle out the yesterdays and tomorrows. Alone, a small unit in a huge universe, and a strange sadness which he could not understand, overcame him as if the whole weight of the world were bearing down on him. Youth's insecurity.

Then the great moon rose over the treetops and golden rays pierced through the branches, down to the leaf and fern-carpeted earth. He stared at the sudden beauty around him, and the dreadful unrest, the melancholy that not only then, but in sudden flashes in the past year, had assailed him, and gradually faded away. Now, he knew. He was no longer a boy but a man.

He stood watching the moon slowly making its course then sat down by his saddle and, head on his knees, everything resolved itself in one blinding realisation. Like a moving finger, all his complexities led and pointed to Becky. Ever since the morning he had carried her into his mother's kitchen, he had loved her.

"Yes, Mr. Moon," Guy smiled at the fantasy as he muttered. "Watching you, I have discovered myself. Dear, dear little stowaway!"

Suddenly he felt the need for action. He picked up his saddle and on the way to his horse he stoped beside Sid and shook his shoulder. "Come on Sid! Saddle up! The moon's up. Time we were on the tracks!"

"By Jingo! Yes!" said Sid, as still almost asleep he stumbled towards his horse.

Again they were on their way, and as silently as they could possibly move through the dense scrub, at some distance apart they approached the drowsing cattle. Pausing at intervals, to allow the already suspicious animals to sense their presence gradually, their progress was slow. At last the whole herd rose and nosed the herbage, then went slowly and calmly grazing ahead, needing little forcing. Just before dawn, in a darkening sky, they arrived at the plateau and Sid rode on ahead to open the slip-rails. When early daylight came over the mist-shrouded hills and valleys, the whole herd, the wild cattle, settlers' and their own, were securely locked in the stockyards at Rock Allen and two very well satisfied but tired young men were asleep in their beds.

CHAPTER 12

MILES AWOKE EARLY AFTER A SOMEWHAT SLEEPLESS NIGHT, thinking of Guy and Sid, and how they were faring out among the tall timber on the mountainside. With utmost precaution, he slipped out of bed and down the wide hallway to Guy's bedroom. The door was ajar, so he peeped in, and a satisfied smile spread over his lean face. He breathed deeply.

"The lads are home an' it's thankful I am", he muttered, then closed the door gently and tiptoed back to his room, dressed swiftly and went outside. He strode across the house yard, past the stables to the stockyards and leaning over the sip panels, stared in delight at the lowing cattle. As spontaneously as the song of the dawn-welcoming magpies, he spoke aloud in the crisp morning air:

"Great Scot alive! Wonders'll never cease."

Excited, he climbed onto the topmost rail to examine the motley mob, and then bounded off to the house. Cautiously, careful not to waken Maggie so early, he roused old Donald. "Father! Wake up!" he whispered. "Come along outside an' be after seeing a grand sight for your Irish eyes. It's sorry I am to be rousing you so soon, an' you need your rest, but I must be tellin' someone. Keep quiet!

Don't waken the others."

But grandfather was, as ever, even at such an early hour, a law unto himself.

"Dash me rags!" he said in a whisper as loud as the bullock bells, "what's doing?"

"Hush! Sh!"

"Don't hoosh me son, find me boots an' I'll be willing to give an ear to whatever's bitin' you at such an ungodly hour."

So Miles found the boots and then Donald clomped down the long hall towards the kitchen, making so much noise while trying to step lightly that he woke Joe. Then Maggie heard him and hastened to find the cause. Grandfather wagged his tousled white head at her in a comical attempt to look sorrowful as he said,

"It's a pity it is to be waking you Maggie. Just you blame Miles for the racket I'm making trying to be quiet. Why didn't he let me go me own natural gait an' I'd be like a trotting horse with velvet shoes. It's so quiet I am as a natural human being." He winked with both eyes and added, "Sure an' he knows that well."

"Yes Grandfather," said Maggie with a sleepy laugh, "but what's it all about?"

"It's Miles you should be asking and not me," tersely said Grandfather as he tried to fix his braces and then found they were back to front – and his trousers also. "Confound it all," he muttered, and looking at Maggie sideways, just pulled the braces on to his shoulders. Using his old device of 'look a persons in the eyes an' he'll notice nothing but the nose on your face' he waited for Miles to explain his early call.

"Come out to the stockyard and see," was Miles' response.

So out they went, and Maggie, shivering in her wrapper, set to work kindling the fire for the early cups of tea. Guy, Charles and the girls, Jinny and Rebecca, who had also come back there from the dance, entered the kitchen.

Soon, the men returned, cold and damp from the early mists whirling down from Old Fantastic, and all very talkative, as they drank their many cups of tea. Out they went again, and when Guy and Sid joined them, there they were, perched on the top rails of the stockyards, discussing the motley mob of cattle. But not Grandfather. He dare not! Or could not.

Guy, just as quick witted and with the same facetious temperament as his Grandad, cast his eyes over the ground at the yards. They returned to old Donald, and a waggish grin spread over his face as he said in a very good imitation of the old man's manner,

"What Grandfather? Are the rheumatics after troublin' ye this morning that you don't join the others on their perch?" The old man looked him in the eye as if daring him to speak of his appearance, which himself, in the excitement had forgotten.

"You young varmint. If you hadn't done such a good job with mustering that mob of mongrels, I'd, I'd..."

"Yes Grandfather? You would do what?" asked Guy merrily.

"Glory be!" old Donald again looked at himself and then at the others and grinned as he capitulated, "I'd be after doing a right about face, bedad! I've seen all I want to see. I'm going to have my porridge," and off he tramped to the house, adding to Guy as he passed him, "an don't ye be too long. I want to hear all about the doings of your trip!"

"Right Grandfather. I'll come now and we'll tell all about it at the breakfast table." Affectionately, he turned and walked beside him. The others followed.

The telling lasted while they cleaned up their porridge plates, while they were wiping up the remains of eggs and bacon off the second course, and right on to the toast and honey. In fact, there were still a few detailed answers to questions on the second and third cups of tea.

"Well," said Joe as he rose and pushed his chair under the table, "I guess you did a wonderful job, the two of you. Much as I would like to stay with you today, I must be off to see about taking over that selection Seth Stride dummied for me. I'm so well fortified with your good cooking Maggie, I guess I'll last until late this afternoon, when I'll be back."

"You'll stay the night Joe?" Miles looked across at him as he filled his pipe.

"Yes! Yes! Then Charles and I will move off at dawn tomorrow. You see he has to be back at his office in a few days, and," he looked around inquiringly, "where is he now?"

Maggie looked at him across her shoulder as she moved plates from the table and said quietly, "Jinny and Rebecca had breakfast with him and they're all gone down to the creek fishing."

"Well, I'll be jiggered," was Joe's rather enigmatical retort, as he took his hat and left the kitchen, with a brief, "so long then."

"Now let's get to business," said Miles. Sid, who had not spoken at the table, but sat moodily listening, was standing at the door. Miles looked directly at him as he spoke, "Sid! You get your horse and ride around all the neighbours with a message." He spoke kindly having decided that if Sid was prepared to behave as he promised, he could stay at Rock Allen until he found other work.

"Yes Boss," said he not too cordially. He waited for further instructions. "What'll I tell 'em?"

"Just tell them of your doings yesterday and ask them to ride in and pick out any cattle they claim as theirs and to take them away. We can't be holding them here indefinitely. We're short of feed as it is."

"What about the wild cattle Dad?" asked Guy.

Miles looked from him to Sid, "I think you had better take them to the market and share the money."

"That's good!" said Sid with a more pleasant attitude.

"Then be off lad. Go on, be off! Standing there will not save grass for stock."

Old Donald turned to Maggie. "Maybe he'd better take some tucker, Lass. Get going man I'll bring it to you when you saddle up!" Sid turned and strode away.

Guy prepared to follow him, saying, "I'll get Becky's and my horses saddled too. They should have finished their chaff by now!"

Grandfather grinned as he said, "To be sure, you needn't be taking Becky along home lad. I'll take her in the spring cart an' save you the time!"

Guy shook his fist at his grandfather. "Now Grandfather! You're much too young to think of taking the lasses home in spring carts and," he stooped and patted the old man on the head, none too gently either, "if it would interest you to know, I'm taking Becky riding. Yes! I've given myself a holiday. We're going out to see the bowerbirds. Becky is most interested in the clutter they have around their nests!"

Donald swung around and caught Guy's hand, "An' ye aren't after tellin' me that you, with a look in yer eyes an' a grin that pumice stone wouldn't rub off on yer face, that you're going to just look at bower-birds, or any dang birds, eh?"

"You're an old rascal, Grandfather," returned Guy happily. "I'll tell you. I'm going just to be with Becky. See?"

"Hm! That's how it is? Well I never! First Jinny; now you! What's the world coming to?"

"It looks to me like a bit of lovin', Grandad!" whispered the young gallant as he went away laughing.

"Lads an' lasses! Lads an' lasses!" old Donald muttered to himself as he grunted with the effort of lacing his boots in the right eyelets. "Rebecca and Guy?" Staring, unseeing, he was very thoughtful. "I wonder just who she is, an' what is her background?"

Behind the small farm in Ireland in which he had been born and reared, was a tradition of good breeding and a more gracious way of life than his own since coming to the Colony.

"Money or the lack of it makes a big difference. Begorrah! It does. No matter what the folks that have plenty of the stuff would be tellin' one." He mused on. If Guy's forefathers had not been gradually stripped of their possessions by greedy self-seekers, taxes and bad laws, Guy would be living in his own country mansion in the Old Country, maybe! "Oh well," he thought, "nothing can take away the essential good of a man, an' where would anyone find a better type of lad?" He thought proudly of Guy. Tall, handsome, long striding.

Then, back came his thoughts of Rebecca. "She's a fine gal with an air of good breedin' an' to hell with the mystery, an' lack of money an' all its trappings." He walked swiftly out the door and across to the gate. Leaning over it he looked around him. Maggie was busy with the usual kitchen tasks but had been watching, like the unseen eye. In the early morning, it had been one long drama. The early rousing, the excitement of seeing the cattle and the story of their mustering. Then Jinny and Charles with eyes only for each other. Rebecca, quiet, self-contained and away from them in her own thoughts as she helped cook breakfast. Sid, unusually moody, an unfinished part of the drama. Joe, off to complete a somewhat shady deal. Miles, striving to do the right thing with everyone, and feeling inadequacy. Then Guy and Grandfather; kindred souls, ready to quip and laugh and, like gunpowder, to flash into fire at the touch of heat.

She sighed as she thought of everything that had happened. "People ask me if I'm lonely on a selection in the forest." Like Grandfather, she spoke aloud, but the unwashed dishes and the thrusting rays of sunshine through the small kitchen window did not reply. "Changes! Oh dear!"

The sun was warm on her head as she turned to work at the table. She looked outside at the shimmering colours on the dew-wet leaves and grass. Beyond the gate, where Donald leaned comfortably, she saw Guy lead two horses to the hitching rails. He left Becky's there and sprang on his own, cantering across to his father. They talked awhile, then went to the stockyard and drafted their own cattle. Maggie, anxious to be outside, could wait no longer; she left her unfinished tasks and joined Donald.

"It's no use Grandfather. I'm sure there's a tempting spirit in the outdoors. It's insidious and keeps beckoning me."

Grandfather spoke gently. "Yes lass. An' all the work in the world will keep, but this splendid glory of sun an' misty horizons, an' old Fanatic's begorrah an' come look at me, will not be doin' just that. You're a wise woman my dear. What do you think of this family of yours?"

She looked intently around her and did not speak for a while. Then she said,

"Grandfather, it seems to me that all is well. I always knew Guy loved little Becky, right from the way he carried her inside as an ailing child. That was a young protective love. But there's a change, and Guy is a man, young as he is. I'll be content. Rebecca is a good girl, and has a great reserve. I'll consider him a lucky man, if eventually they marry. You see? Miles and I love her too."

"Yes! Yes! I'm of the same opinion as you. Rebecca, as you say, has a great potential." Then, he hesitated, "Are you concerned about her background?"

"No Grandfather. As she is, she is. Some day things will be explained."

"Right! Right! I'd trust your judgement any day of the week, but I hope it will not be too late. Here's Guy back from taking the cattle away to the paddock. He's not losing any time. That's a fine little pony of Rebecca's my word, she can cut her sticks, that one, fine long legs she has." He paused and watched the girl race to her house, and mount it in a bound. "It's a fine seat on a horse she has too, begorrah. They're off at a gallop, the young spalpeens. They ride the devil out of their horses!"

"Well Grandfather," Maggie's face wrinkled with a smile, "if there's a devil in those horses, its best they ride it out of them, don't you agree?"

Not waiting for his usual swift retort, she returned, "My goodness! This will not get my bread into the oven. I must go."

As she hastened back into the house old Donald, chuckling in an involuntary surge of contentment, walked over to the stockyards to Miles, who looked up from his work hammering planks on the top of the fence, and lifted his hand in greeting.

"I'm glad you came along Dad. I need someone to help me handle these rails. Mind that bull! He nearly jumped out! He's a mean, unpredictable beast, and ran at me a while ago. It was just as well there was a fence between us. I think he's been boss of the wild cattle until that young Hereford over here found he was the stronger. Hold that end steady Dad! The rail is slightly bent and swings away."

They worked together, easing the ends of the rails, fitting them on the high posts and hammered away companionably. It was nearing morning-tea time when they finished and downed tools. Then they heard a horse galloping down the hill. They stared, intrigued, as Miles remarked,

"Why, that's Joe! Back early? He's certainly sending that horse in a mighty big hurry."

"Or he's in a bad temper," added Donald. "I wonder what's gone wrong! Suffering cats! Why a man can't control himself and act in a quiet peaceable way when something upsets his applecart, I'll never figure out!" He threw down his hammer in very evident impatience.

Miles looked at him, vainly trying not to laugh. They walked to the gate and stood together watching Joe's approach. He was riding one of the young stock horses, and if Joe was excited, the horse was certainly playing up to his rider's mood. Galloping up to the yards, he reined in with all the strength of his saw miller's arms, very fortunate that he completed his unseating right on the horses head. He slid to the ground most inelegantly and ruefully rubbed the part of his anatomy that was most frequently in the saddle.

His face was white and his nostrils almost as distended as those of the horse he had so ruthlessly vented his spleen upon. Miles' nostrils commenced to flare also when he noted the condition of his best hack. Grandfather almost excelled his beaky nose capacity as he strode over to the horse and grabbed the reins. He was too angry to speak, so, patting the horse's neck, he took it to the stables.

Miles and Joe looked at each other in a few moments silence. Then Joe shook his head. "By Joves! I'm sorry Miles. An' it was one of your best horses. I was so furious, that I did not realise how I was forcing him."

"You mean you lost control?"

"Yes, you know, as always, I get mad easy. Now I'll go help Donald rub down and feed the horse."

"Yes. I'll go too," added Miles.

"I'm darned sorry about this," repeated Joe, his fat cheeks drooping like a pointer's jowls, and looking just so woeful that Miles' anger faded somewhat.

"You had better try to appease father. Nothing makes him as irate as having a horse ill-used. We don't like him to be over-excited. He's really an old man."

Miles spoke quietly, evenly, as they entered the wide doorway of the stable. The horse had its nose in the manger, and a quick glance told him that there was a liberal supply of oats in the chaff. He watched Donald gently brushing the horse's flanks and talking to him in a chanting way, full of affection. The old man looked up as the two entered, glared at Joe, and carried on with his brushing.

Joe approached the horse and commenced to smooth it down with his hands. Grandfather's eyes met his blankly.

"Look here," said Joe. "I lost my head in a temper. I s'pose I'm really not a fit person to ride a horse!"

"You bloomin' well said the right thing for once," returned the old man as he lifted the horse's foot, and with a big clasp knife, proceeded to clean the grip out of the frog. Miles saw Joe's face redden. He was about to expostulate. Then he controlled himself. The horse blew into his chaff and shook himself, and Grandfather nodded.

"He's right now. What made you in such a devilish temper anyway?" Miles was relieved that Grandfather had decided at least to be pacified.

For a while there was a pause, stillness. Then Joe looked around the stable, crossed to the doorway, and sat himself down on a bag of oats, while Miles leaned restfully against the big end post of a stall. Grandfather had inspected all the horses' hooves and stood by, gently rubbing the foam-wet shoulder with a piece of sacking, and Joe, head down filling his pipe, commenced his tale of the morning's doings.

CHAPTER 13

"WHEN I WENT EARLY THIS MORNING TO DISCUSS WITH SETH Strife the taking over of the selection, the one he dummied for me, I thought it would be just a simple affair, a matter of half hour or so. Then I intended to come back for young Charles to help 'em out with any hitches that might occur," Joe recounted.

"You were even quicken than you imagined," Miles added evenly.

"I certainly was!" Joe stamped angrily. "Do you know what the pernickety rascal did?" He paused and furiously puffed at the pipe that would not draw.

"Go on! Go on! Be tellin of it!" Grandfather's eyes were gleaming with flashes of delighted impatience and glee. In disgust, Joe put the pipe on an overhead joist and proceeded to walk about, shaking clenched fists as he recalled the morning's argument!

"I had arranged for that Stride chap to dummy the rich part of the river flat down yonder for me! Yes! I paid the survey fees, and the shilling an acre ever since. Three hundred and twenty shillings a year I've paid an' now, do you know what? When I said to him this morning, I've come to take over this place; he glared at me an' said,

"Take over be damned! This selection's in my name. It stays. I've made it into a fine farm. I'll pay you back your survey fees, an' you can wait for the rest!" Then he went and got some money, counted it and offered it to me!" Joe paused to take a breath.

"Did you take it?" asked Miles.

"No! I stamped out of their shanty and he followed me. I said, "I'll set the law on you!" and he laughed at me and said,

"Ya haven't got a let to stand on. Go on, get on your horse an' clear out!"

"So I shouted an' called him every unprintable name I could think of. Then, then…" he spoke with a downcast air, "I galloped all the way back!"

"Took it out of the horse, you did. Brave man!" said grandfather with grim sarcasm and fiercely glinting eyes directed straight into Joe's. Then he walked nearer, and shook his clenched hands in exactly the same manner. "Haven't you lived long enough to know that sometimes a person must do the wrong thing to know what is the right one. Lord knows you've done plenty wrong ones. You should well know the right by now! Joe, you're always just the shyster. You met yourself coming back when you met Seth Strife today. Well, not altogether! That man and his wife have worked like tigers, day and night, and have made that property the most prosperous and the best farm in the hill country. Now, you want to capitalise on their labour and the few pounds you paid. I know you're fast becoming the biggest landowner near and beyond yon mountains, and…" Grandfather thrust his face almost into the others, "I don't like the way you get your land, Joe Crow! Hm! Crow! You're well named. You wait until your prey's almost dead, and then you swoop down for the kill!"

Miles stepped up and put his hand on his father's shoulder. "Easy father! This is Joe, our friend. You're being most unkind to him and…" Joe held up an arresting hand, and, looking straight into Donald's eyes, he said,

"I guess you could put it that way. But it's alright you know, quite legitimate. If a chap fails to meet his payments, well! Someone else gets a chance to the land. It might as well be me!"

"Land hungry! Ach! What about all the dummied blocks you forcibly took over? All their hard work for nothing! Now, one of them meets your tactics as you deserve. Did you offer to pay for the sweat of his brow? No. Colonial fear! You flew into a rage and left!"

"Well, so I did, and I met myself coming back? That's a caution! Do you know what? I reckon you're right. I'll let the matter slide!"

"So the Strifes keep the land and the sum of their years of hard yakka? For once you're out-played! Good, good! An' needs must when the devil drives!" He looked toward the homestead. "There's Jinny calling us to morning tea. Go on!"

Grandfather pushed the horse's oats and chaff into a mound in the manger, picked up and shook a chaff bag, and replaced the rail at the end of the horses stall. Then, first dusting his old hat against the rail and jamming it on his head, he followed the others leisurely, muttering to himself on the way.

Walking along together without speaking, Miles chanced to look at Joe's rubicund face which was unusually serious. He frowned, and then paused. Joe looked across and noticing his expression said,

"Don't be concerned on my account! I deserved all Grandfather said. It was the truth and there's no rebuttal, as Charles would say in his legal lingo! At any rate, it's not anything new to you. Didn't young Guy say the first time we met that I was a shyster? Guess I am, too! But man! I enjoy it all!" Miles intrigued by his unconcern, laughed aloud and remarked,

"Joe, you're really an amoral but likeable scamp!"

Miles and Joe went into the house with smiles on their faces, and Grandfather came in cheerfully. He had talked all the rancour out of his system and looked completely at ease as he seated himself at the table and looked around for his cup of tea.

Maggie watched their faces with interest. Alone in the house for a while she had been thinking of the early setting of her day's drama and wondering just how things would work out before nightfall. Years of experience had taught her to curb her impatience and to wait for just the right moment and place for questioning her menfolk. But youth had that lesson yet to learn, she realised as Jinny, giving Joe his tea, said brightly,

"Did you find the Strife's at home?" The reply was,

"Yes!"

"Then you finished your business early! Charles has asked me to ride along part of the way when he goes back with you. Will you be seeing those people again on the way?"

Somehow, Joe was affected with a very bad coughing and Grandfather said,

"Now Lass, ask no questions and you'll be told no lies," and winked both eyes in ludicrous perversity.

"Oh!" said Jinny in wide-eyed confusion, and Maggie frowned. When Jinny came back with the teapot she whispered,

"Something's wrong! Keep quiet!"

Watching the men file outside, Maggie thought, "Life is strange. Day in, day out, we're just living, working, eating, sleeping and worrying or enjoying our simple pleasures. Then, suddenly, everything seems to be happening!" Something about Joe made her feel uneasy.

She hoped matters were right between him and her menfolk. She knew he was spoken of as ruthless, but to them, he was a friend at all times. She must see Miles and discover just what was happening. Jinny had left the room. She saw her with Charles outside in the sunshine.

Wiping her hands on her apron, Maggie followed the men to the stockyards, curious also to see the cattle. Suddenly the dogs set up a din of furious barking. Everyone looked up towards the plateau. From the outside world there was only one road to Rock

Allen. Next to the Ford's was the Treen's property, the furthermost one into the forest, and facing them on one side was their beloved Mount Fantastic and the source of the two rivers bordering the rich selected properties.

"The neighbours are riding in!" Maggie looked troubled. "All these people an' little enough bread I've in the house!" So she hurried back, and, crossing the woodheap, filled her apron with chips.

"Hot scones, Mother?" asked Jinny.

"Yes! Look at all those men coming to look for their cattle in the round-up!"

"Then you go along and see them Mother. You know you've been trying to get out of the kitchen all morning! I'll make the scones. Even if they eat them here and die around the corner, as Guy tells me someone will one day. She turned to Charles and taking his hand she said, "Come! We'll take the chips and you shall see just how I can cook!"

"I know Jinny," said Charles with a teasing grin. "Didn't you nearly kill me with rock buns years ago?"

"Oh dear! Those buns! Do forget them, but just you see how I've improved, I really have, Mother will tell you so," she repeated emphatically.

"Oh yes!" Maggie agreed, nodding her head.

They went back to the kitchen and Maggie hurried away to speak to Miles, eager to discover just what was the cause of the tension, the tension they had vainly tried to hide from her at the morning-tea table. She went directly to him and broached the subject immediately, as this would probably be her only chance before nightfall.

"Miles, what's the trouble with Joe?" Miles looked around and then replied,

"Come over here. Not that anyone will hear us with all the noise of these bellowing cattle, or that it would be of any account if they did!"

However, they moved away from the others and, looking down

at the cattle, he attempted to send them away from the fence, further into the yard, saying,

"It's nothing for you to be troubled about, my dear. Seth Strife refused to let Joe take over the block, lost his temper. Dad as usual hit out from the shoulder and told him just what he thought of him and his dealings. Joe ill-used the bay hack and you know how that infuriates him. That's what started his tirade, but it's all cleared up now!"

"I'm glad of that. I must get back to the house and help Jinny. These people will be here for dinner. Charles is with her."

Turning, Miles looked down at her. "Charles and I had a serious talk a short time after breakfast! Charles asked our permission to write to Jinny."

Maggie laughed, "Considering that they've done so for years, off and on, I don't see the point."

"Ah! My dear! But Charles added a little to that. The idea is that he wants to marry her. I said they must wait until Jinny is eighteen. I hope you agree, as I have not had a chance as yet to tell you."

"My eyes have told me, and they don't often mislead me," Maggie said as she looked around. Then she started, "Just look who is coming through the forest track, Patience and Gerrard in the springcart, and there's Rhys on his horse."

"To be sure, you eyes aren't misleading you," Miles said, but Maggie did not stay to debate the point. Her face aglow with pleasure she hastened to meet Patience and Miles walked up to Joe, who was leaning over the top rail watching the cattle.

"That old bull's a vicious monster, and will take some drafting. I'll be glad to be rid of him. Here comes the owner, Gerrard Treen."

Miles looked up the hill and remarked, "Sid certainly got around the neighbours. It seems as if everyone is here to look for lost stock. All we need is an auctioneer, and we cold make it a sale day. Guy and Rebecca away riding. Sid hasn't returned yet, so we're short handed for drafting. However, we'll manage I daresay with some of the visitors. What do you think of young Charles and our Jinny wanting to marry, Joe?"

"What? Great Scott!" He paused and grinned, as if enjoying a good joke. "He keeps a close mouth. He didn't give me a hint even. His mother will fold up when she hears this. If he can reconcile her to a love affair before he's twenty-one, he'll make a tip-top lawyer. Joking aside though man, I think it a great idea, but I tell you this, I'll be fighting shy of my sister for a while," and then Joe threw back his head in amusement. "All the same, I wouldn't miss seeing her face when Charles tells her he has a better interest than his studies."

A group of men rode up to the yards, dismounted, and securing their horses on the hitching rails, walked over to Miles and Joe. After the casual bush greetings, they too leaned over the fence, discussing and selecting the cattle.

Ownership solved and proved by earmarks and brands, they squatted on their heels or leaned against posts or trees, and exchanged news and views on every matter of interest that was broached.

Then Rhys and Gerrard came. Patience had climbed down over the wheel of the spring cart to greet Maggie, and they walked on towards the house. They had so much to say to each other, but it was quite useless.

Maggie looked around as she remarked, "Dog fights! Every man has brought at least one dog, and we have four of them ourselves. My! Oh my! Some of them will surely be killed." They looked on helplessly at the dusty melee of fighting dogs.

"This uproar is terrible. Let's get into the house or these snarling tumbling brutes will bowl us over." She shouted, but it was impossible to hear. Barking dogs! Shouting men! Bellowing cattle and cracking whips! So they hastened breathlessly away.

Harry Hall and bullock team early 1900

CHAPTER 14

REBECCA AND GUY RODE LEISURELY BACK TO THE HOUSE YARD gate. They lingered there, oblivious to everything; to everyone. Rebecca – to Guy with his outright and practical aspect on life, this was 'Becky' and he loved her. Engrossed in each other, they talked. At times, peals of laughter, young uninhibited laughter, rang over the crisp mountain air, taking a message which could not fail to be interpreted by the men at the stockyards.

With friendly understanding, they nodded their shaggy heads as if to say, 'Rebecca and Guy! Yes? Wedding bells? Maybe!' Then they returned their attention to the milling, bellowing herd, as they sent the dogs to cut out claimed animals.

Turning at the sudden commotion, Guy swiftly fastened the girls bridle reins to the ring on the hitching post, and, with a gay exclamation re-mounted his horse. He leaned and drew Rebecca against his stirrup, saying softly,

"Becky! Now that all's right between you an' me, I'm goin' to work an' work for our life together. Always, right through eternity, I'll be lovin' you!" She looked at him, but did not speak. She could not. He gently stroked her shining hair, and as he wheeled his horse and cantered away the words she eventually spoke were lost on the wind.

She stood a while, motionless; and then, head tilted back as she watched the fight to the mountain of a pair of whistling eagles, she walked slowly towards the house and entered in contained ecstasy.

At last, when all the cattle were recognised and claimed, there were twenty wild cows and young bulls left for Guy and Sid to share. After much talk and many pipes, everyone came into the big kitchen. They had declared that they,

"Wouldn't think of imposing on the women folk," but Grandfather soon clarified the situation.

He shouted, "Dash it all, fellers! It's only a matter of stickin' a few more taters in the pot. An' it's half a bullock there is to be eaten yet. What's a feed to anyone out here?"

So, somewhat apologetically, they dropped their hats by the bench on the back porch, wiped their boots most assiduously on the old sack, and soon the kitchen was full of men and the air of talk, laughter at tall tales and champing jaws.

Miles looked around. "Sid hasn't returned yet. I wonder what's keeping him!" Each man remarked the time Sid had called in at his home to tell about the round up.

"I daresay he's just taking his time, ambling around the country wondering why all the locals do this an' that!" said Guy looking at the gathering. Then he was thoughtful, and the subject was dropped. But Guy was very quiet for the rest of the time, and looked perturbed.

Soon, each owner left separately with his stock. "That way there's no fear of 'em getting boxed," said Seth Strife as he moved off.

Joe gave him a baleful glare, but there was no dissension, much to Grandfather's chagrin. He watched them both, and was quite prepared to enjoy a good 'go' between that scallywag of a Joe an' a man who could trump his ace! Grandfather loved a fight.

At last there was only one animal to clear; Treen's bull.

"And," said Grandfather, "that's the most pestiferous beast of the whole mob. You'll never get him home on his own. You'll have to take two of the wild cows with him. Go on, go on! Young fellow," he turned to Rhys. "Cut 'em out. You can bring 'em back when you fatten 'em!" he ended with a throaty chuckle.

"All right Grandfather Ford. Watch yourself!" called Rhys as he proceeded to open the rails and cut out two young heifers. With the aid of Guy and Charles he sent them on the track toward the Treen selection. His dogs kept them moving and Rhys sprang on his horse saying, "I'll be back. I just want to see Jinny a minute!"

He galloped to the house and called, "Jinny. Jinny!" She came to the door. "Come here please. Just a moment I'll be keeping you!"

Looking very mystified, Jinny went across as he dismounted and said to her,

"Don't be giving your word. Don't Jinny. Please wait. I'll be back as soon as I can to tell you something!" Then he turned and galloped away, and Jinny, thoroughly mystified yet thoughtful returned slowly to the house.

Rhys, back at the stockyard, opened the rail of the other yard, and the great black bull bellowing and lashing its tail. Careered after the heifers, followed by Rhys with a cracking stock whip. Only the wild stock remained, and Guy, with Rebecca's help, drove them to the river flat where the best sole of grass on the property was so lush and green. Riding leisurely close enough to hold hands at times, Guy grinned in just such a tantalising way as Grandfather and said,

"Becky, little stowaway Becky! When these cattle fatten, you'n me are going to get married!"

There was a brief pause, then Becky's strong laugh echoed through the tall gums, the ti-trees and the wild cherry trees, like the tone of a resonate bell. Guy looked more serious, momentarily downcast.

"But why? Why do you laugh?" he said huskily, his face flushing.

"Oh Guy! Dear, dear Guy. It sounded so funny. When you fatten a bullock you'll marry me. Oh Guy!"

She laughed with a choking kind of gurgle. He then threw back his head and laughed with her. They dismounted, and arms entwined like two children, they led their horses and made their plans.

Rebecca looked thoughtful as she remarked, "I know how it will be. Everyone will say I'm too young Guy. But I'll soon be sixteen and dear Ma Patience will help, I'm sure."

Guy replied, "I'd say it's never too young one is to be lovin' a girl like you," and then loitered a while, in perfect harmony, listening as a golden whistler sent its ringing call through the sunlit leaves of gums.

They turned their young faces toward the treetops, and with loving gentleness Guy drew her closer. "Even the birds agree. Happy?"

"I've never bee so happy, but let's hurry. Ma Patience and Gerrard will be waiting. This will be our very own secret."

Out in the house yard, shaded from heat in the long shadows of the late afternoon sun cast by the old red-gum, Patience and Gerrard with Maggie, Miles and Jinny. Joe and Charles were also there, talking together, waiting. The birds were flying in for evensong and the stockyards, deserted in their deep powdery dust, were silent.

"It's like the days when we first came," remarked Patience. "We're all together again, all but Mary-Ann with her merry little ways."

"She'll be home soon," Maggie told them as she packed some of her home grown fruits and vegetables in the Treen's cart. "She's happy at boarding school in Melbourne and having such a bright time that I fear she'll not settle very well to the forest life again. Mary-Ann likes gaiety and an ordered way of life. She has always loved pretty things and as a child was a perfect little ostrich. She would hide her head rather that face trouble or ugliness. Really, I'm concerned about our little Mary-Ann's future."

Gerrard looked across at Maggie's troubled face. "Frankly! I think you are racing out to the future darkly. Mary-Ann gives promise of being a fine and beautiful woman. With her fine home influence, I can see no cause for concern."

Maggie sighed, "Perhaps you're right, Gerrard. You judge from an onlooker's view. I'm just a foolish mother, but I know my impulsive, determined and rather selfish daughter so very well. Maybe I see my own characteristics in her in some respects. But of this I'm sure, Mary-Ann will set her own course, and she'll have beauty, poise and will carry it with all the elegance of her chiffon dance frock, and, I'm sorry to say, with some arrogance!"

Miles with set mouth commented crisply, "She's alright, my little Mary-Ann!" and for a while there was a lull in the conversation until Patience said quietly as she moved away,

"Here is our Becky. Look! Guy and she are walking beside their horses." They watched speculatively as the young people, arm in arm, approached, not even glancing at their waiting families. The story was there, clear and beautiful in their youthful faces as the evening sun gilded the misty forest beyond them.

"So!" whispered Miles as he bit the stem of his pipe. Patience's chubby face folded in one big spontaneous gasping gurgle of delight and Gerrard offered a briefly expressive,

"Well?"

Maggie reacted in a breathless stream of words, "Oh my goodness! This has been a day, such a long day of happenings. There we have Jinny an' Charles. Now, just look at Rebecca and Guy. It's so exciting to see you Patience, Gerrard and Rhys after all these long months, to say nothing of the cattle muster, the neighbours and all the excitement... Oh dear! Here you are with something to tell us, Guy and Rebecca?"

"Oh dear!" exclaimed Rebecca, "and to think we were going to keep everything a secret. What revealing faces we must have!"

Guy stood stiffly, almost defiantly, as he said firmly, "I'm going to tell the world now. Listen all of you. Rebecca's going to be my wife one day when…"

"Don't tell them that, Guy," she interrupted with an infectious laugh which somehow, in its happy ring, set them all laughing.

"Happiness is in the air, that's why we laugh so easily, I suppose," said Patience.

"Ridiculous! Just ridiculous!" said Grandfather. Maggie re-echoed laughing.

"Ridiculous! There's so much love around, I'm overwhelmed!" and everyone started talking excitedly.

Soon Patience and Gerrard went on their way back into the forest with laughter in their wake. The days ahead held so much promise. They would discuss their problems later.

The next morning at breakfast, Guy came in swiftly and said, "Sid's not here, his bed hasn't been slept in. Dad, I'm worried!" Everyone looked aghast. After the threatening of Jinny and its aftermath, Miles and Maggie looked at each other with a sudden foreboding.

CHAPTER 15

After a short discussion, everyone moved. Guy rounded up the horses and Joe and Charles postponed their departure. Even Grandfather demanded his horse, saddled it himself and set off in the search, with Rebecca who insisted that she too go. Maggie and Jinny stayed at home. At dinnertime, as arranged, they returned. There was no sign of Sid, or his horse.

Guy said, "Lets all go up towards the mountain. It has just struck me that Sid was not happy to leave the place where we saw the cattle duffers, without knowing what they were doing down in the hidden valley. I think we should take our guns!"

"Perhaps you're right, son," agreed Miles. "But I don't like the idea of carrying guns!"

"But Dad! The cattle duffers were armed," expostulated Guy.

"We'll not carry guns," said Miles tersely. "There's no point in killing and carrying a dead man in mind for the rest of one's life! We'll go carefully. If there has been foul play, then there'll be no need for guns, for the miscreants will be gone. If Sid is lost in the forest, where his curiosity has led him, there will still be no need, unless one in each party carries a gun as a signal of his whereabouts." There the matter rested; Miles in one party and later, when the neighbours rallied to the search, Gerrard in the other. They held a consultation.

"Do you think the young fool has cleared out?" asked Grandfather. "Bedad," he answered himself, "I'll go to his hut an' see what he's taken with him!"

They waited around on their horses, and then Grandfather returned shaking his white head vigorously, like a thistle top shaking itself free of seeds.

"Devil a thing's missin' from Sid's hut, but his spurs, whip an' the clothes he stood up in, not even his cash box. An' that's the first thing Sid would think of taking if he had a mind to leave. No! He's lost or done for! I always said his prying ways would do for him one day."

The thought was intolerable to Miles. "Who would want to harm him? Sid was not aggressively curious. It was more of childishness with him!"

Guy was listening intently, and then a swift feeling of panic shook him. He gasped as he said, "I think Grandfather's right. I've a feeling that way somehow. Sid was determined to discover why the cattle duffers were digging. The sun shone on that spade the day we saw them skinning the bally steer. Come on, everyone!" and spurring his horse, Guy led the way up to the mountain, to the secluded valley, guarded as it was by towering blue gums and Blackwoods.

A party of men from local selections joined them and they travelled silently in Guy's train. The recent progress of the cattle had broken down much vegetation, so travelling was reasonably easy until they came to the secret trail along the creek, via which Guy and Sid had travelled, and raced the cattle thieves to the mob of cattle. One suggested the possibility that some of the strangers could still be lurking around.

"Too jolly right. They'll be miles away now if they harmed Sid," said Joe, which was manifestly true for the only sounds that met their ears were bird songs and the lilt of flowing waters. They forced their way ahead. At the top of the escarpment where Guy and Sid had previously hidden themselves while watching, they paused, looked down and waited. In the weird silence, they finally decided the place was deserted, so tethering all the horses, the men scrambled down the rocky, and at times, dangerously slippery face of the cliff.

As they walked across the little green flat, their eyes searched for signs of recent trails of man or beast. The sole of grass was so deep that detection was difficult. Guy walked to the spot where the beast had been slaughtered.

"They've taken even the hide," he commented. "Sid was very interested in that spade. They must have used it, because it was so bright that the sun reflections on it were the cause of us seeing it. Let's look around!"

"Look here," called Joe, "this log has been rolled away from its original position. See how the grass is white and yellowish? Give a hand here chaps!"

"Ahh!" They rolled the log back and noticed that the earth has been freshly dug and replaced.

"This log was rolled here to hide the fresh soil," said one. With spars broken from nearby trees, the men dug a hold but found only an empty tin!

"See," said Miles, "this tin is rusted on the outside, but bright inside which clearly shows that something's been buried here in it for some time, and has only been recently taken out. So Sid must have seen the men at work. I wonder if they came back for it and found Sid."

"Yes," said Guy. "They might have started to dig and stopped when they heard Sid's dog bark. There's a spur rowel." Guy picked it up, examined it clearly and gave it to Miles.

"Yes, it is Sid's," he said. "I know it well. It's from a pair of mine I gave him!"

The men looked at each other. "Now what?" said one. After much conjecture, they decided that by the tracks a little further on, where horses hooves had dug into the turf, there were at least four men. Careful observation up the cliff told its story. Sid had tethered his horse and walked down. Then the others came and after a scuffle he had been forced to travel with them.

Miles looked around thoughtfully. "This is apparently one of the hiding places for the gold, taken in the many robberies from the mines in Walhalla. A better hiding place than this little valley would be difficult to find. It is almost a small canyon, closed in with the cliffs and those huge trees. Chance though is always unpredictable. Trifles lead the way."

"Yes, Dad!" said Guy. "If our fences had been mended earlier, and if our bullocks had not been broken out and a shining spade!"

"Yes, Son! I realise it and," he continued humorously, "If you and Sid had not had sharp ears and eyes, and a thirst for knowledge as you hid along that hill top, well," he laughed softly, "we could go on and on, for its like an endless chain of events, but I hope it has not led to tragedy. This is beyond us," he said. "We must report this to the authorities!"

"They'll be a long time solving this, I'm afraid" said Joe.

"Yes!" agreed another man. "Maybe these duffers are apparently harmless butchers, bakers, candlestick makers, or small farmers milking their cows at this very moment. We have some queer characters beyond these hills, believe me!"

Guy looked downcast. "Yes! But what about Sid?" "What can we do?"

"Och! Some of these quiet fellows aren't what they seem, and they have contacts that fade into the bush for months on end, then reappear and the raids go on. They'll make Sid join them now!"

"Or silence him!" added another.

Miles glanced quickly at the man who had said that the cattle rustlers might silence the missing Sid. "You could be right!" he said sadly. "All we can do now, it seems, is to call in the police and see what comes of this. I'm dreadfully sorry. Come! Let's go home."

Quietly, the men dispersed. Guy and Miles spoke little on the way home.

The next day Miles strapped on his packed saddlebag, and rode out towards the city – Melbourne. Joe and Charles took their departure in the jinker beside him some of the way.

Leaving Miles, Joe ruefully shaking his head declared to Charles, "This has been a darned debacle of a trip from start to finish. I might as well have stayed at the logging camp!" Noticing that Charles made no reply, he nudged him.

Charles faced him with a quizzical grin on his clever-looking face. "It's strange! I seem to have had the only happy episode. Jinny and I reached an understanding!"

Joe's heavy lower lip twisted into a cynical smile. "Is that so? Then my fine young feller, your troubles are right ahead!" Charles' face darkened in a heavy scowl. He turned to his uncle, and said in a harsh voice,

"What do you mean? I shall be able to provide for Jinny quite well in a short time and," he continued in a more amicable tone, "you know that, don't you Uncle Joe?"

Joe flicked the horse thoughtfully with the reins as he replied slowly, "Yes, yes, but it's your mother I'm thinking of by crikey!" He waggled his head. "Wait till she hears of this. She's your mother, but she's my sister and son, she's a holy terror when ya go again' her! I'll wager she'll push a few logs in your way. You need to watch your step for a while, an' let me tell you this, you'll be danged lucky man if you ever put a ring on that lovely lass's finger. Too good for you she is. Yes! Too good."

Charles nodded, smiled faintly, and then was silent. For the remainder of the journey to Melbourne, the talk was of other subjects.

Early mode of transport at Boorarra

CHAPTER 16

MAGGIE, STILL THE SAME ANT-LIKE WISP OF A WOMAN IN HER long, tight-waisted frock, had lingered at the homestead gate watching Miles and his companions until they disappeared over the brow of the distant hill. She turned away disconsolately. Her usually serene eyes were clouded; her lips set so firmly that the fine-textured skin tightened over the bony structure of her face. She sighed, for her thoughts were constantly of the missing lad, Sidney. The impact and uncertainty of his fate had brought a sombre gloom to everyone's thoughts, as a lowering cloud engulfed a pine forest. She remembered his heavy lumbering steps as he entered the kitchen, eager for a meal, his small eyes glinting with avid curiosity as he sought to know the why and wherefore of any recent event of a large or small moment.

With regret, she muttered, "I'll never forget his face when he finally realise that Jinny was not for him, but," she shook her head as if enforcing her 'no, no, no!' to an invisible listener, "it could never be. Never! Their natures and their outlooks, even in this secluded forest, could never meet." She shuddered involuntarily at the mere thought. "And," she thought fiercely, "I never want him to come back to Rock Allen. There's something menacing about him! But," she temporised, "I hope he has come to no harm. Indeed I do!" She walked with dragging steps to the kitchen door, entered and somewhat ineffectively set about her tasks.

Jinny was away, rounding up the cattle to keep them from the broken fences. Grandfather, grumbling into his beard to hide his sheer joy of feelings needed in his advancing years, had trudged across to the stables to fill the mangers with chaff, and a more than usually liberal coating of oats. Gleefully! And the days passed.

The golden-red Autumn leaves were showering the rich, earth of the Rock Allen holding, and in the orchard, apples and quinces were sending forth cidery odours which Grandfather declared made, 'a fellow want to wet his whistle!' and Miles returned from his long journey to Melbourne.

Guy, busy breaking in a young colt, looked across the landscape and saw the lone horsemen against the skyline. So in rare excitement he tethered his prancing pupil, caught his hack and galloped off to meet his father. They greeted gladly, dismounted and walked beside their horses most of the way to the homestead.

As Guy prepared to take them to the stables, Miles said wearily, "A good rub-down and combing maybe you'll be after giving my poor steed? Indeed, an' I declare I could do with just that same myself!" he ended with a soft laugh, a laugh with little humour, as he commented, "it's a long ride to be sure, over a hundred miles in a couple o' days. Go lad! Take the horse an' be quick about it. Then I'll tell of my doings since I left home." He stretched his long thin arms. "Gad! It's stiff I am. Too old! Too old!" He shook his head ruefully as his son protested,

"Nonsense Dad! Grandfather says he's as good as a man of fifty. You're only a boy on that score!"

"Bedad! He also says 'once a man, twice a boy!' So he could be right! Yes!"

Miles had dismounted from his horse, stiff from a dusty ride of one hundred miles. His eager-eyed son Guy said, "Anyway, whichever it is, you're just right for me. But tell me, did you go to Kirk's Bazaar?" He edged closer and watched with the same eager interest, as of his childhood days.

"Not this time. Go on Son! Off you go with my tired horse!" Miles turned away and with quickening steps, entered the house calling in tender, vibrant tones, "Maggie! Maggie me darling." So good it was to be back with his family and to be taking up once more with the familiar routine of daily living.

Maggie had not heard him arrive and, alone in the kitchen, was bending over the fire, stoking it with heavy boxwood Guy had left on the stone hearth. She turned, her thin face alight,

"Oh Miles. I'm so glad you're home." She kissed him and, arms around her, he rested his cheek on her head.

"And so am I my dear. Even the air seems to welcome me. I feel the strain and tiredness rapidly lifting, and to be back with my family, is about everything to me."

"I'll make you a nice hot cup of tea. Just sit there in your old barrel chair." Thankfully he crossed to the hearth, and watched her make the tea and fill his cup.

"There! I've put sugar in it. Drink it up while it's hot. No news of Sid?"

"No! He seems to have completely vanished. The police told me that they've had black trackers out looking for those gold and cattle thieves. Now, they seem to think the scoundrels have disbanded for a while. They sent trackers up here straight away when I told them about his disappearance and the valley."

She clenched her thin hands. "Any news of Sid is better than this uncertainty. There's always been someone on the lookout here but never, never anything!"

"Sometime we'll hear something surely."

"Oh dear! I'm so afraid. This dreadful mystery!"

Miles frowned. "Yes, we're all concerned, but life goes on. There'll always be work to be done, and, by the way, how have you been managing?"

"Fine! Very well, really! Jinny has taken over most of Sid's work, and Grandfather helps. Guy does the ploughing and changing of the stock to the fresh paddocks. Grandfather has engaged a fencer. He says that soon the fences will be secure."

"Certainly you've done well! I'm so proud of you all. It just goes to show that no one is indispensable, not even your husband! Eh?" He smiled, then leaned forward and took her hands, "No! That was not a good thing for me to say. I'm sorry, dear!"

"I know Miles. But you must not say things like that to me, even in jest!" and Maggie's eyes flashed as she continued speaking. "To me, life on a farm is like a relay race. One drops out and the other carries on in his place, for things must be done. But in the end folks meet up again to check the race and each takes successes and failures according to his or her summing up!"

"Goodness! I thought you were going to say death in your analogy, Maggie!"

She shook her head at him. "No. No! Time enough for that. Now I'll pour you another cup of tea, and there's a big pile of letters waiting. One looks important." Miles took the letters and scanned the envelopes. Then he put them aside.

"I'll read these later. Tell me, how is Guy? I've been wondering just how his feelings toward Rebecca are going to affect his future. We'll just thresh this matter out. As things are here, there does not seem to be much we can do to help him financially. There is so much clearing still to be done and prices are low. However, they're very young!"

"Yes! Young in years, but both are so serious-minded and well balanced that they could be years older. Rebecca stayed a few days longer when you left, and helped with the outside work. I think they are very well suited to each other. She discussed animals and agriculture more as a farmer than a young girl. She's very helpful to Patience and Gerrard and often drives the bullocks or horses for them, with the clearing. She prefers being outdoors. That should make them good partners."

"Yes!" said Miles thoughtfully, as he puffed hard on an empty pipe. "But all that would be of no avail without love. Soon, these two will be planning a future together. I believe they truly are of one mind!"

"Yes!" said Maggie. She moved from standing with head bent under the mantelpiece by the fire and watched him intently. Pushing back her hair from her face and fastening it into a chignon on the top of her head, she crossed to the window. Turning back towards him she said, "Oh dear! I wish we had Mary-Ann here. Did you see her in Melbourne?"

"Yes! She didn't seem to be so gay and inconsequential. She said she'll come home next year, and remarked, rather strangely,

"Jinny's having all the fun!" I couldn't understand her, as she never really loved country life. I mean to say, she was never a part of it as Jinny is."

"She loved rambling through the bush, and riding," added Maggie defensively, "but what is the other news?" Miles stared.

"How do you know I'm holding something back?"

"I know you so well," replied Maggie. She stood silhouetted against the window, a thin yet graceful form.

"I've been appointed a Magistrate for all the country between Tangil and Dandenong," said Miles. "The authorities have at last realised that we have no available courts. It will obviate the long rides to and from Melbourne to have people's signatures witnessed and to settle disputes. Also, I've won the district election to our first Council, being the only one nominated."

Maggie said absently, "That's all good!" Still watching outside she exclaimed, "Miles! Miles! Something's wrong. Look, two men have ridden in and are speaking to Grandfather and Guy. There's

Jinny wiping her eyes and coming slowly to the house!" Miles rose and quickly went to the door saying,

"You stay here Maggie!" He hastened outside and went towards the group of men. When Jinny saw him she ran forward and threw her arms about him.

"It's, it's Sid Dad. They found him. He's dead!" she sobbed.

Miles held her closely. "Go inside to your mother dear. Pull yourself together, that's my Jinny. Now off you run!" and Jinny, head down, went slowly on her way.

He studied the strangers as he approached them, standing there, against a backdrop of trees and saddled horses. They, in their silence watched him.

Guy stepped forward, "Dad, these are police officers." He turned back to the strangers, "And sirs! This is my father, Miles Ford." Miles nodded to them as he greeted them and said,

"You have news?"

"Yes! We've found your man, a days march from here. Found him in the densest forest beyond those hills. His body was wrapped in a bullock's hide.

A long silence followed. Miles bit his lip. In the shocked horror of the crime, for a while he could find no words. He stood tense, drawn, then spoke huskily,

"Come to the house. You must have a meal before you return. There's chaff in the mangers. Your horses are welcome to it!"

"Thank you, Sir," said the young officer. "As regards this most unpleasant affair, you'll have no further trouble. Everything's been fixed up. You'll be notified of an inquiry. The greatest trouble's tracking the fiends who did this thing!"

"Yes! I fully understand," said Miles and he turned to Guy. "Help them horses, lad. I'll go ahead."

"Wait! I'll go with you," said Old Donald. "Somehow I find the weight of my years has increased these last days. I must rest a while.

Ah, young Sid! He deserved better than that, to be sure. Still," he shook his head slowly from side to side, "it doesn't signify. It doesn't signify."

Miles looked at him wearily. "What doesn't signify?" he said gruffly.

"It doesn't signify that whatever way we go, we haven't got our marching orders. Let's now turn Sid's page as lightly as possible," and thrusting out his bristly chin, he walked on quickly ahead.

GIPPSLAND STANDARD

July 19/61

"They Came to a Rainforest"

A Novel based on diaries of district pioneers who opened the country

THE EXPERIENCES ARE SIMILAR TO THOSE OF THE FOUNDERS OF FAMILIES WHOSE DESCENDANTS RESIDE IN WOODSIDE AND MORWELL AND YARRAM TODAY.

"IS THIS FOR PROGRESS, BEAUTY SWEPT AWAY?"

—By "Blin Mann"

So, Phoenix-like, the Ford homestead rose from the ashes. It was a large house, spacious enough for all Maggie's needs as mother and housewife.

One of Joe's teamsters gave Miles a very comfortable chair. "Made it out of a beer barrel, I did, and I even made the polish for the wood from yon 'black-boy' leaves, cushioned it with good Lincoln wool too! Just you sit in it, Boss!" He spoke with some embarrassment, yet evident pride in his handy-work. Miles sat in it and sighed luxuriously.

It's a chair fit for a king bedad." he replied; his pleasure showing in his merry eyes. It was a treasured possession; his very own down through all his years a token of good fellowship and a masterpiece in its own way of a bush man's craft.

For some days before Joe and his teamsters returned to the saw-milling area, he and Miles rode around the run for hours. "An eight-thousand acre run takes a deal of ridin' the [illegible]" Joe was heard to comment. When they returned to the homestead, Maggie could not fail to notice their avoidance of her intent gaze. She was intrigued but silent. She could wait. Life eventually settled into the familiar routine. The girls were set their daily lessons, but the call of the outdoors almost defeated Maggie's efforts. Within a few months Joe returned. Again, he and Miles rode the run, and talked to early morning hours.

He left shortly, and nothing said! One morning, Maggie was trimming a newly pressed cheese, when Miles entered [illegible]

[illegible] in assumed nonchalance. He laughed as he linked his arm in hers and firmly, yet gently he led her to her chair at the table, saying "sit ye' down my dear. I came to talk with you while all the others are away in the paddocks. In very faith, there's so much blather with the young folk around the place that we two never seem to have a word alone. Getting too silent you are. You think we don't talk. It's no good between man and wife."

"Then! Miles! You talk and I shall listen, for I know you have much on your mind. I've been thinking it's time you should be telling me what you and Joe are planning!"

"Planning? .... Yes! Yes! but I'm all confused —yes! confused!"

"Then!" Maggie laughed as with gentle sarcasm, she said, "maybe you should bring out your Irish poems. Do you remember how you could fold away your problems and read them to us? After a time your thoughts cleared and doubts settled like dregs in the coffee pot? Then you made your decisions!"

He took her hand and held it. "Yes! I well remember too, begorrah! That a certain fine lady opened a door an' peeped into the future to give me a lead!"

"Now! what have you to tell me?" She looked at the room, frowning at the thought of her unfinished tasks.

"Don't hurry me, Girl! Just listen. Somehow, with all the doings and turmoil we have lost touch. We go on with our work, seeing the waiting task ahead an' just take each other for granted." She smiled faintly. "It's just being there, knowing it. That's the secret!"

"Anyway, overwork, tiredness or family shouldn't be rubbing off the magic of our essential selves. You've disappeared in your silences. Come back my dear!"

With a gentle hand, she smoothed back his thinning hair and laughed softly as she said, "If it's trouble we're well seasoned; we can face it. Confusion? Well! I daresay we'll untangle it with time and patience!"

He rose. "Let's get along outside. We'll drive around the property while I tell you of the way of things as Joe and I see it all. I'll get the springcart and you get your sunbonnet!"

He crossed to the fireplace, took the big black kettle, filled it [illegible] on the crane, and swung it over the fire, which he stoked back [illegible]. With a merry grin he looked at her [illegible] "There now! The youngsters can be after getting a meal for themselves for a change!" So Maggie was soon sitting on the board seat of the [illegible] [illegible]

He touched Maggie's shoulder "Here is the answer, God! Everything one has yearned or hungered for seems to reach out from all that beauty!"

But she was silent; just watching the trees that covered the mountains, rimming the steep escarpments and deepening into the gorges to be lost in the darkness.

The rustle of wind gradually increased and the trees went into an increasingly mad frolic. She moved at last. "Turn away!" So they drove beside the creek in a lofty valley, and, while they determinedly talked of mundane things, the wispy mists veiled the high places.

The spirit of the immensity around them stayed and the frets of every-day living just vanished. But it was not to last, for Miles said abruptly, yet reluctant to introduce the subject, "We have a decision to make. I must surrender the lease of the run. Perhaps I should never have taken such an acreage. It appears that my ideas are larger than my capacity. Distances, pests, stock thieves, our stock that get lost in the forest, or mate up with wild ones, fires, floods. They're all too much for a little Irishman like me,"he ended with a wry grin. "We lose most of our cattle each year, sheep too

At least we fatten the dingoes an' crows in very fast"

So! That's my confusion Girl!" He looked into her face and said "Maybe we should return to the city". She lifted her eyes to the towering mountain. "No! No!" then with a sudden realisation she knew she loved this wild land and here she would stay. And Miles! He laughed in joy. "Such a woman." Now the way was clear. "Bedad we'll select land too. Maybe we have pre-emptive rights. Maybe!"

(TO BE CONTINUED)

Newspaper excerpt from the Gippsland Standard

CHAPTER 17

DURING THE NEXT SIX MONTHS, MANY TRAILS, MANY CLUES WERE investigated, but none shed light on the identity or locality of Sidney's murders. Grandfather declared, with his usual aggressiveness, "To be sure, they might be our next door neighbours… then again, they mightn't. Bedad! An' if I were only ten years younger, I'd be after scanning every man jack in the countryside. Indeed an' I would!" But that was as near as anyone could arrive at solving an apparently perfect crime; the atrocious slaying of a foolish lad.

The placid routines of farm life quietly resumed. "Life's for the living, an' the living have to face up to practical things!" Grandfather, expounding his philosophy of life, pulled on his bluchers, adjusted his bowyangs, jammed on his greasy old hat and strode away, bridle over his shoulder to catch his mealy-nosed cob to amble over the paddocks.

"And who can be up an' confuting that?" said Miles as he too set out to attend to his various tasks. He went across the yard to the stockyards where Guy had been working since early morning. As his father approached, he was greasing the axle of a wagon wheel, and neither by sign nor deed gave acknowledgement of the former's presence. As he carefully adjusted the wheel into its true location in silence, Miles held a steady hand on the rim.

"Now that's set, would you be after listening to me a mite?" Miles' voice held a hint of sarcasm.

Guy turned a grease-blackened face upwards. "Go on! I'm listening!" Surly, grim! And with an impatient grunt, Miles turned, as if to walk away, and then checked himself, thinking,

"This is just no good. The young spalpeen is so unapproachable now. Something's eating at him. He keeps it all to himself and it's building up into a man-sized mass of ill-temper! I'll not be havin' it! I'll try again."

"It's about those cattle!"

Immediately alert, Guy unfolded his long body and with sudden curiosity he looked into his father's then inscrutable face. "Yes? Yes? What about the cattle? I'd say they're doin' just fine!" said Guy, in reply to his father's question. "And I'm pretty busy. I've still to grease two more wheels an' soak them in the creek to tighten the rim."

In a moment of sheer perversity, Miles stepped around the wagon and pretended to be interested in the spokes and slightly sprung felly of a wheel. Guy realised that his father was giving him a subtle hint that he disapproved of his mood, and his news would keep. The next move was his. So, feeling a little ashamed of his moodiness, he said,

"The trouble is, I'm a bit grouchy these days. Yes?" He moved closer, pushed his square chin pugnaciously forward almost to his father's face, and grinning impudently, pretended to shape up to him. They laughed shortly as Miles said, with a rueful shake of his head,

"Son! It's just the last stages of growing up, I'm after thinkin'."

"Quite likely. Now, what are you saying about a letter?" Miles took it from his pocket, and waved it casually.

"Joe says that some of his stock are being taken to the cattle sales at Dandenong in a fortnight, and, if we meet him at the bridge up the river with ours, he'll take them along also. What d'you think?"

Guy stood a while, head down, and tapping his thumb against his strong white teeth; then he looked across directly.

"Dad, I don't want to sell my share of the wild cattle. Sell Sid's an' send the money to his mother. They're fat now. I'll use mine in the bullock team. They'll all go along fine with that old poler and yon tongue. I told Rhys Treen I have no leader, an' he'll send one of theirs until I train one!" He spoke in crisp tones of excitement.

Then, in happier mood, he explained away some of his silences of the past weeks, all the time the wild cattle had been settling down, fattening in the rich river pastures. So, together again, father and son sat down on their heels and talked, while gusty winds whirled dust, dried manure and gum leaves around them, and the dogs slept at their feet.

Three times the big bullock bell, their dinner gong, rang at the house. At last, they stood up and, still talking, walked a few paces. Then suddenly, Guy, happy with the result of their exchange of views, shouted,

"Hoorah! Ah! Ah!" and laughed so loudly and contagiously as he vaulted the slip-rails of the stable yard, that Miles joined in involuntarily and every dog on the farm barked in a mad chorus.

Across the dinner table, Guy said eagerly, "I'll meet Joe with the cattle, Dad." Grandfather looked up, surprised.

"Eh, what's this? What's this?"

"Oh Grandfather! You were up in the paddock with the fencers when the mailman called. Joe has offered to take the cattle to market. His drovers will meet us at the bridge over the river."

"I'll go with you to help with the droving though the timber," said Jinny.

"Thanks my girl, but I don't think you'll be needed," said Guy looking away from her to hide an involuntary grin.

"Then how will you manage?" his father asked. "It does take more than one man to drove those cattle through the tracks as they are at present!"

Guy sipped his tea and eyed the family provocatively. Then he rose, pushed his chair into the table and walked slowly to the door. Laughing over his shoulder at them, as if he alone had the key of happiness, he called,

"So long! I'm going to get my horse and I'll ride through the forest to get me a drover!" Then off he went with a ringing call to his dogs and a 'laugh fit to wake all the ancient kings of old Ireland!' said Grandfather. Everyone said at once,

"Rebecca!"

In a few minutes, Guy was back and reined in at the back porch. "Almost into the kitchen you'll be pushin' yer way to be sure," said Grandfather, pretending to be irate, yet looking with pride at his 'handsome young varmint.'

Guy leaned over his horse to look into the kitchen and called Maggie. As she came towards him, he said,

"Mother, I'm going for Becky. If she'll come, you'll have her here for the night?"

He stroked his mother's hair as he spoke, and answered his own question with affectionate impudence. "Of course you will darling, for to be sure!" and he winked at old Donald. "It's up an' being the second Mrs. Ford she'll be one o' these foine days!"

"Go on! You young devil-skin!" called Grandfather, shaking his fist vigorously.

Maggie, patting Guy's knee, laughed as she said,

"Be off, and bring her along!" Guy wheeled his horse and galloped away.

Riding towards the Treen's selection at Bower Bird Hill, Guy sang to the rhythm of his cantering hack. When he drew rein as the track became rougher, he hummed and even spoke to his horse as if he were a friend interested in all his youthful planning. For his thoughts were rapidly taking him into a rose-coloured future. Yes! Soon he would marry Becky. They could overcome all the hazards of life if only they had each other to share whatever problems came along.

"By Jingo – Yes!"

Approaching the Treen's slab-built but roomy home in the clearing, he stood in the stirrups and gave three ringing cooees. He paused and waited.

"Yes, here she comes," he muttered as Becky, face radiant with welcome, long hair streaming behind her, and arms flailing, raced towards him.

He dismounted, opened his arms, and there, together again, they stayed a while in silence. "Darling! Let's get married. All along the track I practiced flowery speeches for you, and now all it amounts to is I love you! You love me, and let's get married."

"Guy! Dear Guy! Yes, let's get married!"

Entwining arms they turned and walked slowly to the homestead to ask the approval of Patience and Gerrard, Rebecca's foster parents. But, they listened to the young people's joyous plans in shocked silence. Then in his quaint yet kindly way, but with decision, Gerrard said,

"No, no, my children! Married you cannot be at once. Too young! Too young!" Guy and Rebecca stood still, taut with unbelieving surprise. But Gerrard continued. "Marriage money, too, as well as time, you must have. So little we can help you, with such low prices for our few heads of stock. A pity too!"

After further discussion he convinced them, and Guy and Rebecca disillusioned and unhappy in the anticlimax to all their gay planning, rode back to Rock Allen.

Some weeks later, with grim determination and many dark moods,

Guy had made his plans and set forth to make the 'marriage money' beyond his beloved rainforest country, and Rebecca resentfully awaited his return, feeling their youthful dreams were spread on the distant hills. To both of them, it was a period of discontent, but as the months passed, they accepted life as it was, and viewed their future with less resentment and more enthusiasm.

Gerrard said, "They're young. They'll make their own measure of living!"

"But," said plump little Patience, "young they are, but then troubles scar them deeply."

"Age wears 'em off!"

"Maybe, but the present is often bitter!" returned Patience.

CHAPTER 18

"WINTER SEEMS TO PUSH THE SUN RIGHT BEHIND OUR mountain, old Fantastic mountain!" Jinny, looking doleful, turned and walked slowly away from the window. She had been leaning over the sill, appearing disconsolate and tense. "In fact," she said in tones of disgust, "with all this rain and fog we might as well be trying to see through a distant pine forest! It's always raining, raining, raining!"

Her voice became a crescendo of girlish frenzy. Maggie's quiet reply quelled the rising storm.

"Yes! My dear, but remember, we live deep in the rainforest, a world apart. Winter closes the doors, but there are always windows!" Jinny was not done with her complaining.

"Nothing happens here but the seasons, and now that Guy has gone away, and Mary-Ann not coming home until summer, the place seems to be deserted. I wish she would come home instead of staying in Melbourne to study art. She's a little minx. That's what she is studying with Charles and his friends!"

Grandfather, huddled in the old barrel chair beside the log fire, looked across with an unguarded look of sympathy on his sharp old face.

"Draw the curtains, Lass, and light the lamp. At four o'clock, the day's done at this time o' year! But we'll have a grand evening with a game of cribbage, an' out books an' papers." He rubbed his gnarled old hands over his head as he continued. "Yes! Yes! Not to be rushing about an' doing things when you're young, that's mighty hard at times, but have patience my dear. Soon, the clouds will pass, the roads clear up, an' lovers come a ridin'!"

Jinny shrugged her shoulders and, standing there between him and the fading light, she reminded him of a young willow sapling, strong as life itself, yet ready to bend to the winds of chance. His face, fragile and ash-pale, glowed in the light of a darting flame as he leaned forward.

"Step lightly through life, my dear. Have your pleasures and keep your dignity. Don't be afraid to make a decision if you feel it's the right thing to do. You're unhappy, Lass, I see it, and I grieve. But nothing lasts!" Maggie, clasping her hands tightly, watched in grim silence.

Grandfather had spoken where she had not dared. She was momentarily uneasy. Somehow, her fast growing up daughter had built a barrier between them. They had lost the easy mother and small daughter freedom of thought and speech; companionship. She waited, then breathed deeply as Jinny smiled, moved across to her grandfather's chair, and twining her long, slim fingers through his sparse locks, tried to bring them to some semblance of order. She said softly,

"You're a dear, Grandfather. You always seem to understand." She stooped, and looking into his face, sensed an undefined sadness. Her eyes brightened with unshed tears. "I'll remember. You seem to read one's very soul!"

"It's the past telling me things, Jinny-Girl!"

Impulsively Jinny kissed her Grandfather's forehead. Her

mother, Maggie turned away. Somehow, the frets, and undefined anxieties that had troubled her fled, and, with lighter hearts, the three of them turned their faces to the window as the cattle dogs set up a chorus of barking. Maggie hastened to move the big crane and bank the fire under the kettle.

"There's Miles, back from Tanjil with the mail. Now, my girl! There'll be letters to brighten this day!" Grandfather's face beamed with pleasure. There would perhaps be mail from the old country, letters! Papers! Good!

Soon, through the noise of the wind and rain and the rasping of a branch across the old iron water tank, they heard Miles scraping his muddy boots over the old arc of a steel wheel-rim they used as a scraper at the porch door. Opening it, he brought inside a swirl of rain-laden wind.

"Whew! Cold it is and a cruel wind you've brought us!" Grandfather drew his chair nearer to the fire, and Jinny took her father's wet coat and hat, and then hastened to see what the mail bag had to offer.

"Letters! Plenty of them. Here Jinny, two for you. One from Charles, I see. Yes! And some for Mr. and Mrs. Ned Haven. Take them across to the cottage."

"I'll stay and have a talk with Letty a while!"

"Read your letter first," said Maggie. But frowning darkly, the girl placed them against the clock, and putting the oilskin coat around her, she opened the door and once outside closed it with difficulty against a thrusting wind.

At the fireside, Miles turned to his wife. "Jinny and Letty have become firm friends. It was a good move to have a married couple in Sid's place, especially as Letty is fairly well educated and of good family."

"Strange it is to me how these fine girls marry brawn instead of brain," commented Grandfather.

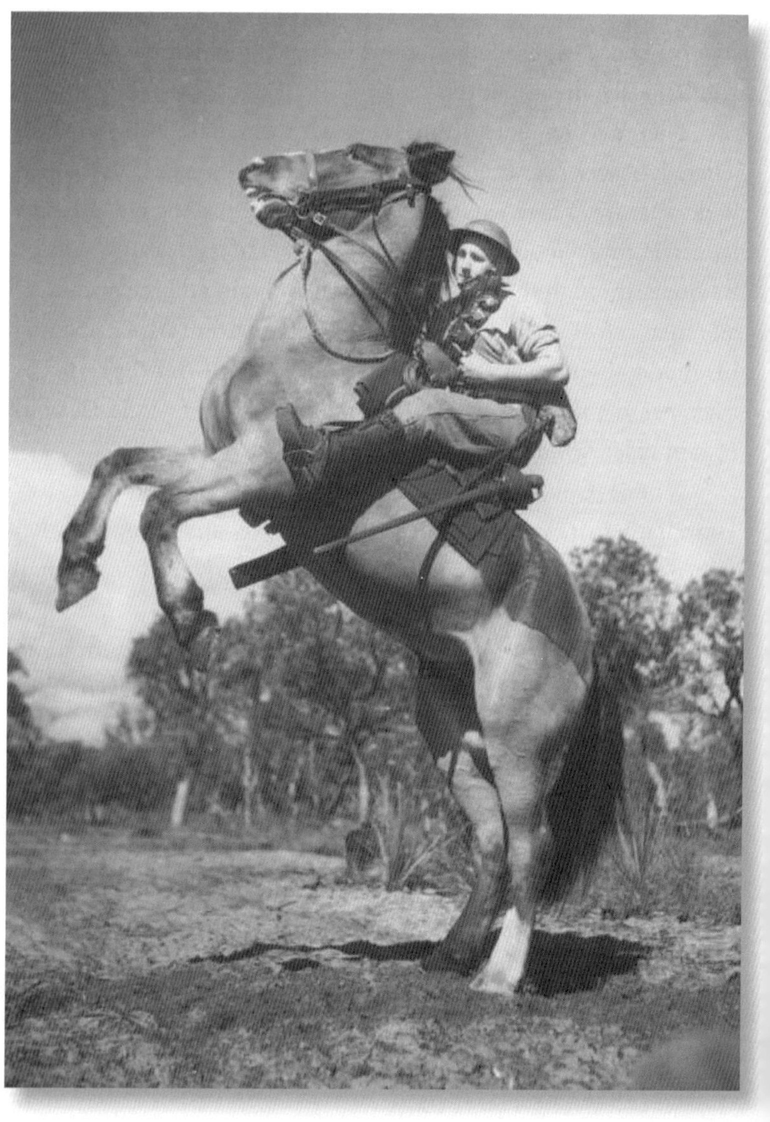

"Ned's a fine honest lad through, and he's so good looking," said Maggie swiftly.

"Ah! That's the snag. He's good looking and bang goes the lassie's heart. If she finds her fine man is 'like a goodly apple, rotten at the core', well she has the rest of her life to digest that fact. Yes?"

"But this doesn't apply to Ned and Letty, Grandfather."

"No! You're right, Letty is slowly winning the battle of inequality by interesting her man in a more gentle way of living, and he even reads some of her books now, she says. Imagine that, out here in the back blocks! And the man's a bullocky!"

"You're being unusually caustic," said Miles listening to them as he scanned the headlines of the newspaper. He looked down at the old man. "We were extremely fortunate to obtain such a good horse and cattle master when we brought Ned and Letty to Rock Allen."

"Ned has done a great job breaking in the bullock team for Guy. When he returns home, he'll be able to earn enough money to marry and keep a family. There's a terrific amount of carting through the Narracan valley with the split palings now that the roads are improved. Joe says that he can scarcely keep up the supply of logs of mountain ash, messmate and blue gum, the demand is so great. The air's ringing with the singing and axes of the paling splitters. It seems a pity to fell those glorious trees, but man must live, and this colony must progress, so that's the way it goes. Something must yield. But, to get back to Guy, here's a long letter from him."

"Yes! Yes! What does he say?" asked Grandfather eagerly. Miles looked pleased as he commented,

"For the only time since he left home three years ago, he has mentioned that very controversial subject, not being able to marry at eighteen. You remember? Gerrard, and I, too, urged him to wait. They were so young, so very unequipped financially. Perhaps we were wrong. It was a fine challenge to their youth. But life is very difficult in these harsh regions, especially for a woman, with the inevitable family and empty pockets!"

"I still think they would have managed," Maggie spoke softly, but with great firmness. With a swift glance at her, Miles said,

"You of all people should have been against the early wedding, for..." but with a very work-worn hand held up to arrest all arguments, she said succinctly,

"I've managed!" Miles agreed,

"You certainly have. However, time has passed, and it's no use doubting one's actions. I'm hoping the young people are holding no grudge! Guy said in one letter that he realised that perhaps it was the right thing to do. It was a good testing time!"

"And Rebecca?" queried Maggie with faint doubt in her voice.

"Well! Guy left home in a fury. His Irish temper just about scorched us all, me in particular! But I think he forgave us! Rebecca, I know was very resentful, very off-hand for many long days. As I have often remarked, there's an unknown quantity in that lass. Now, perhaps she'll be right. Listen, he says in this letter,

"I have my bullock-wagon painted gaily. I want everyone to see and admire it. It must shine in the sunshine, and glow in the rain, just like Becky does, for she's going to marry me, and live in it, on the roads. There are loads of timber to be carried from Walhalla to Port Albert, goods too. So we might as well have a whack at that, and the money to be earned, Becky and me!'"

"Now! Now, that's the best news we've had for a long time," said Grandfather. He could not hide his joy even with the severe look he tried to assume as he turned to Jinny, who came in on a whoosh of wind-driven rain and slammed the door.

"There y'are Miss. Even if the sun's been pushed behind Old Fantastic there's still plenty still in our hearts, and soon the place will be full of springtime again."

"Why?"

"Guy's coming home." Taking off the oilskins, Jinny just smiled, walked over to the mantelpiece, took her letters and crouched inside the big fireplace on a low stool to read them. Then, her face, inscrutable, she folded them and pushed them into her apron pocket. She asked for Guy's letter, and read it without comment, but with an involuntary smile of pleasure. Maggie and Grandfather exchanged a flash of the eyes and the conversation flowed about them again.

Guy's years away from home, much as he had resented leaving, were full of enterprise and variety. His letters were eagerly read for, as Maggie remarked,

"Letters are for days on end, our only contact with the world about us."

Miles added, "If we would only store them with a boon they would be to some scribe in say one hundred years time. By then," he thoughtfully tapped his pipe, "I daresay the whole face of this rich country side with its timber, its river flats and the minerals in yon hills, probably will be changed out of all recognition."

"Yes! Yes, but we'll not be here to see or know."

"Pity!" said Maggie as she nodded in agreement.

Guy had worked as a horse breaker on a large holding where drafts of up to five hundred horses were sent to Melbourne for the Indian market; the way of life he greatly enjoyed.

"Picnic races are to be held soon," he wrote to Rebecca. "I'm practising. Do you know I've discovered that I'm a runner? At least I can race all the lads on the station here. So Becky, if I win, you shall have a splendid present. What would you like best?" Becky's answer was always the same,

"I would like best to see you."

He returned home for a while, and Grandfather said, "Lad! It's given me a new lease of life to be seeing you around the place, an' you can be practising your running as you go up the hills for the cattle. I mind the time when I used to win all the races at the country fairs meself, in the old country that was. You see, all the Ford men were runners, good strong runners. You need some training lad. If only I had the wind, I'd be after training you meself." Guy, busy plaiting some silk for a lash for his long stockwhip looked up at the old man, leaning tiredly against the rail. His eyes held grave concern as he studied his grandfather's face.

"There's a chap coming over to the station each weekend when I return, to train me. I wish you were with me Grandfather."

"Yes, Lad. An' so do I, but be careful. There's a lot of shysters in that game, men who will burn ya out, take the very soul of ya, just for money to line their pockets."

"I'm beginning to realise that. A chap ha offered to pay all my expenses if I'll go to Melbourne and train. He told my mate in the station that I'll be a dark horse and he'll make pots of money out of me. It roused my temper, quite an easy thing to do these days, and I told him what I thought of him. Now I'm just going to run where and as I fancy."

"Good! Good!" said old Donald. "You've already won so many small events, you'll find y'self handicapped in the registered ones. Oh yes! I'm wise to the game. You'll find this's right."

"I'll be right," said Guy.

After old Donald's warning, he went to sports at Bairnsdale. He easily won the first heat of the handicap. After a terrific effort, he won the hurdle race. Barely recovering he, in his own words,

"Up and ran to the starting point for the next heat of the handicap. The starter refused to wait. I was barely twenty yards from the starting point when the pistol went. There was a dreadful reaction between my backers, and the starter and the bookmakers. You're right Grandfather. Shysters! Gosh! I hate 'em. Some bookmarkers offered me up to 40 to run stiff in the heat. Yes! Shysters! From now on I'll only run at small meetings for the fun o' the game."

Shortly after this, Guy joined the military and went into camp.

"You should be a good soldier my boy. All our people were soldiers or jolly good fighters," old Donald declared, catching Guy's elbow and grinning rather fiendishly. "However, you'll be mighty glad to be back diggin' post holes or grubbin' stumps. Take it from me!"

Sometime later Guy came home.

"Had enough of soldiering?" queried Grandfather.

"Yes! That Colonel Price just put the cap on it. I hate it. He gave us hell while we were on duty but plenty of latitude whilst off. Two thousand men were in camp, mostly wild young Bushmen. Things used to hum, I can tell you. We had lots of fun really, open air concerts, band competitions, boxing and wrestling contests and free fights. For those who were interested there was boozing an' gambling in the canteens."

"You were not interested, Guy?" asked Miles. "No! I wanted to save my money. Becky and I have our plans you know."

"You never wavered in your love for Becky?"

"Dad! Becky and I love each other, that is we are like-minded and of one accord. There's never been anyone else and never will."

Somewhat self-consciously, Guy hurried on with his tale of camp life. "After the first big encampment, things were tightened up and we didn't have such a wild time. I had an experience not long before I left. Colonel Price called for twelve volunteers with horses that could jump, to follow him across country to a point on the beach, three miles away, and to do it as quickly as possible. As you know, my horse was a show hunter and I had to volunteer.

We had to carry out kit, that is, heavy rifles and bayonets, feed bags and overcoats, a big handicap. The old Colonel had a fine horse, thoroughly trained. He was a dare devil rider, so you can bet he gave us a lively time. Only seven of the twelve arrived there with him. The others were left at various fences, but unhurt.

D'you know what, Grandfather? Five of the seven were Gippslanders. They have the name of being great rough riders. There was some jealousy between the Northern district men and our lot. The Colonel gave us great praise, which was something from him. He'd only sworn at us until then."

Guy stood up as if to leave the room. "Go on! Tell us more of you life there," said Jinny taking up from her sewing. Guy looked across at her suddenly and his face creased in a grin of expectancy.

"All that lovely white silky stuff! What are you making?"

"Oh! You mustn't look," exclaimed she as she covered her sewing with a scramble of hands and the end of her apron. "Turn away an' I'll tell you."

Guy turned his head but his eyes glanced curiously sideways. "No! Right away. Now," said Jinny, "It's for Becky. You guess why."

"Oh, my goodness! Take it away. I'll never be able to take my eyes off it now."

So Jinny reluctantly gathered her sewing and took it out of the room. "Go on!" she said with a laugh when she returned.

"There's not much to say now really. But I must tell this. While the maritime strike was on, it became known that the strikers were going to march through the city. Colonel Price offered to bring a contingent of mounted rifles to deal with the strikers. A special train was sent for horses and men, and we were all in Melbourne the next day. We went into the barracks where we were held, waiting for things to happen and ready to parade at a moment's notice. The fact of the Military forces being called up incensed the strikers even more. We were stationed at the corner of Elizabeth and Flinders Streets to meet the procession on the way from the wharf. Soon, a moving mass of strikers came. They were ordered back. Their leaders were told that they would be fired on when they got to Elizabeth Street. However, they moved on and heard Colonel Price roar,

"Fire low and lay them out!"

Everyone stood still. The strikers, the riflemen, the onlookers. Not a sound! The silence was potent. The crowd slowly edged back in tension and alarmed horror. There was not a shot fired. Disgusted at such an order, we lowered our rifles, even at the risk of court-martial. But then we were ordered back to the barracks. That was enough for me. Then I hated militia life. To be ordered to fire on our own countrymen who were only seeking a more decent way of living, asking for work to make and keep it at least humane. That was a few dreadful minutes, as if we were standing on an unexploded pile of dynamite with the fuse slowly burning nearer. No more camps at Queenscliff for me! From now on I'm going to be a bullocky."

Re-living the episode, Guy's telling was so dramatic that the family listened hushed, breathless. Then he turned with uninhibited gaiety and they relaxed as she shouted,

"Glory be! Next month Becky's goin' to marry me an' I'm twenty-one, and a man!"

"Yes, my son, a man," quietly returned his father.

"They Came to a Rainforest"

Miles lost no time in selecting his, in his own words: "three hundred an' twenty acres of this fine land, begad; right here at the homestead. Now I see my way clear. How I'll work every acre of this precious soil. Yes! Every ounce of it shall be payin' its way. Now, we can fence the paddocks, an' the botheration of all the wild things of the forest will be over. Post an' rails in the far paddocks. Yes! We'll mortice the posts from the best trees an' shoulder in the rails. Begad! they'll be here in a hundred year's time for our grand children to see how we could work, we, the ones from yonder countries. Imagine that now!" He looked around at Maggie and Guy, his face serious at the prospect of the years ahead.

But Maggie was watching him with laughter-filled eyes, and she nodded gaily at Guy standing by. "It's the Irish of him we're after hearin', he's so happy, excitement is possessing him!"

Miles stared at her, momentarily abashed at her imitation of his accent. Then he laughed with them. Still elated.

"You're right Girl, an' it's excited you should be, too. You with a selection of three hundred an' twenty acres of your own, a feine block it is, right against mine. The only thing that riles me is that you're not old enough to select a block too, young feller."

"I'll soon get over that, Dad. Joe told me he has dummied some blocks, and will let me take over one of them, right on the run here.

"Dummied? No bloomin' fear! You'll get your land in your own good name. I'll have no dummying; no truck with it. Confound it! Now get off with ye an' help Sid move some bits of furniture. It's your mother who's busy preparing a room for your grandfather. He's got a block alongside our's so is coming any day now."

"Is he going to live here always?" "Sure an' he is. "Sure an' it's glad I am," returned young Guy with a pert grin at his father.

"Get off you young spalpeen" exclaimed Miles, a semblance of anger tightening his lean face, at his mocking son.

In a short time, Donald Ford made the long trip from the city with all his possessions, and received a heartwarming welcome from his people at "Rock Allen."

Donald Ford, a man of many parts, as shrewd as any bush lawyer; active; honest as the noon sunshine. Aggressively honest.

When Miles told his father of Joe's land dealings, the old man stood in the doorway, hat in hand, ready to catch his horse to ride around their survey pegs and plan with his son, how best to work the smaller holding. He was impatient to be off, but the story appalled the staunch old man. He moved nearer and stood resting one hand on the table as he studied Miles' face.

"Is this true?" Miles nodded. Grandfather shook a

of a sawmiller to find a way of getting what he wants by hook or by crook! Hm! Well! We'll be afta waitin' to see what comes of it. Bad cess to him an' all" and he thumped one fist into the other in dire disgust, and stamped away outside.

In the earliest days of selecting "Rock Allen", the Ford home became as Miles' father irately expressed it, "alive, too much alive". "Great Scott! This place is just a dumping ground for all those dang fools of selectors. Just look at that conglomeration. Drays, spring carts, wagons; even sledges! The place is like Kirk's Bazaar. How you bloomin' well stand it I don't know!"

The old man shook his head and uttered a loud "C'ark"—a noise resembling nothing so much as the 'squark' of a debilitated crow.

His son looked around and realized that it was a very apt description: "Kirk's Bazaar". "Still", he said, "Dad, you must realise that, as this is the only clear acreage for miles around, and as the selector's blocks are well into the forest, there are no tracks. How far, I ask you, could a wagon go, once it crossed yon plateau? It will not be long before all these vehicles and possessions will be on the new selections."

"Hmm. Well! I grant you that" returned old Donald Ford. "They are all so danged sure that it's the best soil they have ever seen that they're working like tigers. They expect to be independent in less than no time. Gad. P'raps they will too, if they keep on grafting."

"Yes. They seem to be a bunch of honest hard-working folk. These working bees help. They get together somehow to help each other. Guy, Charles and Sid have taken bullocks and pulleys to day to one block. It's just a turn of the wheel. We might be glad of their help one of these days." His father grunted "Why! I don't know. "Haven't you enough for them to do here, with Maggie wanting benches for all those milk dishes, of breaking her back bending over boxes?"

Miles turned swiftly. "By George. You're right Dad. Come on, you and I will be at it now!"

With a secret smile he led the way to the wood heap to get the axes. So Maggie's big flat dishes soon had a rough lap bench to rest their weight upon, in a slab built, bark roofed dairy. This, she painstakingly whitewashed while the men were out in the paddock plowing, clearing, fencing, grubbing stumps or sowing crops. Little she saw of them except hen they came to meals. But Grandfather! Wiry old Grandfather, active and often irritable, yet was of much help to her. He was like an old warhorse scenting battle. Born on a small farm in Ireland, he had migrated tothe Colony in search of gold. "Only gold I got was sunshine" he declared. So like thousands of others with little money in their pockets, he had gravitated to the city. There, he married and brought up his family on the wages he received as a

He had the urge for land and his chance came to get back to the country, when Miles suggested he select some of the run.

"All you need do is potter. We'll do the work," he had told his father.

"Potter be danged! I'm good for a dashed long sight o' years yet. It's not pottering around I'll be doing. To be sure, its break in your horses, I will, and fence with any fella. Aye an' split palings too."

And indeed, the tall lean man was as good as his word.

Charles Day stayed with them for some months and it was "Old Donalds" secret delight to take him out for a day's light work. "Light Work". The lad with his background of little exercise and much study was according to Donald, "green as yon sapling. He'll toughen". He said tersely, with set purpose and a wicked gleam in his old eyes. Toughen he certainly did. But the first stages were torture for the "poor lad, and him so gentle and quiet," protested Maggie.

"Gad, we'll be after makin a man of him in this grand country to be sure," said Grandfather as he rubbed his gnarled old hands together in impish glee.

TO BE CONTINUED.

Newspaper excerpt from the Gippsland Standard

CHAPTER 19

TOUGHENED BY THE VARIED EXPERIENCES OF THE YEARS AWAY from his forest home, Guy had definitely crossed the transient or illusionary borderline between boyhood and manhood. Akin to his Grandfather, he was quick to make a decision and to carry it through. Impatient of interference, he certainly knew what he wanted and how best to obtain it.

"Begorrah!" said his father. "He'll not be making a mistake if he marries yon Rebecca, even if he has empty pockets."

Grandfather added waggishly, "Hard tucker sharpens a man's grinders. Let him be. Let him be. It'll cut no wood if we try to stop him now."

Miles contentedly puffed at his pipe; his thoughts were well into the future.

So, Becky and Guy were married in the quaint slab-built bush church with the fireplace where the forest settlers would worship while dinners sizzled in the big fireplace. But on this sun drenched day, the air fragrant with the scent of musk, ferns, pencil woods and gum-blossoms, with which the neighbours had decorated the church to show their regard for Guy and the once pitiful little stowaway, there were no dinners cooked. Already a grand feast prepared for all at the homestead, Rock Allen was awaiting them.

Some weeks later, Maggie gasped as standing in the doorway she looked beyond the far paddocks. "Miles! Miles!" she stepped back to call around the door. "Just look at our mountain! It's golden in sunshine and seems to be smiling at us like an old friend. Oh my! It just reminds me of Rebecca's face when she stood at the church door and saw Guy waiting at the altar, radiant, like that snowy immensity there."

Miles had left his old easy chair, and holding a finger in his book to keep his place, went to the door. Her little head nodded emphatically as she chattered on.

"Her happiness seemed to reach out to everyone. They all must have held their breath momentarily. Did you hear the gentle whisper of a sigh filling the church as Rebecca entered? Miles! Are you listening?"

"Yes, my dear! I am right now. There seemed to me to be an aura of happiness about the lass. I think that in a second, a swiftly passing era of time, she had reached perfection in mind and from which she might never again possess. It was something potent which touched us all. But I still feel that she has untouched depths of something I cannot fathom."

"Don't be so critical, Miles"

"I think Maggie, that real loving is a projecting forth of one's essential goodness towards another. It is truth and is therefore an insidious force that embraces those around in its supreme moment. It's mystical, wonderful."

For a while, husband and wife were silent. Then warmed by the sun, they went indoors. Maggie seated herself at the table and Miles stood in his familiar attitude at the mantle shelf filling his pipe. He paused, his thumb on the bowl. For a while the kitchen noises alone disturbed the silence. Coals creaked as they fell apart; a bee, captured in a bowl of flowers, escaped with a sleepy hum, flew against the window, and then escaped outside as they watched.

Maggie spoke reflectively. "When Rebecca kissed me as they were leaving, she whispered, "Now I have all I have ever desired. I am rich. Never again I hope shall I be running away, searching or be afraid." I think that was part of it all. She was free, and all they have of material things is a bullock wagon and a team of bullocks. Yet, how very rich they are. So much they have to give each other. They have waited and worked with this one aim, Just to be together."

Miles added thoughtfully, "Guy once said they were like-minded. Good. They enjoy working and relaxing. They are interested in the same things, although Guy will be hard put to it to keep up with Rebecca's booklore. Gerrard told me that, every evening since she came to them, he and she have read together over and over again the few books they had. Rebecca has a deep thirst for knowledge. She told Guy of her life before she ran away from her foster parents and hid herself in Gerrard's wagon."

Maggie, with swift interrogation in her glance hesitated, and then held up an arresting hand, "Don't let us look back. Don't tell me. I've always said, as Rebecca is, well, she is."

"I can tell you nothing my dear. Guy is content to close the past so why should we probe? He did say that she was like a shining star in a murky sky." Then, with an infectious chuckle, he said, "It was quite a dramatic pause in the festivities when old Joe Crow drove among us in that fine new gig and said to Guy,

"This contraption is your's lad, an' the horses name is Shyster." Then he laughed at us all as we gaped in surprise!"

"Yes!" added Maggie referring merrily to the remembrance of Guy who, for a rare occasion, was covered with confusion and wet paint! Joe had re-touched the dashboard with green, sticky paint.

Guy had exclaimed, "There are no shysters here. This horse is

'Joseph' after my very good friend. Come Becky." And together they embarrassed the man with a hand shaking, hugging and Rebecca's grateful kisses, before they seated themselves proudly in their wondrous wedding gift and, looking down, called together,

"So long Joe. Get up Joseph," and they drove around their folk. Then the moment for leaving had arrived. Rebecca jumped lightly to the ground and whispered to Gerrard and Patience,

"Thank you, thank you. Don't forget me." A rare tear coursed down her cheek, but was speedily dashed away.

There, recalling every incident of the first wedding in their part of the rainforest, Maggie and Miles were content. "So, instead of a slow trip in their bullock wagon they left for a holiday in dandy style," said Miles and puffed away at his old black pie awhile. Then, looking around he said, "The house is very silent. Where are the girls and Charles?" Maggie looked troubled as a puzzled frown aged her face.

"Jinny has gone up the river with her fishing lines. She's very reserved and quiet these days."

"Is Charles with her?"

"No! He and Mary-Ann are riding up to the tree-fern gully. She's trying to finish her sketches of the beauty spots before she returns to the city. Charles offered to help carry her materials." Sounds of farm life and birdcalls echoed through the open window. They listened grimly.

Miles moved to the doorway. "Here's Jinny now. Her basket looks heavy. She's a good fisher, our Jinny. I'll help her." As he left, Maggie called,

"Miles! Don't question her."

"Huh!"

He walked away. He took Jinny's basket, lifted the corner and said, "Whoppers! The biggest blackfish since Grandfather's the time he was so mad when Guy left home."

Jinny said shortly, "I just put in the lines an' was so busy thinking, I forgot them until the fish almost told me they were there. Poor things!"

"Thinkin' Jinny? H'm! It must be concentration that does the trick, eh? Come along inside, I'll help you clean them. My goodness! I'm going to enjoy my tea tonight. An' you Lass?"

"Yes Dad! And I worked out all my problems there."

"Good girl! And they were awaiting a solution for many a day I know."

"Yes! Grandfather once told me not to be afraid to make a decision, once I knew the right thing to do. He guessed my problems before I knew they were there."

"Yes! Now I'm afraid he failing. We must face it, but say nothing. It's as he said to me, "Fulfillment for me, my son.""

"I must show him these fish," said Jinny with an effort to control her voice. "Is he resting?"

"Yes!"

They went inside.

The next day Jinny wakened early. In the east, the sky was rose pink. The sun was just thrusting its rays above the horizon. She lay there idly watching the splendour before her. Lights on the distant clouds and treetops appeared to touch each golden fringe and glide away in changing hues. Almost breathlessly she awaited the final stages of the sunrise. It crowned the hilltops and the treetops, and the world was golden-molten gold on the swaying trees – and then, in its paling, came daylight. Soon she must rouse herself and begin her day.

As yet the house was silent. In the distance she heard animal noises and along the wide verandas birds were chirping as they fluttered through the overhanging creepers and the branches of the trees they had all so lovingly tendered over the years. Her thoughts went back as she watched them. The sun was pouring through the house, warming it after the chill of the night. On the breeze was the scent of woodbine.

She dressed quietly and slipped outside, crossed to the harness room for her bridle, then off to run in her horse to ride along the creek in the gully for a swim before breakfast. The horses were in the furthermost corner of their paddock. The dogs barked and a merry gallop was on. At last she caught her hack and, leading it through the stockyard thoughtfully, did not at once notice the solitary figure at the door of the stable.

"Charles!" she exclaimed in acute surprise and some pleasure. "You're about unusually early."

"I slept restlessly. Knowing you have an early swim, I've been waiting since sunrise. I saw you rousing in your hack and so, waited here. Jinny, we must speak together. I've never been alone with you since Guy's wedding. Why are you avoiding me?"

She stood listening. Then, without a word, her face averted, she walked to the harness room. He watched her saddle the horse and mount, but before she could leave he moved swiftly and jerked the reins making the startled horse rear in fright. Being an expert horsewoman she soon quietened it.

"Have some sense! That was a clumsy thing to do!"

She was angry yet sat there in the saddle waiting. To her suddenly critical gaze, his face, which she had always regarded as handsome, lost its appeal. The pale hooded eyes, the straight nose, the small prim mouth, the somewhat superior air of self-satisfaction – all changed in a flash to give a totally different image from her remembrance of a more youthful one. Her spirits rose with a sudden release.

Charles looked up with a smile as if to charm something he recognised in the toss of her head, as she said,

"There's nothing you can say of any interest to me now!"

"Maybe it's the years that have come between us, and we're two different people. It's almost a tragedy, Jinny dearest."

"Don't be such a hypocrite, and don't call me that! You know it's just an idle word. Yes! You're making a screen of words. Charles! Come out in the open. Leave your patter for your unfortunate clients!"

He looked at her confused by the change from the once so happy, pliable country lass to this angry antagonist – a different Jinny from the one whom he had once intended to marry. So, they watched each other a while, like baffled wrestlers. She was determined not to make it easy for him, so left it to him to speak. It was some years since they had agreed that they loved each other and would eventually marry, and this was the final issue. She was coldly angry, her anger over-riding all her past sorrowing.

Her afternoon of taking thought whilst fishing in the shadows of the creek in the gully, and whilst Charles was with Mary-Ann as she painted her pictures of the tree ferns and pencil woods, surely had enabled her to see that somehow, sometime, she had lost his love to Mary-Ann, and that was as it was. It did not warrant a fight. It wouldn't be worth the struggle.

At last he spoke. "Jinny, I love you as a…" but she interrupted harshly.

"Don't! Don't say it, how can you?"

He listened aghast, thinking, "How can I tell her now? She'll break her heart!"

Little did he know her thoughts were, "He's lost in his own conceit!"

He turned away, and for a few seconds the wind movements in the trees seemed to her to say, "Be still and listen." Then she dismounted and he tried to hold her gently, saying,

"We'll get married as we always planned!" She pushed him away.

"I wouldn't marry you, if you were worth all the gold in yon hills! Why don't you say it? Say you love Mary-Ann! Say she's pretty, accomplished and will make a fine wife for an ambitious lawyer. At present I despise you! I don't blame you for loving my sister, but I do hate a person who cannot face things openly and take what comes of them. I myself am almost similar, for I wouldn't believe what my senses told me. I certainly don't grudge you to my poor little sister, but for her future happiness, I doubt."

Looking vastly relieved, Charles preened his scanty moustache, brushed down his waistcoat and fixed his tie, but she had not finished.

"Have you any plans?"

"No!"

"Then make them! It would be intolerable and pointless to drift on indefinitely as in the past." He moved closer, "Jinny! I tried to say, I love you as a sister!"

"I hate you!" she shouted, and speedily left him.

Breakfast that morning was an unusually silent meal. Everyone was secretly disturbed knowing the silent struggle they had recognised, but not commented upon, was nearing a somewhat debatable solution. Rising, Miles nodded to Charles and the left the room, which was a sign for a general move. Mary-Ann disappeared and so did Grandfather, frowning and grumbling inaudibly. Jinny helped her mother, and then she too left.

She heard voices, and steps on the deep verandas as her father and Charles paced back and forth. From her own bedroom, having set it in order, she stood at the window and unashamedly peered through the Nottingham lace curtains. She saw Mary-Ann light and dainty as wafting thistledown when she stepped through a window and joined them.

Jinny could not hear their conversation, but their attitudes plainly told the tale. She saw Miles, tense and angry; watched Charles' face quiver nervously and Mary-Ann restlessly move around them like a young filly in the sale ring. Finally, she and Charles held hands and her father, shaking his head, watched them. Then apparently disturbed, he walked slowly inside.

Jinny turned away, flung herself across the bed she had smoothed down so carefully and, her young shoulders quivering, sobbed! Soon, however, she rose from the bed, washed her face and when she thought all signs of crying were cleared, she muttered,

"I'll go and talk to Grandfather."

Old Donald was in bed. "Age is catching up with me," he told the family, "and I'm not fashing over much about it. For the rest of my time, I'll be after doing things my legs wouldn't let my head do those long years past."

So he had found his hoard of pens and paper to write up some of his memories. He soon tired of that and passed most of his time reading and protesting irately.

"Bedad! An' I'll be makin' me own poetry, seein' as how I can't understand some of that Shakespeare an' his talk."

As Jinny entered his room he raised his head and smiled his pleasure. He looked keenly into her face.

"Come here Lass," he beckoned with is hand, so long and thin, it was like a claw. Jinny kissed his ashen face and he caught her hands and held her near him.

"You're troubled, my girl." He moved his head so that he could study her face. Then nodding gravely he said, "So you've made yer decision. I knew you'd do the right thing. It's so very right too. Yes! Yes! Don't fret my dear. It was bound to be this way. Y'r mother an' I saw this comin' many long days past."

"Oh!" Jinny stared in surprise as he continued.

"Little Mary-Ann marked Charles out for her own, before she herself even knew it. This day had to be. Jinny I'm so proud of you. Y've held yer head high and shaped yer own path. Although, perhaps y'don't realise it."

The girl spoke in husky tones. "Thank you. But how did you know Grandfather?"

"My dear! I know you, and I know our self-willed Mary-Ann. Neither is to blame, really, and in fact it's all as it should be. You,

Jinny, are a child of the crests of the mountains, the fields and livin' things, not of cities and man-made canyons. Mary-Ann, bless her little buttercup of a heart, is a child of laughter, of fine ways, of cities. Charles? Well! Charles'll do as Charles' wills, always. He'll be right with little Mary-Ann at his side, the gomeril," he ended fiercely.

"But where do I go from here Grandfather?"

"Dear! Just bide your time here with your folk and one day, you'll wake up and say 'everything's just grand.' An' sometime, somewhere, you'll meet an' marry a man who will be up to your measure. An' to be sure he'll be dandy. Begorrah, he will, the fellow who can be that."

"Oh, Grandfather! You make me add up to more than I am and I have been so angry, so bitter," protested Jinny, "and anyway, where shall I meet this dandy fellow you speak of?"

"Ah! That's just as I say. Bide your time an' to be sure, if y'stick your head up the chimney, you'll get who's for ye. An' God bless you my darlin' grand-daughter." With the utmost weariness he lay back on his pillow.

"Oh dear! Now I've tired you with my troubles. I'll get you a nice cup of tea."

With troubled gaze she tried to make his head comfortable on the pillow. He winked with all his past vivacity as she turned to go and whispered,

"Forgive 'em. They measure alike."

With lighter heart and swift steps she went to the kitchen, and old Donald muttered, "Maybe years will come an' go before yon lass makes another choice. I'll not be here to see how the pattern of the future works out, but I'll warrant there's certainly someone in yon forest who's my choice for Jinny." He shook his head rather sadly, "Time will pass and time will tell its own story. Begorrah it will!"

The busy years passed. Looking back, to Maggie, they seemed

to have fled with the swiftness of the shadow of a cloud over the countryside.

It was late spring and she stood in the garden, in a moment of stillness, alone. Her thoughts took her back to the earliest days of Rock Allen. She studied the homestead with its high walls, its spacious and deep vine-covered verandas.

"It's a far cry from the bark, slab and sapling hut," she thought. "How the years have changed us! Sometimes, though, I could well return to the days when the children were small."

She smiled while the sum of many of their doings passed as in a momentary phantasmagoria. Then her glance took in a belt of tall timber where a mass of scrub and saplings had once been. There was a small plot at its edge. The sun glistened on the white painted railings.

"Dear Grandfather! It's so long since you left us. But we still think of you," she whispered. Only the birds and a fat blind old dog could have heard her there, and little they cared.

The trees he had cherished caught a freakish breeze and, as she watched, the leaves seemed like merry spirits dancing to the memory of his volatile and happy, yet fighting spirit. Somewhat sadly, Maggie turned through the overgrown garden into the house: the big silent house. Trying to still her restless feelings, she walked through the empty rooms, but it was no use. Her children of the yesterdays were adults making their own lives.

Well, that was as it should be. She had enjoyed their formative happy childhood days with them. Mentally reproving herself as over-sentimental, she returned to the garden to await Miles' return with the men from his daily ride, around the stock. As she walked, the laurenstina showered her with confetti-petals and the racemes of the laburnum, like long gentle fingers, caressed her white head. Perfumes hung in the air.

Across the house-yard, Letty Haven was waving a farewell hand to her sons as they rode off to their work in the road-construction gangs. Ned was away with is bullock team carting on the roads. Ned, still hale and hearty and strong as his own bullocks.

Still her thoughts returned to the past. "Sidney! Poor, harmless Sid, so brutally murdered and his killers never brought to justice! Grandfather had once remarked,

"He didn't of his curiosity die in vain." The cattle stealers never returned. So he left us a gift, security."

Jinny? Yes, she, in time, married Rhys Treen. Happily. And she was content to move even further into the green forest. Mary-Ann and Charles Day were fast rising in the social set of Melbourne. Charles' ambitions were insatiable. 'Excelsior' could have been his daily slogan for his pride of place, for position meant more to him than even his bank account. But Mary-Ann, whilst enjoying the gaiety and glitter of city life, was not solely materialistic. As she recalled the past, Maggie was perturbed about her daughter. She remembered Grandfather again. How he had often remarked,

"That Charles! Y'know. He doesn't come of the kings of old Ireland like our little Mary-Ann, (Maggie smiled at the unconsciously arrogant pride of the old man) an' all the polish in the world cannot be turning brass into gold."

Mary-Ann, in her letters, often mentioned the delightful drives into the gullies and hills around Melbourne. Maggie pondered,

"Did Mary-Ann at times subconsciously yearn for the old familiar ways, riding through the splendid forest, swinging on the branches, riding the young sapling until her weight bore them to the ground, of piling into heaps the long strips of bark which hung mournfully from the giant trees, or climbing up the strong vines, the monkey ropes they called them? Did she remember the pungent scent of the pencil woods especially after rain? And the big grey kangaroos and wallabies, the little paddy-melons that would silently or with thumping noise cross her path? The gang-gangs and black swans calling weirdly, and the whistling eagles that sent their messages across from the tallest trees as she rode along?"

Again. Did she remember the whirling mist from the white-topped mountains, enfolding clammy ghostly arms around her whilst they adorned her young head in diamond droplets which gleamed in the intermittent shafts of sunlight?

"Ah'h!"

Then Guy! "To be sure there is no problem there. With Becky alongside him going into new ways on strange roads." She smiled at her mood of retrospection and went back into the house.

There was a pile of letters stacked up against the clock, the old Ansonia, and as the pendulum struck its resounding strokes, they flittered on to the hearth like gifts from an invisible hand. Maggie, gathering them thoughtfully, decided to make a clearance. She piled some of the big hob for burning, others she gathered to place in a drawer in the old cedar chiffoniere. Many papers, undisturbed for years, rustled under her hands.

"What a jumble," she muttered, as she ruthlessly threw them aside. "Oh! Grandfather's memoirs!" she whispered. She opened a tattered notebook, flipped over the pages in a hurry to scan them. "Poems!" she read on and smiled at light-hearted verses he had copied from long forgotten books. Then there were pages of his own efforts.

"Many the time he had grumbled about the cutting down of those trees," she thought and read his protest.

– MY PROTEST –

Once they were trees, spreading and beautiful
Resonant with bird-song; fragrant grand
Growing for centuries, though not immutable
Then pioneers rung them and left to stand
Like stark, grim tombstones.

Bare-limbed supplicants, eloquent of tears,
Of seasons. Upholding prayerful arms
To unheeding skies. Patterned by the years
Albeit, proud and majestic. Butchered on farms
Left as grim tombstones.

Shapes graven with epitaphs of fugitive race
Of ancient ill-fated men. Showing signs
Where primitive axes of stone left trace
Of shields, lithe canoes and vibrant times,
Now! Soulless tombstones.

Bow! Bow to the pioneer's inevitable fight
But speak to this generation and say
We heed the dire urge to put forests to flight
But you purloined beauty. You must repay
Repay trees for tombstones.

She read slowly and thoughtfully. Then the door opened and Jinny stood under the lintel smiling at her.

"Mother! Whatever are you doing?" said Jinny.

"Old letters! Papers! Why do you live in the past so much? It's no good. It's like trying to relieve one's life and that's impossible." She stooped and gathered a few loose papers. "You should burn and be rid of them."

But her mother just shook her head in negation and back went the papers in a jumbled mass. Then with a flourish of her hands said,

"How did you come?"

Jinny laughed tolerantly as she replied, "I rode Rhys's hack. He's so fat that Rhys is afraid of him foundering so I offered to use him. Rhys is busy ploughing for cropping. Grandma Patience is teaching the children to carve pictures on emu eggs. They're most interested and it will keep them out of mischief," she added. "They really are so energetic that they must be employed."

Maggie, watching her intently, remarked, "Jinny, you're a very happy wife and mother. You waited a long time before you agreed to marry Rhys. He was a very patient lover!"

"Yes! I was living in a bemused mood of bitter reproach about Charles and Mary-Ann. Silly. Now! I'm glad. Glad, that things happened as they did." For a few seconds the room was silent. Then Jinny said abruptly,

"Where's Father?"

"He went with the men to watch them draft our cattle for the sales. He has been away for some time, so he should be back soon. He's probably yarning with someone."

"Yes! Many people are coming to this district. There's so much gold being found at Walhalla that many prospectors are lucky and carriers are making a good living on the roads. It's not so easy to get farm hands, and Miles needs them. He's ageing. There's a time for a man to stop strenuous work. Life seems to be like climbing mountains. We struggle to the peaks, then slowly return, back to the levels, the starting point. There we stay and gaze at the place where we used so much effort; perhaps for nothing."

"Oh Mother! You are in a mood today. What of the fun we had climbing, the wonderful times we stayed on the peak, or the crest of the ridge? And the pell-mell scramble back with so much to think about? The richness of the valleys and gullies, and the hazy blue veiling over it all? We turned away so satisfied, so uplifted with all the panoramic beauty. Yes! It's the coming and going that counts. We could never remain on the crest. It's as you say, like life. But the moments of rare beauty! Well! We have reached the ultimate and should be eternally glad."

Maggie's eyes opened wide as she listened. "Jinny how right you are! You sound like Grandfather. Philosophy?" Maggie's tone was quiet as she remarked, "You'll understand Jinny. You and

Grandfather were good companions. It's not often I'm sad for him, for his life was complete. He welcomed his rest, but somehow, your plot seemed to beckon me. Imagination!" Her glance moved as she crossed to the open doorway. "I see your father is coming."

"Then I'll walk across the house-yard to meet him. Are you right now, Mother?" They smiled at each other. Maggie nodded. "I'll go then. It seems like old times when as children we ran out to meet him. How is he today? He appears to be aging quickly."

"You realise he is an old man," said Maggie easily, "but he'll be a changed man when Guy returns with Becky and the children, from Port Albert with the load for Walhalla. Bullocks are so slow. It generally takes six months to travel each way. So it's over twelve months since we've seen them and Miles is watching anxiously each day!"

With a gentle laugh Jinny returned, "And you Mother?" She caught Maggie's hands affectionately then examined them with troubled gaze. "Oh your poor hands. So twisted and roughened and once they were so slender and shapely." Maggie withdrew them and put them behind her back. "Yes. All the harshness of the early years hasn't altered you. You were so patient."

"No! No! My dear. I had many lessons to learn. Many times I rebelled, often loudly and indignantly at the lack of amenities. How I hated taking the washing to the creek and hanging it on the bushes to dry, making pounds and pounds, and pounds of butter in the hottest of weather and seeing it melt to grease in the burning heat of the drought years even before it could be taken to the stores! Then the times I shed tears over the floods and their damage, drowned or starving lambs and calves, and the times the men were so far away in the forest, splitting palings! No! I'm just an average back-block wife and mother. It would be too dreadful if advancing years did not add some measure of good from life's experiences."

Maggie was watching Jinny keenly. Suddenly her own face appeared to close. She turned away with widening eyes and quickening breath, gripping her hands until the knuckles were a whitened ridge. Swiftly she commenced her tasks around the fireplace.

"Hurry to meet your father, dear," and Jinny, unaware, went outside.

Maggie stood stiffly there, her eyes unseeing. Then relaxed. "It was one of those black moments. So senseless, so awful!" She whispered as the indefinable depression and desolation, which had suddenly gripped her, faded away. She felt as if she had been projected into some future happening, bleak and dire, which oppressed her with unrecognisable fear.

She roused herself and strove to clear her mind and body of the effect of her black moment.

"Silly superstitious old woman I'm becoming, maybe I'm in for a bilious attack," and she bustled around doing whatever task happened to catch her eye.

Outside in the clear sunlight of the highlands, Jinny hastened to meet her father. His weather-tanned face broke into a delighted smile when he saw her, and dismounting swiftly, bridles over his arm he walked on. His spare frame bent forward in his hurry to greet her.

"Jinny-girl! It's good it is to be seeing you! Did Rhys and the children come?"

She shook her head vigorously. "No! I planned that this would be my day alone with you and mother. It's little chance would we have to talk with those noisy rascals besieging you. I thought too, that Guy and Becky might be along."

Miles's smile faded a little as he said, "They're later than usual. There! It's impossible to gauge time on roads such as they travel. Mere bogs or quagmires in the rainy season! Dust heaps in the summer!"

They walked on, arm in arm, deep in conversation. At the garden gate Jinny took the reins.

"You go inside Dad. I'll unsaddle Bonnie." As lightly as in her early girlhood she sprang into the saddle then rode towards the stables. Dismounting and leading the mare to the harness room door, she unsaddled and ran the currycomb over the long sleek coat. Then she filled the manger with oats and chaff, accompanied by a progressive hinnying at the first rattle of buckets.

Closing the stable yard gates, Jinny looked up towards the sliprails. Suddenly she tensed, shaded her eyes and peered through the quivering haze of distance. Then she turned, and ran to the homestead.

"Come! Come quickly!" she called and at the urgency of her voice, Miles and Maggie hurried outside. "Look," she pointed up to the wide plateau where, what was just a dark blur before, was being delineated in the nearer approach, as a titled wagon.

"Becky!" they exclaimed in unison.

Miles exclaimed excitedly, "I'll go and meet them! Faith an' it's a good day this is. At the rate they're after travellin' it will be a full hour before they arrive. Those bullocks make their own pace an' it's a long journey they have behind them to be sure."

"So Bonnie can finish her chaff," said Jinny, "and you have time to have your rest."

"Come along in," added Maggie. There was no holding Miles. Soon he was cantering through the sliprails, up the track and out on to the plateau to Becky and her children.

When at last they arrived, the Rock Allen kitchen was alive with sound. Children were moving about, restlessly curious, anxious to tell of their life on the roads and to show their collection of insects, animals or seashore lore and preserved wild flowers. The shrill young voices dominated until Becky held up a long commanding finger.

"Quiet now small ones. Eat your dinner and begone." She pointed to the door and peace reigned for a while. Her children knew that she demanded obedience or the consequences were not to their own liking.

"Now!" She hid a smile at the children's sober face – Davys, Guy, Richard and Narissa! And continued, "Guy will be here in about two days, he thinks. He suggested I travel ahead and said, 'Dad will we wearing the track into holes as he rides along waiting for us, and you'll be keen to see Ma Patience and Gerrard.'"

Miles smiled, thumbed down his pipe and waited for more news of his son. "We were delayed by thieves on one of the loads of hogsheads of beer! As the roads are so rough and hilly, Guy often had to brake and make holes in the casks to free the gasses. Then he plugged the holes with wooden chocks. Along the tracks, people got to know when the bullock teams were passing the densest parts of forest, for they sneaked up at these places, pulled out the chocks and held cans to catch the beer as it spurted out! So there were many short weights amongst the hogheads! The Publicans were very hostile! Guy was furious! He's so fiercely honest, and it's almost impossible to find the thieves. They even put finer river sand in place of the stolen beer to make up the weight! Now the whole situation is solved. Guy has..."

She was interrupted by Narissa. The little four year-old, flaxen-haired child had quietly returned to her mother's chair. Standing behind it, open mouthed with interest, she listened to Becky's strong voice, but she could remain quiet no longer. She shrilled,

"We've got Sky," and like a flash young Richard, peeping around the doorway, dashed up and in his hurry to complete the tale, jumbled his words,

"Blue-blue Sky Queen-place."

Even Becky, striving to appear stern, had to laugh at the sudden diversion and explained, "They mean we have a dog. He's a blue Queensland heeler. Nobody dares approach the Ford family or their possessions when he's there. Sky! Everyone avoids him because he's a man hater, a one man dog, Guy's!"

Becky turned to Narissa and Richard, "Out!" and off they went like stones from a shanghai.

Bullock team with covered wagon

CHAPTER 20

MILES LOOKED ACROSS AT MAGGIE WITH LIFTED EYEBROWS. When the meal was over he took his book into the quiet of the drawing room, which with the heavy saddlebag furniture was rarely used, except for its coolness during summer, or as a retreat from the clatter of voices and kitchenware. Deep in his reading, he did not notice time passing, until Becky came into the room with the usual brisk stride. She was so thin that she looked taller than she was. Her face had almost emaciated in appearance, but the bone structure was so well proportioned that she would always have a claim to good looks, despite the freckles and suntan and the hair pulled so tightly into a bun on the nape of her neck. It was a strong face. Becky had no halfway characteristics. Her anger was knife-edged; her love was deep, lasting, yet fierce. Rhys Treen had often declared that he would rather be her friend than enemy.

"To meet the sharp edge of your tongue is fearsome," he had told her once and she answered,

"Then let those who are afraid of it keep their distance!" So Rhys had pretended dismay, "Not those I love, Rhys. Not my own kin, for," she spoke with a depth of gentleness in her voice, "you are my very dear, kind brother. Never shall I sharpen my wit on you."

But that was Becky, and as Miles looked across the room at her, she gave him the image of a handsome and capable young woman looking at him with smiling eyes.

She said, "Were going across to stay with Ma Patience and Gerrard now. Your man has attended to the bullocks and harnessed old Joseph in the gig for us. He's so fat, it will do him good to trot through the bush to Bower Bird Hill. As Gerrard would say, "Good you are to have taken care of Joe's wedding gift, the gig and 'Joseph Shyster.'"

They laughed together at the memory, and Becky continued, "We'll come back to Rock Allen in two days. Then Guy should be here. Good-bye Grandfather Miles." Miles made an effort to rise. "No, don't disturb yourself. The children will be along to say good-bye and Jinny has her horse saddled so we'll go along together". She kissed his forehead as he said sadly,

"It's my dearest wish, Becky that you and Guy take over this property."

"Leave it to Guy, he's not ready yet!" She smiled as she turned to go, and the four children rushed in, kissed him goodbye and were away in a matter of a minute – off to Bower Bird.

In two days Guy arrived and Becky certainly was there. She rode his old hack along the track to meet him.

"Getting old he is, to be sure!" she remarked. "The old gelding has stumbled a few times!"

"He was so sure-footed in the days when I rode through the forest to court you." Guy grinned as he added, "Pity we grew old!"

He tied the bridle on the side of the wagon and they walked together, arm in arm beside the bullocks up to the homestead.

Leaving the children at Bower Bird Hill with Ma Patience, once the team was rested, Becky accompanied Guy to Walhalla to dispose of his load. On their return, they remained a few weeks, as it would be another year or so before they could be with their home folk again. Then, looking back somewhat sadly, they coo-ed and waved goodbye as they disappeared over the brow of the hill.

Tall and slender, his tawny hair long and unkempt, dressed in patched dungarees and shabby shirt, and wearing his old blucher boots, in all their leathery impaired state, with absolute unconcern, Guy yet made a handsome figure as he stood examining his loaded wagon.

Becky watched him intently, her pride in her man shining in her eyes. He grinned across to her as he said,

"There's a fine load to be sure. Wattle bark, timber, and goods to be delivered on our way. It's a slow journey but we'll make Port Albert in good time. The bullocks are rested, so let's be on our way Becky me love!"

Smiling happily, she turned back to her charge. The covered wagon was their home. Soon their small cavalcade was on its way, moving slowly along bush tracks and corduroy roads. When the children were snugly asleep under their possum skin rugs, Becky and Guy would spend the velvet starry evenings beside the camp-fire in companionable silence, listening to the myriad bush sounds or talking the hours away. All so satisfying.

"Things are going to be alright. All we need is time. Time! Then we'll return to the land!" Guy in utmost contentment leaned back on a mossy log. "Land! I love it, and always it was so. I mentioned to my father that back loading from the Port is most profitable and soon we'll take up leasehold of our own. I thought he would be pleased, but no! His face tightened. He looked desolate and was very quiet. Then he said,

"Surely you're not after thinkin' to settle away from Rock Allen Lad! It's dreamin' I've always been, ever since you were a whippersnapper that you would work this place beside me an' your grandchildren with you in the years ahead. You must have had your fill of bullocking. Come back, back here where there's room an' to spare for you!"

Guy paused thoughtfully and kicked a log into the campfire. Watching the glittering sparks thrusting like yellow diamonds through the darkness, Becky shivered as she drew a shawl tighter around her shoulders. She waited. Staring into the red coals he continued,

"I see Dad's point of view. I said to him, "Becky and I have three sons. There's much good land open for selection in South East Gippsland and for them, I must be reaching out. One day we'll return to Rock Allen."

"What did he say?"

"Nothing. He looked so sad. I felt torn apart in sympathy."

"Leave it to the future, Guy. Only the present is ours."

"Yes! But in fact, I'm tired of bullocking. It's time we had a more settled way of life. These children will grow up as complete savages if this nomadic way of life continues. But come. It's been a long day and I'm mighty tired. Are you Becky?"

"No! I could sit by the fire all night enfolded by this darkness, with you beside me."

"Come. Come away. To sleep through the night is best. I'll leave ahead of you in the morning to unload at the Port. Wait for me at Lily's Leaf. There we'll head back home. Come, sleep my Becky. The future looks so bright."

But only the present was theirs.

In the next evening when Guy pulled in at the wayside hotel with his bullock team, Lily Leaf was a scene of activity. Weary bullock teams lined the roadside and their drivers crowded the low verandas of the country roadside pub.

The boats of the Port had unloaded their cargoes and the wagon drives were the first stage of their return trips. Piled high with goods, stationary there and covered, they resembled great humped mountains and monstrous animals, with long shafts like horns dug into the soil. Noise of voices, cattle and bullock-bells filled the salt-tanged air and in the distance, birds calling their evensongs and the boom of the distant ocean. Guy stood beside his bullocks, watching them feed and, at times, searching the distance of a sign of Becky. While he unloaded and again loaded at Port, she had paused beside a billabong to wash the children and prepare a meal.

"Ah!" he muttered in relief. The wagon, silhouetted on the brow of the hill, came slowly nearer. He looked around for a sheltered place for Becky to draw her vehicle, and chose a big she-oak.

"She'll listen to the weird whistle of the wind through these needle-like leaves," he thought. He looked back at his bullocks then, passing by the crowds of men around the hotel and the numerous wagons, he walked along the blue-metalled road the early convicts from Tasmania had made from ship ballast. He gathered odd-shaped pieces of basalt and put them in his pocket for playthings for his children; Davys, Guy, Richard and Narissa.

"They can play 'how many eggs in the bush' with these," he muttered with a smile on his tired face.

He stooped, and groaned in sudden pain. For a few seconds he remained head down, motionless. The pain eased. He breathed deeply. With slow, tentative steps he walked on. Becky was already speaking to him as he approached. The children were hailing him joyfully. With concealed effort he managed, in his unaccustomed weakness, to appear as normal. Becky jumped over the front wheel of the wagon and took hold of his arm.

"Guy. Guy. What's wrong? You look ghastly. Tell me! Tell me quickly!"

She looked anxiously into his greying face which she tremblingly touched. He took and kissed her hands with a tension which, more than his appearance, told her that all was not well.

But he laughed, his usual gay uninhibited laugh. "I'm just a little over-tired my dear. It was heavy loading, a long day. That's all. Come along. The children must eat and it's time they were in bed.

Then you and I will eat and I'll tell of the day and my load."

The next morning, Guy certainly was ill, much too ill to rise and yoke up to set out at first light on the long trail back to Walhalla. Still, he insisted that they leave later in the day. He must complete his contract, on time, well or otherwise. Arguments were of no avail. So, Becky, with sharpness in her voice, engendered by anxiety, declared,

"Yes! We'll leave right now but I shall drive the loaded wagon." Then ensued a battle of wits but finally, weakened by pain, Guy capitulated. He would ride in their wagon home and Davys, their eldest son, would take care of the bullocks.

"But Becky, my bullocks are like myself, tired, and you will find them difficult to push along. If only we could get some green feed into them they'd improve," he needled with a return of his merry smile, "and anyway, how can you make those lazy old polers and leaders pull, to say nothing of the tonguers, without some healthy swear words? I ask you, my lovely Becky?"

"Guy, you know I often drove lethargic bullocks at Bower Bird Hill."

"Yes! But they were in good heart on those lush green flats in the deep forest. These walking hat-rackers! You'll never send 'em."

"Just you listen to this, Mr. Guy Ford. Hup! Hup! You lily-livered Curts. Up! You blocks, you stones, you rocks rolled into a bog. Get inta ya yokes you belly-pinched brazen faced varlets, knaves, eaters of broken meats, puppy headed monsters, a plague on you, Poltroons…!"

"Oh Becky! Becky! You tear me apart! Those animals will gallop right past Rock Allen and end up to Walhalla in less than no time," Guy laughed until he subsided in utter weakness. "Tell me! Where did you learn such words? You who once disliked even your own voice when raised."

"Shakespeare, my dear," laughed Becky as she rumpled his hair and kissed him affectionately. "You're satisfied I can drive your bullocks then?" and, she added with a slow smile, "I'll change my voice."

"Darling, I'm so relieved that I'm a well man already," said Guy.

"You'll now be well in bed in that wagon. So let's get on the roads," said Becky. She turned and saw four curious little faces. "Get back into the wagon you varmints, an' look after your father for me. One word out of any of you and I'll cut all those golden curls off your heads with my bullock whip. Now get!" she shouted in such a voice that they turned and ran to obey screaming in pretend terror. "Davys, take up that whip."

From then, Guy's health delayed them in their travelling, and Rebecca had perforce many times to take the charge and trudge along the dusty roads. They decided that it was time to make a permanent home. Land was being opened for selection some miles from the Port. So they paid their fees, drove in their pegs and took over a block.

Guy remarked, "We must still carry on with the team, but eventually our land will keep us in all we need Becky. This is good country, and we'll make it better every year, so our children will have security."

"Guy! There's no doubt that you're stout hearted. Just look down at those gullies. The trees and scrub in this windy district look like a surging sea."

"We'll quiet 'em sweetheart. Just wait an' see. You and I together can do everything we want to do, just everything. We've made quite an amount of money on the carting with the team, so that's a keystone in the lintel of our future. Yes?"

Becky smiled happily. "Whatever you do is right with me. So long as we're together, I don't care if we have to chew cabbage stalks and camp in hollow trees."

"Becky! Becky! Cabbage stalks! You're a caution, but I love you from the crown of your head, along your freckled nose, right down to those awful blucher boots of mine you're wearing to go slogging along, and just you go an' take 'em off. They could be oozing water on our good earthen floor." Laughing together, they called the children to a merry dinner.

"Not cabbage stalks, my love?"

"No! Good boiled beef an' turnips," laughed she.

Guy's health improved, but one day they brought him home to a broken-hearted Becky. He had died on his horse. For her, the world seemed as a ruined waste – devastation. His heart had failed and she was desolate. Four young children were her sole cares. She rallied outwardly. Sympathy she turned aside. She was completely apathetic.

Men, in time came and offered to marry her, only to be met with white-hot anger and a lashing tongue. They called the tall, handsome, fine-boned woman a cold-blooded, fierce termagant. She had a grudge against the world. Embittered, hostile. Life without Guy was just 'a nothing.

At last she came back, a very changed Rebecca! (Never again was she called Becky). People opened their eyes in wide surprise; Rebecca Ford took to the roads again.

"There's good money, carrying, and my children must have the best education and land in this country." She could wield a stock whip as well as any man on the roads, and made her power felt in any argument. Her strong voice shouting all the classical epithets she gleaned from her reading, drove men and cattle to do her bidding. None but her children knew her tender tones, but even they dared not antagonise her.

Bitterness in her lonely soul drove her. She could drink with any man, but with aloofness. Men watched her striding vigorously alongside her bullocks, and marvelled. In the rough hurly-burly of life on the roads, she went her way regardless, even without haste at any time.

One day she picked up an old newspaper and reading it suddenly tensed at a notice of a search for a small girl who had disappeared some years past without a trace; the daughter of a French woman and Englishman.

"Francoise Evans – Me!" whispered Rebecca. "No! No!"

Then, realising that her father, the last member of an aristocratic family in England who had deserted her mother, had died, and she was an heiress to a large sum of money, she was interested. She had a small store of papers and trinkets to prove her identity, so decided after much thought to claim her heritage.

"I'll not use his money for myself but my children will have the best education and meanwhile I'll buy land. Yes, my children will be the largest land-owners in the country."

So the children were established in boarding schools and she, strong in her decision not to use for herself the unknown and deeply resented father's money, returned to her carrying. She was still bitter; still carried her grief for Guy as a flagellator, and still impelled her team with epithets gleaned from the classics read by dim lantern in the long sleepless nights.

CHAPTER 21

"I'LL NOT BE SHORT CHANGED," REBECCA'S STRONG VOICE RENT THE silence of the tree-clad distance. She stood, poised and erect, outside a bush shanty where she had just delivered goods from her wagon. The bullocks stood patiently by, glad of a respite after the long day's journey in the stifling dusty heat of the roads. She was furiously angry at the discovery of a shortage of her payment.

Her face, deadly pale, was set in cold anger as the burly publican paused, grinning at her, on the doorstep of his long low built bush 'pub'. He could not apparently, envisage the idea that a mere woman bullock driver would have the temerity to question his dealings. So often he had successfully taken advantage of the men coming and going. He stared open-mouthed as Rebecca's voice, strident and firm, continued.

"Man! You paid me half you owe me. Step over here and I'll give you a receipt."

With a contemptuous grin on his puffy red face, the man bowed like a giant frog trying to reach its feet over a gigantic paunch. Then, with a blatant sheer, he lit his pipe. With much deliberation, Rebecca counted the money she held then deposited it in the dust at her feet. Eyes slitted, and hard as flint, she watched him, then raised her long whip. With an insulting cackle of laughter and puffing unconcernedly at his pipe, he leisurely walked towards her. She whirled her whip and cut the offending pipe to the dust.

"There's a receipt for half my account. Pay the full amount or I'll write the figure on your back." The whip whirled ominously. The shaking bulk of the man disappeared with great alacrity back into the saloon. Rebecca's account was paid in full. Swiftly.

Like smoke under rain clouds, the story of how Rebecca reprised the cheating publican's pockets open with her whip, penetrated every logging camp, every pub and slab-built cottage. Many stories, some sheer fantasy, were told of the 'woman bullock driver, Rebecca Ford'. But she went on her way, unconcerned with the image she created, and with only one aim; to amass money. Money to buy land for, and when the time was ripe, for her children to take possession of it. None dared question her integrity.

On and on she travelled through the muddy or dusty roads, driving herself even harder than her bullocks. But under the harsh façade, she was still a woman; a woman with tenderness and compassion.

Once as she approached a wayside shanty at dusk she heard sobbing screams. Halting her team, she strode ahead. A stripling boy was being unmercifully beaten with a chain by the uncouth shanty owner.

"Stop it! Stop it!" she shouted. But the man, frothing and dancing in maniacal joy, continued. Her whip flashed in the long dusty rays of the evening sun. She tore his coat to ribbons and coiled the whiplash around his legs until he cried for mercy. She gathered the unconscious boy in her arms, marched into the bark shanty and bathed his many wounds, then placed him in the owner's bed and dared him to enter. She remained in her wagon outside there in the outback until her charge recovered. Then she fed and trained him until he was strong and able to work. He made himself a hammock of sacks which he hung under the bullock wagon at nights. 'Dusty' was the only name she knew him by, and he was a good handy man.

Each trip brought experiences, happenings. The English cricket team had been entertained at a fine country station, during which time a big kangaroo hunt was held. The hunt over, the happy cricketers rode on the swing-bridge and over the wide river with an almost military formation and clatter of hooves. They cantered up the gravely corduroy road and pulled in at the local hotel.

Fastening their bridles to the hitching posts, laughing and discussing the day's sport, they walked across the dry tussocks to a long veranda, then into the bar-room. The carriers and farmers leisurely drinking there ceased their yarning and, as one man turned, observed the strangers and with natural courtesy moved aside to clear the bar for them. The clamour of voices slowly resumed again though it all penetrated the noise of horses on the bridge.

Soon the double doors swung apart and in walked a huge man. He stood and looked about him; hatless, coatless and with shirt-sleeves folded carelessly over his elbows. A plaited rawhide belt supported his trousers – and his hands. His hair was wind-tossed and looked like a furry cap above his keen eyes, which glittered through his over-hanging eyebrows. He looked like a big friendly mastiff standing guard in the doorway. Ned Haven!

Then he said in his booming voice, "Good-day to you all!" as he strode to the bar and nodding to the barman said, "Give all these chaps a drink, on me!" He turned and saw two men in a far corner conversing very intently; an Australian farmer and an Englishman. "Who's the whiskery old bludger over there?" he shouted. "Give him a beer. Go on!"

"Be quiet Ned!" said Rebecca, the only woman there. "Don't you know that's The Honourable W.G. Grace, the best cricketer in the world?"

"I don't care if he's the Prince of Wales himself. Give the poor whiskery bludger a beer. Come on feller."

Consternation! But Mr. Grace, vastly amused, asked to be introduced to the genial giant. They conversed and drank together and when Ned announced that he had to be off, Mr. Grace walked outside with him to watch him harness the four ponies to his trap. He was most interested as Ned led one pony to each side of the pole, and then attached the other pair to the singletree ahead of them.

In the strong sunlight, the great cricketer and the burly bushman exchanged ideas and views for almost an hour. Ned had forgotten he had affairs to be attended to at the Port, and a long journey ahead of him; and Mr. Grace was most intrigued with Ned's views on life and living in the Australian outback.

Later, as he ran his hands over his unruly hair, he remarked to his wife, "Gad Letty! I was really careful to speak as you've been trying to make me all these years, but he was such a fine bloke, an' that's good enough for me. I'll tell you later of the chaps I met there. A whole cricket team! Imagine that! But I didn't think much of 'em as shots!"

"Ned! Ned! Will you ever learn to be discreet?"

"I'm just me – and Mr. Grace was just W.G. Grace an' there it was," replied the graceless Ned.

Amongst the carriers that day was the tall and weary Kemp Mallow, a very successful and shrewd man who would have married Rebecca, for he really respected and loved her. Numerous times he said,
"Next trip, again I'll still be asking you!" The man was loath to take her repeated refusals.

As he became more and more financial, he was even more insistent until he finally realised that there was nothing else but to accept that Rebecca Ford's "no" was definitely "no". Regardless, they remained very good friends.

Kemp Mellow was of good family, fairly well educated. Reading and increasing his bank account were his main interests. 'Carrying' was but a means to an end with him. His nickname was 'Copper'.

"Copper Kemp, he likes to pile up the coppers y'know," said Ned Haven once to Rebecca when they met at the small country township.

Rebecca said briefly, "They grow. He'll be quit of the teams soon!"

Ned had take up leasehold in the vicinity of The Port and eventually turned his interest from being a bullocky carrier to breeding horses.

"The best horses on the roads. Mind I'm tellin ya!" he was often heard to boast.

As this was certainly near the truth, no one contradicted him, for genuine horse lovers admired his animals. Rebecca was always happy to meet him when her team pulled into Longford. In fact Ned kept his 'weather eyes open for her' and if there were any hogsheads of beer or heavy goods to be unloaded he saw to it that his were the strong arms to help young Dusty. In the evenings Rebecca would spend much time reading by the fires in the big parlours of the various outback pubs or shanties. Here, Ned would join her.

"It's Rock Allen doings I'm pleased to be hearing of," he would say, and smiling at his eager face she would delve into her capacious pockets for letters from Ma Patience or Maggie. Then they would discuss every angle of the doings.

"When I get back there, I'll write to you and your wife Letty and tell you all there is to be told!" Rebecca said as she was on the point of leaving one morning.

"So long!" she said with a casual finality and turned abruptly away, walked a few paces. Then, just as suddenly, she returned and looked almost fiercely into his face, saying as if it were something defying contradiction, "I'm going back to Rock Allen to live. Yes, I'm going to be a farmer. There's no place like that rainforest country for me!"

Ned grinned at her as he slapped his leg gleefully. "Good on ya Missus. Good on ya!" Then he shook his head woefully, "I'm sorry I ever left the mountain. Maybe one day I'll go back!"

She looked at him with speculative and narrow eyes, "Maybe you will," she said. "Its land, land and more land I'll be buying. My children will be the largest land owners in yon green country, just you wait Ned!"

He nodded his head, "By criminy, I'll wait an' I reckon I'll see!"

Rebecca waved a hand and again turned away. "Well, we must move!" and she nodded across to Dusty who shouted to the bullocks.

'Hup'.

She whirled her long-handled whip and off they went along the corduroy road. Ned Haven pushed his hands through his rawhide belt and watched them wistfully until a turn of the road hid them from his straining eyes.

"Tough as dried beef she is, but a woman in a thousand. God pity her," he muttered and strode over to his horses.

CHAPTER 22

This was Rebecca's last trip with her bullock team. Although young Dusty was so useful and did the heavy work, she had had her fill of the roaming, restless life on the roads. She returned to the forest!

At Rock Allen, Miles and Maggie were almost pathetically pleased to see her. Much aged since Guy's death, Maggie was also very subdued. She had repeatedly said to her husband in the past,

"I should have known. I should have known there was sorrow coming to us, after that black moment that so distressed me one day when Jinny came across from Bower Bird Hill. Too young he was to die, too young."

Weeping, she was repeating this so often that saddened as he himself was, Miles had to remonstrate harshly, "Quiet! Quiet I say. Ye should know that life goes on an on, all we can do is accept our boy's passing. Calm yourself. I've had enough!"

Maggie, shocked into realising that grief was not hers alone, too heed. They were prepared to make their son's wife welcome in their home, and for a while all were content.

Looking around at the rich pastures Becky thought, "Yes. I'll live on here at Rock Allen alone but for my children I shall be. I must talk to Grandfather!" So, one day, she saddled a hack and rode out to the hill paddock to help him muster cattle. On the homeward ride, behind her slow moving stock, she reined in closer to Miles's mare and said without preamble,

"Grandfather Miles! Guy told me, many nights ago when we were camped beside a wayside camp fire, that you had asked him to bring us all back to live at Rock Allen and that you would give him half the property!" Miles looked across at her with a hesitant air, taken by surprise out there in the pleasant surrounding so full of colour, the movement of gentle breezes in the tall trees and quiet, fattening cattle.

Disregarding him, Rebecca went on, with her eyes intently narrowed, "I told him that I would not live with another woman in my kitchen. I might seem harsh," she hastened to explain, "I greatly respect Grandmother Maggie, but I shall not live with her, especially now Guy is no longer with us. I must rear my children alone." Her voice quavered, and then she said harshly, "Alone I say!"

Miles, involuntarily tightened his hands on the reins and the young mare responded by rearing in sudden alarm. He spoke gently.

"Steady girl, steady!" He patted the mare's quivering shoulder and for a few seconds there was a pregnant silence. Sitting there in the saddle, still running his hands through the mare's shaggy mane he waited for Rebecca to continue. He was puzzled to understand, "Just what's the girl driving at?"

There she sat erect and tense on her horse, looking like a latter day Boadicea. A shabby felt hat folded into a peak hid most of her hair except for the prodigious bun at the nape of her neck. A lightning thought stilled Miles,

"This is not the Becky we have all known and loved. I must be careful. That indefinable, latent force I once detected is emerging."

So, he waited, watching her with intent eyes, yet impassively.

She exclaimed with some impatience, "You must understand. I mean what I say. I intend to rear my children with hindrance from none. Not from you, nor Grandmother Maggie nor even my dear Gerrard and Ma Patience!" But he was still provokingly silent, determined that she would declare herself there and then. However, he was somewhat dazedly struggling for the best answer. She flashed him a wry glance and continued with sharpness in her voice, "My mind's made up, I shall live on the tilted wagon as I've done all these years past until you decide what your plans will be."

Then her expression changed and to Miles's discerning eyes the resemblance of the once 'quiet little Becky' returned momentarily. She came closer to him and looked into his eyes,

"Try to understand, I must go alone, that is my only way!"

Miles, still lost for words, looked around him, saw the swaying, sunlit branches of the tall gums, heard the busy, noisy honeyeaters fighting over the sweetness in the blossoms and watched the cattle lethargically grazing, tentatively attacking the silver tussocks. Somehow then his thoughts flew off at a tangent,

"There's little food value in that stuff for them!"

It was really only a matter of seconds, but Rebecca's voice seemed like a distant descant among the myriad noises of birds, insects and beasts as she protested harshly,

"Grandfather, you aren't even listening!"

He roused himself, turning to her saying, "Rebecca, I'm a bit confused! It's sorry I am, but give me time to think." But she was determined to have some kind of answer and said briskly, her softer mood gone,

"Are you unwilling to face facts?"

A slow rage crept into Miles as he thought, "Why in hell must she being so pugnacious?" He shrugged his shoulder as if to push the subject away. He said, "to be sure, it's not so ancient I'm after bein' that I can't make up me mind, and that same I'll be doin' in me own good time!"

He pointed to the straying cattle. "Come girl, or we'll be having to muster yon cattle again. I'll talk to you later," he said over his shoulder as he spurred the mare into a canter to round up the herd.

So, nothing was said until they had driven them into the fresh pasture, closed the gates and cantered back to the stables. As they unsaddled their mounts, Miles leaned across the mare's neck saying,

"I see your point but it seems to me to be a foolishness you're havin?"

He got no further. Her mouth set hard in straight line, she strode swiftly away without a backwards glance. He stayed there, leaning against the mount and thought,

"It's me that will be interested to see just how that lass will be arranging matters when the four children, older now and wiser in the ways of living, return from that boarding school!"

The next morning Miles and Maggie were in the kitchen where all the main episodes of their lives seemed to be debated, when Rebecca came in with an armful of vegetables from the garden.

She proceeded to shell peas, and told Maggie of the talk with Miles the previous day. Miles puffed away at his pipe, listening intently. When Rebecca had finished, Maggie rose from her bent-wood chair, ran her hands over the smooth wood and in dismay, stared with half-parted lips. All she said at last was,

"Rebecca, you must take your own way!"

"Didn't Grandfather tell you?" returned Rebecca in surprise at Maggie's paling face. Maggie looked across at Miles and shook her head. Feeling the need for action she took a broom and vigorously swept ashes from the cobbled hearth.

Her sudden tear-brightened eyes caught his, asking his help to say the right things to Guy's widow. Miles moved in evident impatience as if to say, such damned nonsense! Rebecca noticed, and her thin face hardened. Plop, plop! The shelling of the peas and their bouncing into the billycan were the only sounds that they heard in the suddenly silent room.

Rebecca had thrust the can down noisily and stood up. Her face contorted in anger as she exclaimed, "There's no need to be dramatic about this. It's merely a reasonable thing to do!" Then gathering up the pod angrily, she continued; "I have quite an amount of money now. Carrying on the roads was very rewarding, and there's a large sum from England. I've set it aside for my children, to buy land. I intend that they will be the greatest and most prosperous landowners in Gippsland!" She calmly walked to the open doorway, looked across the paddocks then came back and stood beside Miles saying, "I'll buy this property first, Grandfather. You should take life more easily!"

Then, she waved a hand nonchalantly towards Maggie, who was standing by, aghast. "This house is much too big for an old lady to keep in order, even though you now have help in the kitchen," she added, referring to the buxom lass from the township who had been with Maggie since Jinny married Rhys Treen. "I shall keep young Clara!" She ended suddenly as Miles, furiously angry, swung around at her with,

"Be damned! Keep you out of my affairs!"

Maggie was visibly distressed, yet angry too, at this audacious proposal. Miles, first filling his tobacco pouch from an old pewter bowl on the mantle-piece, strode to the door, paused a moment saying,

"Woman, we'll discuss this when I can contain my temper! Until then, you have a lot of thinking to do!"

Maggie said softly, "I'll help finish the peas," and Rebecca flushed, shrugged her shoulders most expressively. They finished shelling the peas in heavy silence. At last Maggie, the usually gentle one, almost bursting with exasperation exclaimed, "This is all too ridiculous. Let us speak at least!"

"Yes," returned Becky, "speak of anything but this contentious subject, you may be doing!" Maggie looked at her, shocked at such rudeness. She could scarcely believe this was the same person. Becky, in a rage, followed Miles example and left the room, closing the door with a resounding slam.

"I'll help finish the peas, and I should have answered the girl reasonably," Maggie told herself, "but somehow I had no words. It's all too sudden. So awful to be arguing with Guy's Becky!" Then, wiping her eyes on the corner of her apron, she shook her head and went on with the preparations for a dinner that nobody ate but Clara who was busy in the dairy.

A week went by, a week full of tension. Yet three people had time for thought. At least, Maggie said, "Rebecca was right. This house is much too large for two old people!" Miles had struck a match to light his pipe. In surprise, he held it until it burned his fingers. He threw the remainder of it into the fire with the force of his irritation.

"Faith and begorrah girl," he burst forth. "Is it going yon stubborn lass's way ye are? Leave be I say! There's room an' plenty in this house for all of us an' well she knows it!"

"Let me see." He splayed out his fingers, ticking each off in turn. "All those empty rooms. Mary-Ann's and Jinny's, Guy's, Grandfather's and that big sunny room old Joe Crow built for Charles Day many years ago, after the bush fire! Clara has her own little room off the back porch. Now, Rebecca knows this – still, she's making all this song and dance. You listen here. It's my belief she wants this house, but to be rid of us!"

"Oh surely not, Miles. Don't be so unkind!"

"Well, just you wait!" he said firmly. "Let her, if she's so minded, live in yon wagon. This house was built for you Maggie, an' here you stay until such time you will, to leave it! Now, let's put the whole confounded muddle out of our heads an' you be tellin' me of the doings over at Jinny's!"

Maggie did not reply to Miles immediately. She watched him with meditating eyes, yet with signs of deep unrest. His thoughts were concentrated on a single trend.

He repeated, "Tell me of Jinny. When is she coming with the children from Bower Bird Hill? Rhys is busy clearing virgin land with Gerrard, I know, and has little time to spare. They're doing a fine job with the Barger plow and bullocks and the Trewhella jack. It's a fine property now, to be sure, but so it should be with all their slogging an' sweating in the hefty forest it was when they selected it many years gone."

"Indeed! They worked no harder, nor consistently than you, Grandfather Donald and our dear boy Guy!" She turned away in sudden intensity of feeling.

Miles's kindly face seemed in a tangle of wrinkles as he grinned provocatively. She had, unawares, reacted to his subtle plan to turn her thoughts.

"She's been sad and remembering too long," he decided and became acutely angry. "To think that, after all the years of making-do, the hardships, isolation and sorrow, any member of the family could add another furrow to her face!" He glanced through the window as his old dog barked, and he frowned. "Yes?" he muttered and watched Rebecca striding towards the homestead. She was wearing a long full skirt which flicked the tops of her laced boots as it flapped from side to side. Her dark hair pulled tightly into a coiled bun shone in the sun, and gave her face an alabaster pallor, he thought, "There's no doubt, she's still a very fine looking woman." He watched until the corner of the house hid her. She entered the room, her face appearing more real and natural than it had since her return to Rock Allen.

She approached Maggie and said swiftly as if to check interruption, "I am sorry for this tension between you and me". She paused, as if the measure of her condition had taken her breath. Then she turned to Miles with a friendly gesture.

He nodded calmly, waiting, for he sensed there was more to come. She said with quiet determination,

"I have decided to take over Ned Haven's cottage and set carpenters to enlarge and improve it, and…" she got no further. Miles was furiously angry.

"The devil you will! An' where will Dusty go? Into the covered wagon?" He shook a clenched fist as he shouted; "Now just you listen to me young woman! We're your people! Yes, nothing will change that, but don't try to rule us!" He hurried on, avoiding interruption, aggressively, he thrust his hands forward, "You have a big problem. The futures of four young people depend on how you handle it! We wish to help. To be sure we do, but you know well that this's my property! You must have my approval before you interfere even with the shed!" He paused, breathless in his anger.

"Yes, yes!" said Rebecca flatly.

"Then," Miles relenting, said shortly, "Go ahead. Do what you like with yon cottage an' let us have peace!"

"No! No!" Maggie protested. She turned to face Rebecca, "It's time this thing was settled for good an' all. Shame on you girl, thinking to take Guy's children to the cottage. When they come, it must be to their father's home. Now! Have done! There must be no friction, for this IS home for them." She turned to Miles. "You and I will go to Melbourne to visit our Mary-Ann, as we have so long promised. When we return, we'll have clear minds and settle things peacefully, maybe!" Rebecca and Miles stared at her in surprise.

Maggie flushed and shaking, stamped in rage, which was a rare occurrence for the often almost annoyingly prosaic woman. However, she won her point and, head erect, Rebecca nodded to them and left the room, her face a mask.

Miles was stern. He swore softly but with unusual ferocity, and, putting a hand not gently on Maggie's shoulder, said between clenched teeth,

"Were ye after seein' the glint in her eyes? It's using us she was. An' she got her way, by Jove! Leave her to her victory for a while!" Then he laughed grimly. "In faith, my dear, it was a rare lift to me heart to see you not so soft. Gentleness can be softness y'know, an' it's often too gentle you are!"

"Get along with you man!" she replied and Miles, somewhat baffled, regarded her intently, but waited. "I've been planning this holiday for a long time," said Maggie thoughtfully, "and now's the very time to have it!"

"I should have known," laughed Miles.

The next day Maggie set about her preparations for their first holiday since they had taken up their freehold. She was excited. Her way of life had changed so utterly since her youthful days, and somehow, she imagined returning to the city would turn back the years. She was in a ferment of conflicting emotions. Dubiously, she regarded her few frocks. The best one was of heavy silk, voluminous, greenish black, very old and made by a country dressmaker. She shook her head slowly in chagrin, remembering the just right wardrobe of her early girlhood.

"Not that I mind so much really," she said aloud to the motes in the shaft of sunshine in her room, "but I'm afraid I'll look a queer one in Mary-Ann's splendid home! I'm just a dowdy old lady now!" she told Miles later as she spread out her best frock ready to fold for packing in the straw hamper.

Miles was very indignant. "Och, to be sure, you're still my Maggie, and Mary-Ann's mother. A ten-year-old gown is right with me an' I'm sayin' no more!"

Maggie stood immobile a while as she looked at the motley pile of clothes. "However," she said slowly, "I'm still a woman with the average amount of vanity." She moved closer to the array and again inspected her frocks, holding them away from her. In a little flurry of sudden disgust she turned to Miles with, "We'll stay home!" She impulsively spread her arms, picked up the heterogenous pile of garments, flung them pell-mell into the big old walnut wardrobe that had been her mother's in England and, with a satisfactory push, closed the doors on them. Miles stared, amazed. Then, a look, as when sudden sunshine had rolled away a clogging mist, overspread his face. He laughed aloud, and humming a doubtful tune – if any – danced a few steps of the Irish Jig.

Panting, he said, "My, oh my! What will Rebecca say? It will fair do me heart good to watch her face when we tell her of this latest move of yours. Is it disappointed ye are?"

"Yes I am, but also, I'm relieved!"

"Women!" added Miles desperately, "to be sure, it needs a Solomon to work 'em out!"

When he told of the change of plans, Rebecca made little comment, but thought as she turned away, "Things happen," and waited.

So, in the course of events the four children arrived home for the school holidays and outwardly at least there was harmony at Rock Allen. When the time came for their return to Melbourne they all begged to be allowed to travel on their horses to the bush school the Treen children attended. But Rebecca had made her plans and was adamant. However, Richard developed pneumonia and Narissa too, became ill. So the two young ones had their own way, and with much hilarity, eventually saddled up and romped through a few weeks of bush schooling with their cousins.

Then, two rebellious youngsters were sent back to boarding school. Miles, needing to attend stock sales, suggested that he and Maggie have their deferred holiday and took them to the city. Rebecca was satisfied. The plans for her children's futures were based on their schooling at, to her, the best schools.

So, according to Miles they had a 'foine holiday' and were

'dashed glad to return to the bush'. As they drove back through the countryside, they relived their long past odyssey to the rainforest. The time passed swiftly as anecdotes brought laughter, more memories, and to Maggie, at times, steady tears.

"I wonder what Rebecca's doing in our absence?" Miles reflectively remarked. "You know Maggie, I always thought there was a latent violence in that one. She came to us all a waif with nothing else but clothes on her skinny little body an' a pitiful bundle of trinkets and old papers. She reached out for love and to be sure, she got it. She still was a lone soul. When Guy died, Guy, the only person who really belonged to her, she changed. Now, she clings to her children so jealously that she possesses them. That's not good. It's a weakness, unexpected in so forceful a woman. She's building on a vision, an' it bids fair to become an obsession." He rubbed his fingers through the reins and his dark eyes took on a puzzled expression as he turned and looked inquiringly into Maggie's face.

She shrugged and drew her heavy cape about her thin shoulders. Miles whipped the horses and little more was said along the lonely bush track. When they arrived home tired, yet mentally refreshed, they found Rebecca in a much more amenable mood. So, the next day without delay, not wishing to leave their problems in such an equivocal position, Miles said,

"Rebecca, we want to do the right thing by you, Guy's widow, so have decided to give you half the property. Hush," he held up a hand in sharp remonstrance as she commenced to speak. "Let me have my say. I had intended to do this for Guy, so I feel in duty bound to do it for his widow. Had you been less aggressive, I would have done it sooner, but lass, you fair aggravated me with your bullock driver manner! Bedad; you did! And as this is the last time I'll speak of the matter, you can darned well live where you please. Here, with the little ones in comfort, or even over in yon wagon. The cottage must be kept for the workmen. Yes, an' its expecting I am that, before many months, we'll be seeing Ned Haven back. I'm after hearin' that his good wife Letty has died."

The three remained in uncomfortable silence for a while. Then, Rebecca said, "I'll take your offer an' help you with the outside work. I can break in the young horses and be a good stock-woman, but I'll not be a kitchen maid!"

Maggie nodded. "Then we're all served, for I too, like to work alone in my kitchen when my maid Clara is elsewhere!" Rebecca continued as if she had not heard,

"Then it's agreed?" She looked quietly at Miles. "We must put it on paper and I shall take my half share of all profits!" She laughed harshly, "You see, I am not a trusting person. Life on the roads certainly sharpens my wits. I'll make every penny a prisoner for I intend to buy and buy land! My eyes are already on that fine place over the river, Seth Strides! One day it must come on the market, for he's an old man with none to follow. It will be a start on the properties for my sons. I read somewhere that Cicero said, 'There is nothing more fruitful, nothing more delightful, nothing more worthy for a free man, than farming!' So that's the future I plan for my family.

Tersely Miles commented, "You plan?"

Blackwarry School 1906

CHAPTER 23

"YOU'LL BE DEALIN' WITH PEOPLE THERE," SAID MILES. BE careful. That's all. Now, we must draw up our agreement and you can make your way as you please then. But let us have peace."

That was the way it was arranged, and that is the way it was and Rebecca was, as she said, "Again a free woman." She worked like a man. True to her word, she handled all the young horses, saw to it that the cattle were rotated from poor to good pastures and fattened quickly. As time went on, Miles was, in spite of himself, leaving more and more to her commonsense ways of battling with the elements and animals.

"She has brains an' in faith, she knows how to use 'em," he once commented in satisfaction but with cold expressionless eyes, for, although he never regained his early affection, he had full measure of respect for her. Age, sorrow and the years of heavy toil had undermined his health, so, Rebecca, suntanned and as sinewy and strong as a man, delighted in taking over an increasing amount of management of the property. Things were going according to her plans.

When the boys came home from school, she drove them from one task to another, from daylight until dark.

"It's all in your own interest," she told them. Narissa too, was expected to do her share of the outside work, but she strongly objected, until, at last her mother said, "Well, you shall stay at your ladies' school until you make up your mind that it's a farmer's girl you are, and then, back here you shall come and stay."

But Narissa had other ideas. She certainly had no objections to staying on at school for she enjoyed the company of other girls and the times she spent at Mary-Ann's luxurious home in the city, and the many parties given for her cousins, Virginia and Jasper Day. She was her mother's daughter in as much as she had the strength of character and a defined will of her own.

Miles, somewhat grudgingly, agreed with the many comments of others, "Yes! Rebecca's a splendid manager of the Rock Allen property. It certainly has increased in productivity.

Ned Haven eventually returned from the coastal country, having lost his wife Letty. His family were adults making their own ways in life, so he was content to work with Dusty in the old familiar routine. Miles was happy to have him around.

Watching Rebecca one day, Ned said, "She's dynamite! A fine business woman! Strewth! A man would have to be as slick as a snake's tongue to get the better of her in a deal!" He paused to watch her selecting cattle for the stock sales from the herd they had just rounded up, and then continued slowly, "Dash me buttons! She turns a penny an' there, Great Scott, it's a pound!"

Turning to help with a troublesome beast, he muttered, "But she's' got me thinking. Something's at her." He shook his tousled head as he moved his greasy old hat around in puzzled thought.

Some days later, resenting her autocratic and possessive plans for her family, Miles said, "Begad lass! You can train stock. Yes! There's not a man in the hills able to gentle a rampageous colt nor a breakaway steer. But humans? No! They'll not indefinitely respond to the snaffles, curb or stockwhip manners. Use these and I'll bet me bottom dollar you'll get trouble. Leave those youngsters alone a bit."

"I know the way I'm going," and Rebecca turned away. But he added fuel to the rising fire of her anger,

"Guy would never have used such tactics."

Then she haughtily held up a quivering hand to check him. He was deeply irate.

"Snap out of it Rebecca. Guy was my only son. I too, loved him. His memory is bound up with all the happy companionable days of his youth. But to you, it seems to me, it is a scalpel flaying your very soul, contorting your every view of the lives of your children. They're people, people I say, with their own concepts of life. Don't destroy them or their love for you, or your own future." A tense and pregnant silence held them both.

Without a word Rebecca left him. For that speech she did not willingly look his way nor speak to him for days. Then her family returned for a while and the many complexities of dealing with them and their leisure cleared her mind of that assault on her devotion.

One morning, when the air was crystal clear and crisp with the scent of gums and acacias, Rebecca and her eldest son, Davys, saddled their hacks and paused when mounted to look across paddocks of waving grass and crops, towards the misted green-brown of the mountains. The grazing sheep in the far paddocks and cattle in the near distance added to the scenic beauty. Of a sudden, sensing a feeling of deep satisfaction, Rebecca laughed softly.

Davys turned in surprise. She touched his arm with gentle insistence, "Soon you will be taking over the management of some of my properties, maybe this one? I've often thought of you here at your father's home riding your long stepping thoroughbred hack after your own stock. She looked with rare excitement into his face. She waited and the stillness of the immensity before them suddenly became menacing to her excited brain.

The lad was immobile. His clenched hands and whitening knuckles were the only signs of his inner turmoil as he returned her gaze. Gradually her smile froze.

"What is it Davys? Why do you look at me like that?"

"Mother," said Davys gruffly, "I have no wish to become a farmer, much as I love you and this property. I intend to become an architect."

She stared at him, then she laughed, a soft breath of a laugh, but not with one iota of amusement, and she waved a strong brown hand as if to brush aside such rash folly. Davys spoke with outward calm.

"I've told you often mother that I AM going to be an architect. I want to design and create beautiful buildings, even bridges. Yes," he added with a flash of humour, "I'll even bridge the river between Rock Allen and Old Fantastic for you sometime in the distant future."

He stood there straight as a young sapling, his face bright with assurance as if he were endeavouring to sweep away the look of fury he saw swiftly changing her face. Her eyes were bleak, her tones icy, as she said with slow deliberation,

"Davys, don't be so utterly foolish. You'll enjoy your studies in architecture, yes. Pass your examination certainly, but be content to return to the land. Believe me my son," her voice became soft and she smiled with all the charm of her first youth, "the land will give you all the joy of creativeness you could ever desire."

But her son was not to be persuaded either by honey or gall. His face clouded and in cold anger matching her early fury, he said through clenched teeth,

"No! You have made my decisions all my life. I intend to be an architect so nothing you will say will make any difference. I'll no longer be forced to do tasks I hate in all weathers and conditions, when all I crave is my drawing board and the great books of the masters of literature and art."

Rebecca's eyes were wide open with dismay for she realised at last that her son's willpower matched her own. She moved closer to him and looked into his face distressfully,

"But Davys! Davys! I have bought more land and stocked it with pure-bred cattle thinking that it would be a wonderful start for your future accumulation of even finer holdings." She added persuasively, "Change your mind my son and come back to Rock Allen.

He shook his head. His decision was made and they both realised that no amount of argument would change it. They stood quietly, still. Then, his face crinkled with a mischievous smile as he put his arms around her shoulders, drew her towards him and rubbing his face on hers, said with a teasing voice which at the moment was so like his father's that she relaxed with a long-drawn sigh listening,

"Never mind old lady. Now. We'll be after saddling up the horses in faith ye can be showing me around the property. Then you might tell me how much money you'll be making off it for me."

She laughed in spite of herself. "You'll come to the land eventually young man. Everyone seeks to own even a few acres in time, it seems to me."

"Not me mother. Keep it for Guy and Richard."

"Start the horses," she ordered tersely. So they rode out towards a different future relationship and Rebecca had, perforce, to realise that her eldest son was indeed a man, no longer a malleable boy.

Davys had made his point and back he went to his study.

The day came later when young Guy too proclaimed his disinclination to be a farmer. All Rebecca's vehement protests, rages, promises of rich lands and money, even her painful loss of dignity were in vain; her coaxing could not sway him either. Guy continued his studies in law.

Rebecca looked imploringly at Miles, "Grandfather, you must try to convince this stubborn boy that to be a land man is best of all the ways of life." But the old man Miles had become, looked steadily at her, his deep-set eyes bright with intensity, said,

"No! No lass! Ye must mind the time when the children were small, you issued a keep off, my preserve order about their upbringings. Maggie and I were to have no truck with them. Begorrah! We've stood by your ruling all these years. Not so easy it's been at times but I admit it was the wisest thing after all. No! This is your problem. You have a wise head. You'll solve it in time I'll be bound."

So Rebecca fought her bitter battle alone. However, Miles was deeply perturbed. As he ambled his old hack around the property he stroked its shaggy mane and in his habit of thinking aloud said,

"A man plans an' builds all his life thinking to pass his gains of land or business on to his descendants, with the feeling that he then has reached his goal. There's Davys, now Guy, both fine lads who could carry on here. But no, they have other ideas. The Saints preserve us, Bedad!"

He dug his heels not so gently into the slow pacing horse. "Come on ye lazy old varmint. I daresay we aren't meant to live our lives over our children's children. But," he added, with a resounding whack on the patient steed's withers, "there's still Richard."

Rebecca, perhaps with the same thoughts, continued buying hopefully every farm or farmlet that came on the market. Her returns showed that she bought wisely and sold well.

"Yes, there was still Richard," and again, "Yes! Maybe Narissa!" Rebecca was like a person walking up a long dark road with eyes only on a bright light ahead, never even glancing at the possible treasures of the sidetrack. That bright light was "land, land and more land." The neighbours watched and judged with a degree of wonder and envy.

"To be sure," they commented, "she's lucky, she can't go wrong. She fair hits the market every time. Her stocks are always the prime ones and top the markets."

But all that concerned her was property for her boys who, she was to realise, did not desire it.

In her quiet and thoughtful way, Maggie watched the unfolding drama of her family's lives. Her busy years were fast lapsing behind and she had much time to think. More and more, her tasks were taken over by the strong and willing Clara, and Maggie enjoyed almost the grace of living as in her youthful days in England. She, however, felt very perturbed at the trend in Rebecca's planning. Was Guy's widow heading for heartache?

Still Rebecca consoled herself with the thought, "There's still Richard." Maggie, and Miles too, waited expectantly.

"Young Richard is so different from the others. Maybe Becky will have him to stand by her."

Spring merges into summer and youth attains adulthood with all its problems, but young Richard, as it happened, was solving no problems but his own. Life was not a serious business to him. He was the essential hedonist.

Rebecca's hopes for his settling on her spacious acres were met with frustration.

"Mother; you sent me to expensive schools. You have educated me for learning and fine living. I'll not be a land man in this wild country."

"Then," she asked in consternation, "Just what do you propose to be?" He gave a sudden abrupt laugh, and as if there were only one answer to that question, said swiftly,

"I aim to travel, to study culture, fine arts and enjoy the way of life of the world. You realise that you have since our early childhood impressed on us the necessity to appreciate the beauty of form and colour, to read the best books we could lay our hands upon and behave as young gentlemen. So, my dear Mother, I intend to do just that and on your head be the results," he ended flippantly.

Rebecca's fine eyes flashed, but for once words failed her. She was suddenly in a state of shock at the impact of her son's declaration. Unaware of her reaction he continued,

"Later perhaps I might return. Then I'll watch your sheep and cattle fatten and your men sow and reap your crops, cheerfully, most cheerfully my dear Mother, but," he added firmly, "I shall not live here."

Her face darkened in violent anger and not trusting herself to speak she glared at him, but Richard talked on regardless.

"It's a big world Mother. You are very wealthy, why don't you leave this dank country and take your fill of the good things in life?"

He had touched her deeply. Her face appeared to tighten as she said with seething emphasis, "Indeed?"

Then she walked a few paces from him and, hands caught together, exclaimed, "Land deserves better service than you would give it, by just absorbing the profits. You must give as well as take from it." She clenched her whitening knuckles. "Now after all your people's toil you would allow this heritage to resemble the grains of sea sand in the hand as they are trickling irresistibly back to their source."

She turned away from her son and with almost shambling steps dragged her drooping body through the doorway up the wide hall to her small office.

Back in the living room, Richard watched her departure with almost amused nonchalance. The matter of land-ownership was of so little importance to him that he barely understood her deep distress.

"Much ado about nothing," he quoted aloud and scornfully. Alone, Rebecca stood beside her desk, head down, her tall, spare body bent slightly forward.

Later she realised that she had felt as if she were on the crumbling escarpment of a mountain, stumbling helplessly down, down with the scree into a limitless plain of disintegration and waste. She did not hear Richard's entry into the room. He watched her slightly uncomfortable silence until, raising her head, she saw him and commenced to speak slowly, huskily,

"When the wind is strong it is better to travel with it than breast it. I'll go with it Richard," she nodded slowly as she fixed her glance on him. "I have decided within the last few minutes that I shall give you your share of my wealth. You must not expect, nor will you get a penny more, for I shall be generous. You can take it and set out on your travels. You agree?"

Richard laughed gaily, "I'll hold out both my hands my dear Mother." Rebecca impassively searched for her cheque book. At last she realised that dreams and actual happenings worked adversely.

Shortly after that day, 'Young Richard' left Rock Allen, left without one sign of understanding or pity for the bitter heartbreak he should have seen drawn in the lines of his mother's strong face.

For some days, Rebecca scarcely spoke to her workmen but from daylight until late night she worked unceasingly at book work and planning. Yellow lamplight shone dimly through the windows until early hours of the mornings. She sat alone, immersed in the affairs of her properties. There were new pastures to be cultivated, old ones to be sown down with grasses, spring crops and later, harvests to be arranged, stock to be sold or mated. She was curt with the men and rode or drove her horses until they were in a lather of spume.

Then one day she saddled a young gelding, rode at breakneck speed towards the mountain and spent the whole day and night in the densest part of the bushland. She returned haggard, red-eyed and hungry, but, as she said grimly to old Ned Haven, 'with the devil exorcised at least,' and she gave him her old comradely smile.

So he trudged back to his cottage thinking, "Now there'll be peace here an' a decent body can sleep o' night. Good riddance to that young scamp of a Richard."

Nevertheless, her son's apparent defection was no check on Rebecca's property sense. In fact it almost became a collector's obsession. Soon she was again bidding at all land sales. She conditioned herself to think of her son's dislike of farming as just a phase of their youth. In time the land would claim them. Their success at their chosen professions she accepted as just fitting returns, quite normal results for intelligent young Fords, but of course not to be reckoned with ownership and developing of rich broad acres.

"Lawyers, architects, world travel, ach!" Even so she followed their progress with growing pride. There was Davys, her eldest son about to graduate, with Mary-Ann's only son Jasper, who had spent all his school days with the young Fords. Mary-Ann and Charles Day had opened their home to their nephews and niece Narissa from the time Rebecca had first sent them to boarding school.

In fact, young Richard and Virginia Day had been dancing and skating partners for many years, both taking life lightly and happily, giving the minimum of time to studying or serious thought. But Virginia fell in love. Richard went abroad, and the carefree companionship vanished. Then Virginia's wedding plans at the Day's home brought the young people together in a rush of hectic planning and excitement.

Even the saturnine Charles Day relaxed and took full measure of enjoyment out of all the doings, but his wife Mary-Ann, knowing that there were limitations to his complacency, shrugged her elegant shoulders as she watched him – and waited.

At their very handsome suburban Melbourne home, Charles and Mary-Ann Day were in accord.

"Yes. Our only daughter Virginia must have a splendid wedding." So, as the wedding day approached, the excited younger people filled the fine home with happy conversation and laughter. Mary-Ann enjoyed every minute of it but Charles managed to elude most of the turmoil; the office, the club, his refuge. One morning Mary-Ann, busy at her writing desk, looked across the room with surprise widening her eyes.

"Charles? This is an unusual time for you to come home."

"Yes! But I'm not staying. I came for some papers. They're most important. I don't know how I happened to forget them. Its all this confounded coming and going upsetting the whole household." He spoke with frowning impatience, but Mary-Ann ignored his mood.

"Charles! You must help me with these invitations. You are most inconsiderate holding me up so much. There are so many of your friends you say must be invited. Definitely I think you should leave some out. Really this wedding is almost getting out of hand."

"Then delete some names from your own list, my dear. I have included only people whom I feel it to be essential they should be seen here."

"Yes! But they are not friends of ours, just business or social connections, and it certainly IS Virginia's wedding."

"Of course, yes! But it also the biggest social event of the season." Mary-Ann picked up a letter and waved it.

"This is from Rebecca. She'll be in Melbourne next month for Davys and Jasper's graduations. She writes that she will be sure to be at the wedding. I'm so pleased."

"Pleased? Great Scott alive! Surely you aren't inviting HER? A female bullock driver, a walking scarecrow of a woman, who once drank whiskey with any tramp? Ridiculous!" Charles paused, as if checked by a silence in the room. His thin face creased into a mass of frowning lines.

As Mary-Ann sat rigid and aloof, Charles, quite out of keeping with the pose of a dignified gentleman, snorted,

"Her family, having had good college educations, yes, invite them if you must, but a bullock driver! And a woman at that! God!

I can't even begin to imagine what my colleagues' wives will say behind their hands."

"Charles!" Mary-Ann rose and facing him, stamped her foot in cold fury. Her voice, however, was controlled. She spoke through almost clenched teeth. "Rebecca was a bullock driver, yes! And if she were charwoman or a street woman, being our Rebecca I would still have her here as a very important guest at our daughter's wedding. She is Guy's widow! And although I'm ashamed to say I have not met her all these years, I am still excited at the thought of seeing her. So there!"

"You're still a little spitfire, but," somewhat startled he moved over to stand by her side at the desk, tipped up her head and roughly kissed her forehead, "you're very lovely and very unpredictable. Go ahead. Invite even your washerwoman if you have mind that way, but," he added in a swiftly changed tone, "forgive me if I just say the minimum of polite phrases to that Rebecca!"

"Oh, you're impossible!"

She turned away and took up her list of guests and read the names aloud. Charles crossed the room and took the papers he needed from his own desk. Frowning impatiently he fastened his brief case as she said with emphasis,

"You must give me a few minutes of your time to check this list. I've been waiting far too long now!"

So, with an exaggerated sigh he pushed his case on the desktop and sat down. With tantalising care, she read numerous names and he listened in an uninterested pose. He moved impatiently as she remarked,

"I'm so happy that my father and mother, although so old, will be here. Now that Rebecca's living at Rock Allen she makes life much easier for them."

"It should. Living in the bush at their age! Just as well their health gave out!" grunted Charles. "They needed something to stop their senseless working! People so old should give way to the young!"

"You're a very heartless man. Someday old age will catch up with you. To be able to work on the property is a joy to them. And, and," Mary-Ann sighed, "I would just as soon not be here when you are their age. You will not grow old so graciously!"

"Mary-Ann! This is not your way. What has come between us?" Charles' unusually haughty face looked very concerned.

"Ourselves! Just ourselves, Charles! As Grandfather's Shakespeare said, "'Tis in ourselves we are thus or thus" or words to that effect, and I've been seeing myself lately. Yes, and seeing you too. Grandfather once said, "all the polishing in the world will not make gold out of brass," and I'm tired, deadly tired of all this polishing of the brass!"

She looked around at their beautifully furnished and decorated room.

"All my life, I avoided ugliness. I always wanted the best, the smoothest. Well! I've had my share of it all. Charles!" She rose from the chair and moved closer to him. "You are a very wealthy man. Let us sell all this," she waved her hand about, "and get away from the tensions, the mad keeping up. We could even go back to the country, back to the hills, the fern gullies and the tall timber! It's so lovely there, and people rarely talk behind hands. I'm tired of living on the edge of insincerity, of being afraid to be natural."

Charles stood aghast. "Leave Melbourne? Go and live in the bush! My God! Mary-Ann have you gone mad? I always hated it, even at Rock Allen when I went as a young boy. And I well remember that you were not sorry to leave it all behind you to follow the trend of city life."

She started, "Maybe, but I was so young, and strange to say, in love. You said you hated it? Then why did you go so often, and accept my people's hospitality?"

Charles laughed sarcastically. "Uncle Joe. Yes. My Uncle Joe was a very wealthy man. You remember? I looked to the future even then."

Mary-Ann recoiled, her face paling. "Yes! Money! Of course I should have known. I think that I have never known the real you." She shook her head in disgust as she slapped down her list. "What's the use? We'll leave all this conversation as if it had never taken place, until Virginia is married, married with all the ostentation and deference so dear to your heart. Then, well!" she laughed harshly, "We'll see!"

She rose and walked swiftly from the room. Charles, with an explosive oath, gathered his papers and left the house. The slam of the front door almost broke the nearby window.

A township near Port Albert

CHAPTER 24

VIRGINIA'S WEDDING DAY WAS BRIGHT WITH SUNSHINE AND COLOUR. The crimson and gold of autumn leaves and flowers gave the scene an air of gaiety and carefree joy. Mary-Ann and Charles, the extremely handsome parents of the bride, moved amongst their guests in the rooms and gardens of their mansion home, giving everyone the image of perfect marital felicity.

A guest tapped Charles on the shoulder. "I say old chap! Just who is that woman over there? She has quality, that one. I would like you to introduce her to me. Come along." So the head of one of the city's biggest organisations and Charles forged their way through the guests.

Rebecca, who did not usually give much attention to her appearance, had been taken in hand by her daughter Narissa and outfitted by the most exclusive shops in the city. Still tall and slim, almost angular, her face showed clearly its fine bony structure, and her complexion, although tanned with harsh seasons, yet had a fine satin texture which added to her air of good breeding. She stood apart, by a huge lilly-pilly tree, lost in appreciation of this lovely native, thriving abnormally in an old city garden. With head

Summer heat

angled gracefully backwards and her body relaxed, in sheer joy of the living beauty above her, she herself was just that. The native with the patina of the years; the essential Rebecca again; totally free of all past slogging on the road and its harshness.

However Charles saw nothing but the woman bullock driver; the only image his small soul could perhaps conceive. Rather reluctantly he approached and spoke to her.

"Rebecca, this is my friend Kemp Mallow. He would like to make your acquaintance. Kemp, this is Mary-Ann's sister-in-law, Mrs. Ford." He turned and left them. He wanted no part of the woman from the distant bush.

Rebecca had turned with casual glance, and then a marked change came over her face. The stern aspect slowly changed and suddenly her strong laugh startled the people about her. Forgetting their veneer of gentility, some of the wedding guests were openly startled. Her gaze travelled coldly around and dwelt on their faces with expressionless concern. Realising their lapse in good manners, they turned away with swift assumed nonchalance.

"That uninhibited laugh!" She understood their cold glances were 'you are not one of us surely'. She ignored them. So often she had met their counterpart in her lonely days as a bullock driver. With an overtone of pleasure in her voice, she turned and exclaimed,

"Cooper! Copper Mellow! Yes! And I didn't recognise you, so grand you are. Say! Where are your bullocks?"

"Rebecca! Cripes! I should have known there would be no other woman as handsome, even in this city." He took her hand and they looked at each other in delight at the memory of long, almost forgotten friendship. He looked beyond her at the sunlit lawns and gardens, almost obscured by people. "Come, let's go somewhere quiet, were we can talk, anywhere out of this menagerie."

So they walked towards the ornate entrance of the Charles Day home, entered the hall and, still talking, up the parquet hall in search of a quiet room, which they found. Settled in the comfortable leather chairs they relived the past.

Eagerly, Kemp leaned forward as he said, "To think that the last time I saw you up there on Walhalla road we, you and I, were dusty shouting bullock drivers. Now look at us! What a change. Come! Tell me of the years between."

Rebecca looked at him appraisingly. "Yes! To be sure, the years have certainly added something to your labours. You have come through amazingly well."

"Indeed I have. But then, what of you? You look splendid. But back down the years, even in your bluchers and that dreadful Tasmanian bluey you always wore, you looked regal. Tell me! Do you still swear in Shakespearian language? My! You were a tonic. You knew just how to rule a man an' beast, and by Jove every man on the roads was wary of you."

"Ach!" Rebecca shook her head and their laughter filled Charles' den. "I have no need to swear now. My children are grown up. One boy is an architect, one is a lawyer and the other has gone to England."

Kemp's big hands, broadened by the heavy work of his early

years were continually rubbed together in sheer pleasure. Once more in retrospect he, the urbane city financier, walked beside his bullocks through choking summer dust, or coiled his long whip around his head, spurring his team to pull almost beyond their strength through clogging, slushing mud. Prim secretaries and balance sheets – Pah!

Time passed rapidly as they recalled the past. Suddenly, Rebecca sprang from her chair.

"We must go back to your zoo, as you have so facetiously named it." He agreed glumly and they reluctantly returned to the guests.

Immediately, Narissa moved swiftly toward them. "Oh Mother! Where've you been?" She gave Kemp a fleeting uninterested glance. "I've been looking everywhere for you."

Rebecca was very amused. "You thought I had run out of this jungle. Yes? Dear daughter?"

"Well, knowing you I did think just that."

Rebecca gave her daughter a quizzical glance. "No! I was talking to an old bullocky I used to know, my friend Kemp Mellow." She turned to him with a slightly ironic smile.

Narissa in quick surprise, exclaimed, "Oh my goodness! Nick's father." The young girl smiled as with a sweeping bow, she said saucily, "How do you do, Sir Kemp? I'm sure it's a weird state of affairs that having a bullocky for a mother, I now shall have a bullocky for a father-in-law!"

He stared, speechless at such audacity. "Well, well! So you're the one Nick calls Rissa?"

"Yes!"

Kemp turned to Rebecca with sparkling eyes. Whether it was the light from the setting sun or just plain excitement was a problem no one even thought to work out but he certainly looked happy.

Narissa stared. She could not hear his faint whisper. Indeed it was difficult for Rebecca, as he said almost to himself,

"To think I loved you so devotedly, so long and hopelessly! Now, this, your daughter and my son!"

She answered quietly, "I could not give you less than a shared love, Kemp my good friend, and I shared my love with one man, Guy, for all time!"

"Yes! I always knew that you were a 'one-man' woman. I wanted a home and so married another, a good woman, but to my shame it was not as you say it, a shared love!" As they stood there, interested only in each other, in the tense moments, Narissa stood, open-eyed wondering. Tears came to her eyes. This was a new aspect of her mother and not the reserved, aloof and at times highly unpredictable woman, with whom no liberties could ever be taken, even by her children who knew of her love, ambition and deep bitterness.

Sensing Narissa's perplexity, Rebecca spoke with speedy change of mood. "So you have not met my 'Rissa? Well, I know your son Nicholas!" Her fine eyes sparkled, "But had I known he was this 'brazenfaced varlet's son', this -"

Here, Kemp Mellow's head went back and his wide mouth opened to its limits as he laughed aloud and long. The bystanders turned in amazement and looked at each other as if to say,

"Is this the urbane Sir Kemp Mellow?"

It was indeed, and with hands aloft, he exclaimed, "Great Caesar's ghost! Stop her! That Shakespeare's got at her again!"

Then he paused, looked around rebuking at the curious guests, and said to Rebecca and Narissa,

"Come, let's walk together by yon lily pond. Perhaps the fish will not stare at us!" So under the shade of an immense Moreton Bay fig tree in the spacious grounds, they talked with the young girl and listened to her youthful plans.

After some time, deciding they must return and mingle with the wedding guests, Kemp bowed with exaggerated dignity to Narissa, as he said with assumed gravity,

"Miss Narissa Ford! I am delighted to think you are to be my daughter, and I hope you will accept this 'base, proud, shallow, beggarly three-suited hundred pound, filthy worsted-stockinged knave' as a father-in-law!"

Narissa stepped back in confusion, but Rebecca laughed and exclaimed, "So you acquired Shakespeare also with the years? Still gathering, still the same old Copper piling up wisdom instead of copper are you? Dear! Dear!"

They laughed together, then she looked at him seriously, "I shall answer for my daughter and say that I'm sure you will make a very good father-in-law!"

She looked around at the placid waters of the lily pond and then caught her daughter's hand and his, looking from one face to the other and said,

"Such a happy day it's been, and to think I really tried to avoid being here for Virginia's wedding. I hope it will be a good sign for my niece's future. I'm glad I came." Narissa took her arm affectionately as she looked at Kemp and said,

"Thank you for bringing the smiles to her face. I think I am going to like being a bullocky's daughter-in-law."

She turned suddenly. "What's that you're saying, darling?" Nick Mellow had come up unobserved, and rested his chin on the crown of the girl's head. With an audacious gleam in his eyes, he demanded to be told just how these three had met together and the meaning of the few words of their conversation he had overheard,

"A bullocky's daughter-in-law! What ever are you talking about Rissa?"

Nick Mellow, immaculately dressed in the latest fashion of the wealthy young men-about-town, swung his tall hat to and fro as he waited for an answer.

Kemp looked at his son gravely. "Nick, this lovely young lass has just tole me she is going to marry you."

"Yes! We have mother's permission and we're going to discuss it with you at the earliest opportunity. You see, we have just arranged it. It must be this wedding. Romance is in the air."

The flock

He turned to Narissa. "Now you have met my father 'Rissa, what is this I hear about a bullocky's daughter-in-law. Some book you've been reading darling?"

"Nick! Don't you know?"

"Know what?"

"Easy now Lass," said his father. "Nick knows nothing of my past days of bullocking." He turned to his son. "You see Nick, when I met Narissa's mother here today, all the days of my youth which I had almost forgotten, in my efforts to amass money, came back to me. So much I tried to push the past beyond me that I did not tell you or even your mother." Then he laughed grimly. "I dare say, being in her social set, she would never have married me had she known I was a bullock-driver."

"Dad! You were never a bullocky! That's wonderful! Now I know what's been at the heart of me ever since I was a little whippersnapper. I always envied the folks in the bush. So you were out there in the forest, hauling great logs. Man! You were lucky. Why did you leave them?"

"Money. That's why I was there. When I got it, I left!"

"Just for money? Dad, how could you? And I would leave all this just to live the kind of life you left. Gosh! Things are topsy turvy."

All that afternoon, the pattern for Rebecca seemed to be apartness. They stood, a little intense group in the beautiful gardens. She thought, "It's in keeping with my life."

The sound of music floated through the greenery and people moved around more quickly as the shadows were lengthening, and the sun was warm and clear in its oblique beams. Kemp Mellow looked at his son and shook his head slowly.

"It's like a puzzle where the pieces don't fit. On person goes through life obsessed with an idea, a goal he's thrusting everything else aside to attain. He reaches his goal, and with loving pride holds out both hands to give it to the most precious ones in his life. Suddenly, what he has in hand has very little place even to himself. The others see it as something not worth a wink of the eye. I wanted money, money for life and possessions and to make my family happy, myself too," he ended dryly.

He sighed, and Nick said, "Well Dad! There's an old saying "one man's meat is another man's poison" but that does not altogether fit your case and mine. I've never had to fight for the things so important to most people in the way of life at whatever time in history one life's; therefore to me those things just don't seem to be so important.

Kemp agreed, "They say the very wealthy person declares money is a small thing. So is one's apple on a prolifically yielding apple tree. The one and only perfect apple at the top of the trees precious to the one who desires it greatly."

"Dad, you valued that apple at the top of the tree until you grasped it. Then you wanted the tree, more trees laden with fruit, until you had the trees all about you. All you wanted then was to give the whole orchard to the ones you loved; and do you know what they wanted? The ground the apples grew on. All I want in life is to start right back to the earth as you did."

"Strange!" whispered Kemp.

"I like to think that you were a bullock-driver, Dad."

Feeding the chooks

"And so do I," added Narissa, who had been listening keenly. "And I love you Darling Nick, even if you do speak in parables and with your head in the clouds, either planning to be a farmer or a writer." They held hands and looked into each other's faces, parents, garden and wedding guests forgotten.

Rebecca and Kemp stood quite still watching. Suddenly, laughter, clapping of hands and high voices broke the tension and turning they walked together rather hurriedly around the gardens and lawns just in time to cheer Virginia, the bride and her new husband on their way.

"Let's be married soon, 'Rissa," whispered Nick.

"Yes! And go back to the bush where I grew up, an' live happily every after?" she said.

"Yes! Yes!" he answered, kissing her shamelessly. Then Narissa added gravely, "But you cannot be a writer and a farmer too. Farming is a full time occupation mother says, and she knows. Let us start our married life there all the same."

"We'll see," added Nick.

Hearing the girls' reply, Rebecca, amazed, thought, "Life in time flows a full circle. I tried to force my sons to a life on the land and here is my daughter planning her own future there!"

CHAPTER 25

THE FOLLOWING WEEK, MARY-ANN, WITH CHARLES' SOMEWHAT grudging co-operation, arranged a dinner party as it was one of the rare occasions when most of the Rock Allen and Bower Bird Hill folk would be in the city.

Charles, trying to be facetious, which was his pompous manner, unconvincingly said, "Wedding and funerals seem to be the only time we meet our bush relations," and he muttered as an aside, "just as well too perhaps."

Mary-Ann angrily retorted, "You should be ashamed to speak in that way of my people. How one's thoughts take shape in words eventually! This will be a special occasion! Narissa's engagement to Sir Kemp and Lady Mellow's son will be announced." She added with a touch of malice, "That at least should please you."

Charles flushed angrily, "Huh! The Ford family is certainly rising in the social scale!" Mary-Ann thought swiftly,

"Why must we be like this?" Then, furiously angry at the impact of his retort, said, "My people place more value on human relationships than on social prestige, which I assure you has been much more rewarding than you could begin to understand Charles! I pity you. Myself too!" She ended slowly and her voice sounded flat and dreary.

Suddenly, everything seemed to lose colour. Mary-Ann experienced a vague feeling of depression, as when a child the clear light before a storm with the backdrop of dark clouds, delineates every detail of the landscape in bleak clarity. Walking towards the window she looked back at him, her face a cold mask,

"Years ago, Grandfather said you did not measure well. Now I understand! My people are wholesome and honest. Homely folk! They have worked strenuously all their lives and have contentment."

She paused. There was a charged silence in the lovely room, then in bitter tones she continued, "Jinny after all was the fortunate one."

Charles stared in chagrin. His mouth was drawn in deep anger.

"Jinny and I were in love, yes, but I left her for you. Your meaning is clear, your memory also but much too late. You have reached your decision. Maybe we both could have regrets."

"Yes, but not Jinny. She is satisfied with her lot. Quite."

He moved towards her as if to make their peace, "But Jinny would never have been the social success you are, my dear Mary-Ann, even married to me." He ended with a would-be forgiving smile. But Mary-Ann turned away uninterested. The atmosphere between them cooled considerably from then.

Despite Charles' somewhat boorish acceptance of the suggestion of a family dinner, he quite enjoyed being host at his well-appointed table.

Before dinner was served, Miles grey-haired and much aged, still relishing the magic of a quietly drawing pipe, sat with Maggie, Patience and Gerrard in the supreme comfort of the early Victorian chairs, gleaming in their rich brocade upholstery. They watched the younger folk in deep interest.

Jinny, across the room, smiled at Rhys as she nodded towards her parents. “Look at them there. The dears! So proud, so shrewd yet for all their years, vital and interested as if those years had touched them with blessings.”

“Maybe they have my dear. To me, they have the strength and vigour of their rainforest. Blessings are as you value them though. Some people know they have them yet look for more. Now! There’s Charles over there. His blessings are there for all to see an’ he certainly likes ‘em to be seen. A fine home, a lovely wife, a family to be proud of, beautiful gardens and money, money galore. But these are just bones of contention, because they aren’t giant size.”

Jinny laughed spontaneously as she said softly, “Mary-Ann too?” and he joined her, but continued seriously,

“Everything’s gone sour on him. He lives in a circle, a revolving circle with Charles as the pivot, the whole thing. See darling his diet is all wrong. He feeds on power. Organising other people’s lives in his main interest, and amassing money. Cold comfort that!” She took his hand and looked seriously at him.

“You could be right, but let’s leave it at that.”

“I would like to read Mother’s thoughts just now,” she continued. They of one accord turned to watch the older ones. Maggie, as in the days of her busy youth was looking around with appraising eyes.

Miles, a straight, almost stomach-less grey-bearded man, was talking to Gerrard. She listened a while and when Gerrard and Patience rose to speak to Rebecca who had just arrived, she said,

“It seems we have almost completed a pattern, Miles. Years ago we left Melbourne together, and now we are back, back with a difference.”

“Yes my dear! A big difference, a lifetime of happenings. Here, under our youngest child’s roof, are our best beloveds. Jinny and Rhys with their family, Andrew, Margaret, Morris and Donald,

young bush folk grown up and building their own tracks. Rebecca with her daughter Narissa and her sons Davys and Guy. Such fine upstanding lands. See! Taller than their mother!"

"I'm sorry young Richard, her youngest boy is not here also."

Mary-Ann came across the room to them and hearing her mother's remarks said, "Yes, Rebecca would have liked every member of the family to be here for Narissa's engagement announcement." She turned to her father with the same love in her eyes as when a child. "Are you going to make a speech Dad?"

"Not if I know it. Still I'll wish our Narissa well."

"In as few words as possible, I would say, knowing you," Mary-Ann whispered as she bent and kissed his forehead. He patted her cheek and puffed gently as he nodded, "Quite!"

Maggie put her hand on his, as if to say, "Dad's alright, leave him be." She said, "Young Richard is such a wanderer. He wrote to his mother and told her that when he sees every country in Europe he will return. He has met some of Rebecca's father's relatives and of course is very interested in tracing more, "just for the excitement of it all," he writes. But she's not very pleased. She'll have nothing to do with her father's folk. Still bitter, but that's her way. Richard discovered his relatives by tracing the source of the money that was left to her and which she invested for her children. She herself never touched a penny of it, you'll remember."

Mary-Ann said slowly, "I remember the day she first came to Rock Allen. She had hidden in Patience's wagon. Do you remember Mother?"

"Of course I do my dear, but hush, here they come. Davys too, so like his father."

"Dear Guy! How proud he would have been of his lawyer and architect sons," said Mary-Ann as she watched them approach.

"I think, had he lived, he would have preferred them to be farmers." Maggie spoke in a soft quavering voice, more quavering even than usual.

At that moment, a maid came to Mary-Ann and indicated that dinner was served. They went into the dining room.

With Narissa and Nicky were his parents, Sir Kemp and Lady Mellow. Virginia and her Scottish doctor husband, Paul McGregor, came back especially for the day and were leaving the following week on a world tour, later to return and decide on their future home, Australia or Scotland.

The beautiful Indian rosewood table gleamed softly under the glittering chandelier. It was a happy gathering, yet for the older ones there was just a tinge of sadness. Never again would such a gathering be! Somehow, they knew. They felt some pride as they watched the young folk all facing futures of their own making, branching out like young shoots from the sturdy parent stock. Life was good – the future so bright.

But then came war – 1914.

Some weeks later Davys and Guy went home to Rebecca on holidays. Early one morning, young Guy rode up to the house-yard gate and shouted,

"Here's the mail Ma."

"What's the latest war news?" called Davys.

"I daresay everyone in Australia is saying the same thing every day," said Rebecca dryly as she opened the mail bag. Down in the stables the boys had furtively cleaned guns for target practice. Up towards their mountain Old Fantastic they rode through the rain and fog-engulfed gullies, discussing their plans and looking like medieval warriors as they emerged through occasional illuminating shafts of sunshine to spend the brief span of time in target practice.

They were in a state of subdued excitement. The future to them held nothing so much as a promise of high adventure. Youth! But Davys, the serious one, tired of this and saddling his fine bay gelding, rode alone for long stretches over the most difficult terrain, thinking deeply to clear his indecision. Then! The war news became grimmer and grimmer.

The continuous call was for reinforcements for overseas.

"Keep the home fires burning."

"Tipperary."

"Come on boys, we're needing you all." The songs with their psychological impact penetrated the furtherest corners of the outback.

Davys walked in to the homestead and firmly spoke to Rebecca, "Its no use Mother! I'm going." Guy then declared his intention likewise. She was shaken.

"No. No!" But that was all. She thought, however, "They're men! I'm only a woman. War! Confound it. Men to fight, women to agonise."

Davys persuaded Guy. "Young feller! You stay here. It's food that's needed. In the meantime, the world will go on without architects, and if I get knocked back, you can take my gun." Guy agreed finally.

Rebecca listened amazed, heartened, as Davys turned to her.

"He's as tough as a young bullock Mother. Use him well." To Guy he said, "I give you my horse." Stroking the beloved hack in distressed affection he added, "Never sell him. Let him die on the place. I've had him and the old mare since they were foaled, both of them. Let him die on the place. Good old Dandy!"

So that was it. Dandy lived the years on lush pastures. Davys died in France. Young Donald Treen also left his rainforest home to lie 'forever in Flanders' Fields.'

When peace was declared, Jinny, as it happened, was at Rock Allen visiting her parents, much aged; and Rebecca who commented tonelessly,

"We've spared Guy and you Jinny have Morris and Andrew to return to you."

"Yes! And Richard?"

"Now he's Captain Richard Ford, in the British Army. I daresay we'll not be seeing him for years, if ever. He is more English than the English, by the tone of his letters." Rebecca's voice held a depth of bitterness. "Richard said he would come back to us, when he left Australia."

"He'll come," commented old Miles with set jaw, denoting his disapproval of any doubt on the matter. But Rebecca was non-committal. Jinny, in tears said,

"Those dear boys, Davys and Donald! Life will never be the same."

"There are many others to grieve," said Rebecca.

"Yes!" thought Miles. "She'll not even share her grief," and he said to them all as they sat around in brooding silence. "We have boys to return. Mary-Ann has lost her only son Jasper. He went with Davys."

"They were always good companions. I'm sure they would be happy at least, together," Maggie added sententiously.

"War!" was Rebecca's reply in deep, disgusted bitterness.

The boys returned in time and in the forest, country life flowed on with many adjustments. As the ripples on the water after a stone is thrown slowly spread and spread and finally the surface again becomes placid, so it was everywhere; and thus it will ever be, everywhere.

Eventually Mary-Ann and her husband Charles just agreed to part, so she went to England to Virginia and travelled Europe later with Richard Ford; and the years passed like unforgettable whisperings, wafting away the memories of pioneers down the vistas of time.

CHAPTER 26

WITH ACQUISITIVE EYES, REBECCA CONTINUED TO WATCH EVERY property that came on the market. She certainly had a land-hunger. It was also a painkiller. She was a legend in her own time. She had attained her goal. She was the largest landholder. Land, land to pass on to her sons, but the ultimate gain was a hollow victory. Possessions lost their savour. Finally her urge, her obsession dwindled away. She spent hours alone in the distant forest – the forest the settlers had so consistently cleared further and further back to the mountains.

She had come to a time of summing up. "All the years! What of them? All my work, my planning! My objective was to pass all to my sons! Now! Davys is dead, Guy and Richard rejected my offerings. I planned their futures so extensively, so carefully. It's all so futile. Now I realise as Miles once said,

"No person can live another's life!" I feel like a donkey, alone, lost, loaded down with treasures that nobody can claim or even have responsibility for." She smiled reluctantly and turned to look thoughtfully up at the mountain.

Suddenly, she tensed, as an illuminating thought gripped her.

"Maggie, Jinny, myself, Narissa and perhaps who knows, Narissa's Elizabeth! My granddaughter! Maybe Rock Allen has a definite affinity for woman. Ah, it's foolish I'm becoming. It's no more I'll be tormenting myself. I feel my resentment of the happenings of my childhood has faded away. I shall let things bide, but at first I must put them in order. Guy and Narissa will inherit all, for I am sure that Narissa has a land feeling. In fact, pioneering in these hills would never have been so grand if the womenfolk had not worked so faithfully and arduously with their men. Men's work they did, to be sure, and well they did it." The lines on her face smoothed and a calm eased her moments of grieving.

"Ah," she breathed softly as if some weighty problems had been solved. "Now I'm content, I see the pattern through the haze and confusion, the dusty roads an' rain soaked hills of the past. Miles, Maggie, Gerrard and Ma Patience all gone with the years! But surely their rainforest work will be their everlasting memorial. They loved it so, and I realise that I had a deep-seated grudge against the world in general when I lost Guy, my husband. Now I'm at peace. I'm glad he's at rest."

Even though life has made Rebecca pause and had given her a clearer vision of self, and a time of summing up, the pattern of her life was so firmly set that almost involuntarily, she gradually returned to it. She had to have some tangible aim each day, something to tire her body and in more particular, her mind – but with a difference. She wore her regrets and illusions.

Boxing Day picnic races were always held some miles toward the mountain and all the Rock Allen hands were there. The hot sun shimmered over the countryside.

Suddenly the old dog in the shade of the Banksia tree in the garden gave a staccato bark. Busy at her desk, Rebecca impatiently put aside her pen and papers ad went out into the garden. Again the dog barked, then as if reluctant to farther exert himself vocally, looked across to the stock-yard as if to say to the other canines there, 'you youngsters carry on', and he circled, shook himself lethargically, and lapsed into his dreams again. Not so the pack of sheep and cattle dogs; the unchained ones rushed up to the gate leading to Bower Bird Hill and the others strained at their bonds.

A solitary horseman on a fat old mealy-nosed cob approached. Old Rhys Treen! Rebecca, by this time at the garden gate, opened it and her long stride with her full skirt swinging about her old-fashioned boots, button-ups with some of the buttons missing, soon brought her to the stockyards. Her face flushed with pleasure as she watched him approach. She was slightly stooped and her shoulders, bent by years of bullocking, had thickened. Nothing could alter her fine facial structures. She still had some claim to beauty in her lighter moments especially.

"Time," she remarked with a wry grin, "has jammed the brakes on me." So she had perforce to lead an easier life, much against her will.

Rhys, his kindly face flushed with the effort of dismounting, said as he led the cob through the gate to the stable, "Good of you it is to meet me."

"Indeed, an' good it is of you to come to Rock Allen," she replied with a humorous quirk around her mouth.

"So!" Rhys nodded in snowy pate. "Now! Happy we both are." She walked beside him as he took his pony into the stall. While she spilled a liberal supply of oats over the chaff, Rhys talked and answered questions. "Yes, everyone was well. Jinny had been intending to drive across with him, but their daughter Margaret had persuaded her that she should be at the picnic to meet old friends, and to be sure, Becky that's where you should be this day, instead of glooming here alone." She shook her head and he continued as if to himself. "I thought it best I stay around in case of bush fires. Now the wind has changed its safe we are. I knew we would be alone. So I came." They walked to the house slowly, talking intently. Rebecca soon had the old black iron kettle boiling and in the dusky coolness of the old living room they settled down to rest and talk.

She said seriously, "Did you receive my letter?" Rhys nodded vigorously,

"Yes! Yes my dear. That subject I'm coming to. Sorry I am to have been overlong in comin'. You see, not every day do I feel up to exerting myself, but I'd not forgotten. I suppose," he rubbed his head apologetically, "being a happy an' contented man, I tend to be selfish. A pity it's so," he ended ruefully. "I realise the restlessness that's always been tearing you apart, Becky, but had hoped that now you have reached your goal, that you're the largest landholder, ay' an' the richest, you would be content. Now," he drummed his gnarled fingers softly on the table as he watched her, "tell me more of what you barely mentioned in your letter." He spoke half facetiously. "What's eating at your peace of mind? Contentment will you ever know? Is it that you are still runnin' away?"

There was a moment's pause. She spoke slowly and in a husky voice.

"Running away? You say I have reached my goal?" Somewhat impatiently, she caught the curtains which a sudden change of wind had billowed above her head and there was a brief silence in the old house. Rhys waited deliberately. Rarely had anyone dealt out home truths to the strong-minded Rebecca, and he was rather enjoying himself in his quiet way. But to her this was Rhys, her long-loved foster brother, and she took it.

She nodded, "I've reached my goal. Yes," she added bitterly, "but somehow, I'm like a traveller who has lost his way, yet pushes deeper into the unknown." She held her worn hands toward him. "Tell me Rhys, what is driving me?"

He shook his head slowly, "Lass, there's nought driving ye. It's runnin' away from yerself, ye are, and this you've done since ye were a waif of twelve. It's time for you to stop."

"I stopped when I was married!" she whispered.

"An when Guy left? As if with chain mail you enclosed yourself an' self took over. Cruel I am but this I must say." He looked steadily into her widened eyes. "Shame on me that I didn't say it many years past. Forgive me lass."

"I do," she answered simply.

He continued. "You're a very fine woman all the same, and I have been selfish in contentment. So happy have I been all these years with my Jinny an' my family, and now we're old. I'm so fortunate too. My sons are carrying on the property".

Rebecca rose and moved closer to him. "I have something to tell you – I'm going to England to see Richard. Then I shall visit my mother's people in France. You remember that he traced them from my old papers?"

She gave a bitter laugh, and Rhys smiled rather grimly, waiting for her to continue. After a resentful pause, she said, "Yes, I know! It's a complete turnabout." The muscles of her face working, she still faced him. He watched her with a concerned expression in his quiet eyes.

Slowly shaking her head, she went to him and gently touched his arm.

"Forgive me, Rhys. Do you know? I think I am going to cry. I can't remember ever doing this in my life. Look, the tears are streaming down my face. Oh dear! I'm an old fool."

She laughed shakily as he said in his quaint way, "Good it is. You should have done it many years since. Not even when you ran away in such blind terror and hid in our bullock wagon did you cry. You should have cried those grey-green eyes dim when Guy died. But, not a tear did you shed. You shrivelled your beautiful soul in bitterness. Becky! Becky! Cry, cry all those bitter tears away. Then leave this rainforest country, travel the world, and come back to us, not as the land-obsessed, harridan image of a woman you have been given to world so long. Give us back our dear, dear Becky."

"Yes! Rhys," she said in broken tones.

"There! There lass," he said thickly. "You're facing yourself at last, an' it's headlong you're goin' but don't be too drastic."

She smiled as she said, "I always believed in a sharp knife," and her tanned face wrinkled like old chamois skin. He grinned as a young boy and he said,

"Changes we old 'uns don't like, but this, I think will be a good one. Go! Go, quickly, but come back to your part of this forest country. For this is our land. This is Australia," and the gaunt old man bowed his head to hide his emotion. "Our children are building their lives in their own ways and land is always land whoever uses it."

Then they heard a honeyeater in the old woodbine and from a tall mountain ash the whistling eagle sent his call.

To them, all was well.

ORDER

		QTY
They Came to a Rainforest	$24.99	....
Postage within Australia	$5.00	....

TOTAL* $________

* All prices include GST

Name: ....

Address: ....

Phone: ....

Email Address: ....

Payment:

❑ Money Order ❑ Cheque ❑ Amex ❑ MasterCard ❑ Visa

Cardholder's Name:..

Credit Card Number: ....

Signature:..

Expiry Date: ....

Allow 21 days for delivery.

Payment to: Better Bookshop (ABN 14 067 257 390)
PO Box 12544
A'Beckett Street, Melbourne, 8006
Victoria, Australia
Fax: +61 3 9614 3250
betterbookshop@brolgapublishing.com.au

Be Published